VANISHING ACT

M.L. DAVIS

BOTWRIGHT
— PUBLISHING —

Botwright Publishing

VANISHING ACT

For Toby
Forever and after.

Prologue

The sun dipped behind the clouds, but the cobbled streets of Bath city centre still glistened with the warmth of the day. She stood at the front of a gathering crowd, trying to block out the muddled hum of voices muttering in several different languages. She only wanted to hear her little boy, who was stood on a wooden box, beaming up at the man stood beside him.

'What's your name, little dude?' the man asked, crouching to match the child's height. Despite his wild hair, sharp eyes, and jet-black suit, he was not intimidating. He was a showman, and the skill of his performance extended to much more than magic tricks. It was the finesse of his rapport too. He knew how to speak to people, how to speak to children. It was natural, like watching a father with his son.

'Alfie,' whispered her boy, tucking his head to his shoulder.

Her stomach lurched when he announced his name, loud and clear, to the ever-growing crowd. She tried to ignore the anxiety, determined to let her boy have his moment. *Nobody knows us here. We are safe.*

'And how old are you, Alfie?'

'Four.'

'Four? Wow! Four is the very best age to be. Did you know that?'

Alfie shook his head, his dark curls bouncing as his gap-toothed grin widened and his shocking blue eyes gleamed. It made her heart roar with love and pride.

'And tell me, Alfie,' continued the performer, his Australian accent buoyant with enthusiasm, 'would you like to be a magician?'

'Yes please!' Alfie gasped, lifting his head and straightening his spine.

That's the real magic right there, she thought, pressing a trembling hand to her chest. *Taking my quiet boy and melting away his shyness.*

Alfie was staring at the magician, his fingers wriggling at his side, his body rising with every bounce of his legs as he pushed himself onto the tips of his toes. She took her phone from her pocket and snapped a photograph, even though she knew she would never forget that moment. That image of her usually reluctant son, stood confidently before a crowd of strangers, would burn bright in her memory forever.

She and Alfie often stood in that spot together, the square in front of Bath Abbey, where ancient architecture met modern life. Where the hordes of impatient shoppers bumped into those willing to stand still for a while and take in the beauty, the buildings, and the street performers with their unique talents.

She had to be careful with money, so the bigger forms of entertainment were never an option. But sparing loose change for the street artists was an affordable way to have fun. Alfie never seemed to mind that he didn't visit any of the bigger attractions.

He would stand happily for hours, his small hand warm in hers, his tiny body tucked against her side. He rarely stood too close to the act, but he always watched on with a smile nestled between his chubby cheeks.

That day though, the magician caught his interest in a way no other artist had and Alfie pulled her to the front of the crowd. She could not fathom what had taken his eye. If anything, the man looked more like a surfer than a magician, with blonde hair in a top knot and a thick sandy stubble grazing his chin. He wore a black suit with a silver tie, yet there was nothing showy about his style. She supposed it was the way he moved that was mesmerising, the grace as he twisted his body, the quirk of his sharp features as he seduced the crowd.

When the show started Alfie had let his hand drop from hers and taken another step forward. And when the performer asked for a volunteer Alfie darted towards him, which had both shocked her and filled her with joy.

She watched him, her baby boy, take an oversized plastic wand from the magician, his mouth a perfect O of excitement.

But as the trick got under way, a woman pushed in front of her, blocking her view. And before she could say *'excuse me!'* a hand landed heavy on her shoulder, a warm tickle of breath grazed her cheek.

And when a voice whispered in her ear the one thing she was most terrified of in the world, she had no choice. She turned and walked away, legs numb and heavy, leaving her son performing magic against the towering backdrop of the gothic abbey.

By the time the act had finished she was gone.

And she crumpled beneath the horror of wondering if, by the time night fell, Alfie would have vanished too.

Now - Austin

The soundtrack to Austin Jackson's life had become some kind of permanent ticking. The second hand on the clock above his desk, making its slow and repetitive journey. The clacking of fingers on keys as he and his colleagues tapped and clicked their way through another eight hours. The dodgy chain on his bike as he pushed the pedals, and his will to live, towards the office. The clattering of passing trains.

The office building backed onto a railway and from his top floor desk Austin had a perfect view of the tracks. Whenever a train zipped by, he fantasised about jumping one and riding it well away. Some days, he fought against the urge to jump under one instead.

How has it come to this?

It was a question he asked himself every day, even though he knew the answer would crawl into his thoughts and leave him guilt ridden and sick with rage.

Nothing like a solid routine to keep your 9-5 on track

And the routine was unrelenting, consistent:

Nine o clock, make a coffee as strong and as bitter as his thoughts.

Twelve noon, eat lunch, and wash it down with a large side of self-loathing.

Three o clock, ask how it had come this and wallow in the answer.

Four o clock, fall into the trap of reminiscing, remembering a life that didn't involve counting down the minutes that made up the final hour of work.

Austin never wanted to live a life of routine and, above all else, he never wanted to work in an office. He'd decided as a teen that he could cope with bar work, and during his years at university he did just that. Yes, he could work behind a bar, he'd be a waiter, could handle giving out leaflets for sleezy nightclubs on cold streets in the middle of the night. But whatever happened he promised himself he would never spend his days at a desk.

And yet there he was, thirty-five years old and tap, tap, tapping away as he inputted feedback from surveys into databases and charts. That was his routine, Monday to Friday, nine to five.

What a bloody way to make a living.

He tried not to be resentful. He was lucky to have his job.

Lucky.

He repeated the word in his head, trying not to puke. He was fortunate, *blessed* to have a friend who owned a business and was prepared to let him in. No matter how hard he tried Austin struggled to believe the lies he told himself, found it hard to be grateful for his circumstances. It had been nearly a year since his world turned to crap, and the career he had worked so hard to achieve burst out of his life and slammed the proverbial door behind it.

In the early stages of studying for his degree, and even after he graduated, Austin had not intended to become a street performer. His sights were set on the stage, and he pulled pints at a busy West End pub, while trying to make it from behind the bar to under the spotlight. He allowed himself a small smile as he remembered the man he was then, optimistic and driven, even as dozens of failed auditions slapped him in the face.

Desperate to succeed in one way or another Austin developed a new approach. He'd performed some basic magic in a part time job as a children's entertainer and it had been well received. So, he took more training to hone his skill, transforming his image along the way. He let his hair grow to his shoulders, where the tips turned fair in the summer, especially on visits to Australia to see his parents. He grew out his beard, endured the prickly, itchy stage until he had enough facial hair to craft the perfect goatee. With the carefully angled beard, his knotted mane and his razor-sharp eyes, Austin looked like a dare-devil illusionist. He pictured himself immerging through flames before an awe-struck crowd, who would breathe a sigh of relief at his safety before erupting into applause.

That's how he'd pictured it. The gasp, the sigh, the applause. The perfect tune to match the rhythm of his heart. It hadn't quite turned out that way. He was no great illusionist, no escapologist, no Derren Brown. But as he grew in confidence he took to the streets and performed fast paced comedy magic that left the crowd in stitches and the tip bucket full.

The crunch of wheels as office chairs slid against the cheap linoleum pulled Austin from his memories. With a lurch he came crashing down to the stone-cold reality that he was no longer a magician, but a data administrator, who had finally reached the end of his Monday shift. The sliding chairs were the daily signal that the working day was over. Regular as clockwork.

Only four more days until the weekend.

Austin grunted a goodbye to his colleagues and hurried down the corridor, bounding down the stairs and out onto the street. It was a relief to breathe in the fresh Spring air, away from the stale office atmosphere that reeked of old coffee, egg sandwiches, and a lack of ambition. He bent down to unlock his bike, pulling the straps of his rucksack tight, ready for the ride to his flat.

'Excuse me? Are you Austin Jackson?'

Austin leapt upright and turned to face the source of the voice.

Oh christ. Not another journalist, please not another journalist.

It'd been months since the press had last accosted him, but Austin's chest still tightened whenever somebody addressed him by name.

'Yeah,' he replied. There was no point denying it. They'd obviously done their research to find out where he worked. It can't have been a coincidence that somebody had passed by the dingy office block just as he was leaving, and he had no friends in Bath. The woman was a stranger, as far as he could tell.

Though the more he stared it became apparent there was something off about her, halting his original assumption that she was a journalist. Her pale brown hair was swept into a messy bun, her face bare of makeup. She wore plain baggy clothes, shabby in comparison to the white designer sneakers that looked several sizes too big. She'd pulled the laces so tight the leather wrinkled, the fabric cuffs loose around her skinny ankles.

'I'm Amber,' she breathed, trembling as she spoke. 'I'm Alfie's mum.'

There was no pause, no need to take a moment to allow her words to register in his mind. Her announcement sunk in within seconds and Austin's hand flew to his mouth as his stomach convulsed, sending a hot stream of bile into his throat. He swallowed it and gaped at the woman before him, a creeping coldness gripping his neck so he couldn't breathe.

He had wondered about her every day for eleven months, her faceless existence had haunted his nightmares for nearly a year. It was almost more disturbing, having a face to put to the mystery. Pale skin, high cheekbones, startled brown eyes and dry lips dotted with red grooves. He had her face, and he had her name too. After all the time he'd spent searching, wondering, *loathing*...

He had planned over a thousand things he would say to her if he ever found her. But with the moment finally upon him, his words would not form. He couldn't even muster one of the thousand things he had to say. Not even the most important of all.

I am so sorry. I am so sorry I lost your son.

Then - Amber

She'd been drawn to Ray the moment she saw him. At least that's what Amber told him whenever they recounted the story of how they'd met. It was a lie, but she bargained it was a harmless one. In fact, it gave Ray confidence, in her and in their relationship.

The truth was, Amber had not noticed Ray until he approached her through the pretentious crowds of a club in central Manchester. It was just a week after New Year's Eve, and anybody who'd resolved not to drink or not to spend too much money was at the bar. It was an upmarket place, sleek black surfaces, attractive lighting. There was no tacky haze from a smoke machine or over excited booming voice from the DJ booth. Just ambient music and glazed glass tables, a canvas of class.

Amber sipped on her drink, swirling the refreshing tropical juice around her tongue and wincing when the vodka seeped through. She'd made no resolution to stop drinking, nor to stop spending money. The only thing she had vowed was to finally settle into a relationship, and no longer with the kind of men who would rather do shots of Jägermeister down the pub than visit a cocktail bar.

Usually, Amber had a type. It wasn't that she was shallow, or at least she hadn't intended to be. The men she dated were chosen as much for their personalities as their looks. She liked men with a playful side, a laddish sense of humour and an eagerness to impress. She chose men who enjoyed watching football with their mates and didn't take up all her time. In a relationship she liked to spend enough time together to be a couple, but not so much it was stifling.

Unintentionally, her type did extend to looks as well. She'd had three boyfriends since starting university at eighteen, and if they all stood side by side they could pass as brothers. Tall and tanned with dark hair, brown eyes, and muscles that strained against white tops. They all had the same trick; buy a size too small so the thin fabric pulled taut over their arms. Desperate to impress.

The similarities didn't end there. All three relationships had ended in disaster. Dishonesty, disloyalty, and disgrace.

Ray couldn't have been further from Amber's type. He asked to sit beside her at her table in the bar and she'd said yes. Why not? She was alone anyway, perched on a high stool with a large and colourful cocktail in front of her. When Ray sat, he placed a glass of whisky beside her own drink before turning away, his fingers drumming against his leg.

He was older, she could see it in the gentle creases beneath his eyes and the flecks of grey hair above his ears. Amber soon learned he was thirty-eight, but she considered his age probably wasn't a bad thing. She was fed up with the immaturity that lingered in the men she chose to date, and at twenty-six she wanted to think about settling down. Thirty loomed over her, four short years away, and there was so much she wanted by then. Marriage, children...wouldn't an older man be more likely to want the same? She hoped that by breaking bad habits, she'd finally start a new chapter in her life.

She'd asked for his name, and he stopped drumming his fingers and turned to face her. He was a serious man, with intense blue eyes, as light and as startling as a husky's. He had a small round nose, and lips that protruded into a permanent pout. Amber came to realise the pout wasn't deliberate, but the result of slightly crooked front teeth that were almost too big for his mouth. He kept his lips closed over them, his hand raising to hide his mouth when he laughed, but Amber didn't find them unattractive. They gave him charm.

He was a professor of History at the University of Manchester, where she herself had studied art. He didn't make jokes but he was profoundly intelligent, his stories captivating enough without humorous quips or comedic value. And, so unlike her previous men, he did not have the needy desire to impress. Why would he? He was effortlessly interesting.

Admittedly, while Amber was not prepared to pile all her hopes and dreams on somebody so soon, excitement fizzed alongside the buzz of too much vodka. And in the following weeks, she fell for Ray so hard and fast it was like riding on an upward spiral, and she was soaring dizzily towards cloud nine.

Yes, she'd been well and truly drawn in, like a moth to a flame. Like a stuntman to danger.

Now - Austin

'You have to help me find him,' Amber urged, still gazing at Austin with eyes the colour of autumn leaves. 'Please. I've done my research, you're the last known person to have seen Alfie, the last known sighting. And although you probably don't think you can help, you can! I need you to.'

The words spilled from her, a turbulent river of thoughts that Austin suspected she'd rehearsed for a while, just as he had. But where her words cascaded from her quivering lips, his remained stubbornly still. He had so much to say and yet nothing to say at all.

Instead, he studied her face, searching for some resemblance to her son. While Amber had always been a faceless figure, an image of Alfie had been all too clear in his mind. Unfaded, despite the months that had passed, Austin could recall the boy's joy, excitement and wonder as he'd taken part in the magic act. He could also remember the wrinkled brow, the worry etched into his tiny features, once he realised he was lost and alone.

'You left him.' Austin's voice cracked as his words made their appearance, slow and stiff.

Amber tilted her head to the ground, eyes pressed shut, teeth sinking into her lower lip. She rubbed at her arm, and Austin shuddered as his eyes were drawn to the trail of bruises dirtying her skin the way mud spoiled snow. Amber breathed a sigh of composure before lifting her gaze back to his.

'Will you help me find him?'

Austin fell silent again, a waging war of emotions battled within him. In the pit of his stomach it was rage, a fiery resentment bubbling at his core. In his trembling fingers it was sadness and shock. In his heart it was terrible guilt, the kind that had destroyed his self-respect, happiness and certainty.

'I want to help you,' Austin said, his guilty heart pulling the words from his numb brain and forcing them out of his mouth. 'But I can't. I wouldn't know where to begin. If I could've found Alfie by now, you have to believe me, I would have. I gave all my information to the police. They're your best bet now.'

'No!'

Austin was not prepared for the strength Amber mustered as she yelled her response to his suggestion. He reached out and gripped his bike handle, glancing to the left where one of his colleagues had immerged from the office block and scuttled away red-cheeked. The street was filling with people finishing work and Amber's shout, which was bigger than she was, had drawn a dozen pairs of eyes their way.

'No,' she repeated, calmer now, her own cheeks glazed a dusty pink. 'No police.'

It was instant, the effect those two words had on him, the memory they evoked. *No police.*

They sent a cold wave crashing over him.

Eleven months earlier Austin had been packing away his kit, satisfied at the end of a long and successful day performing magic on the streets of Bath. His tip bag was bursting with change, and he was bursting with joy. The school holidays meant bigger crowds and more kids, who always took to his act with an unashamed enthusiasm that most adults held back.

''scuse me?'

A tiny voice caught Austin's attention and, stood alone, was the dark-haired boy who'd taken part in his last act. At the end of the volunteer segment, Austin sent the lad back to his mother in the crowd, as he finished the final five minutes of the show. Austin looked for the mother, expecting her to be at Alfie's side. But the spectators had moved on and the only other people he could see were passing by, not stood watching or waiting. The boy was all on his own.

'G'day, Alfie!' Austin said, keeping his stage voice in place to mask his confusion. 'Did you enjoy the show? Where's your mum, champ?'

'Gone.'

'I'm sure she hasn't gone far,' said Austin, scrutinising the street again. 'Perhaps you've just lost sight of her.'

'She was gone after I did the magic.' Alfie's voice shook, but he steadied himself with a sniff, a tiny hand reaching up to wipe at his nose.

Austin's skin prickled, a cold rush that cooled his skin beneath his hot heavy jacket. He'd known from the moment he looked at the boy something was up. The skin beneath Alfie's eyes was red, his hands balled into fists which he rubbed against his face, his cheeks damp. But he'd hoped it was nothing he needed to worry about.

Austin peered at the people walking by, although he had no idea what Alfie's mother looked like. He was expecting to see somebody frantic, somebody distraught, grabbing stranger's arms and asking questions, calling Alfie's name with her hands cupped around her mouth. He longed for that person to appear, imagined how her body would weaken with relief when she spotted Alfie, safe, at Austin's side. But there was no-one. Surely she wouldn't have nipped off, even for five minutes, without him? What mother would?

'Tell you what, Alfie, why don't you help me pack away my stuff? Just like how you helped with the magic trick, you'll be helping me again. And by the time we're finished, I bet your mum will be right back here.'

'Okay!' Alfie bounced on his toes, his fear dissolved instantly in the distraction.

Austin hoped he was right, and Alfie's mum would be back by the time his kit bag was full and ready to go. But, when they finished, there was still no sign of her. With nothing left to distract him Alfie turned silent as he chewed on one of his fingers, his blue eyes round and glazed with tears.

The streetlights flickered on though the sky was still a hazy orange. It was not dark yet but the evening was underway. Families browsing the shops were replaced by glammed-up guys and girls heading to bars and posh restaurants. Signs in shop windows were being turned from *Come In We're Open* to *Sorry We're Closed,* and the great gothic buildings were bathed a faded peach from the sinking sun.

What the hell is that woman thinking? Poor kid's bloody terrified.

'Tell you what, champ,' said Austin. 'I think we're going to need a bit of help to find your mum. But that's okay, it'll be an adventure. We're going to go see a police man. Or a police lady. Maybe both. How does that sound?'

Austin had not expected resounding enthusiasm, but he was startled by the response he received.

'No!' shrieked Alfie, bringing his hands to his head and shaking it until his dark curls quivered. 'No police!'

Austin insisted it would be okay, tried to reassure Alfie the police would find his mum, that they would look after him and make sure they were both alright. But Alfie's face was putrid red, he flung himself onto the pavement, rocking back and forth while he chewed his finger so hard it bled. The whole time he muttered the same two words.

'No police. No police.'

'Hey, come on buddy, don't do that. You're going to hurt yourself. No police! Okay? No police.'

Alfie took his finger from his mouth and let out a small sigh. Austin was stunned by the child's strange reaction, and with the mother still absent, he took out his mobile and rang his girlfriend. Jasmine would know what to do. She always did. When the phone clicked to voicemail Austin bit his tongue to keep from swearing and tried again. For a second time the phone trilled with ringing until her answer phone message took its place.

Uncertain, desperate to help, and knowing it'd be easier with Jasmine at his side, Austin did the unthinkable.

He told the boy to come with him, bought two tickets for the bus, and took Alfie back to his house.

Austin blinked away the memory, letting his focus return to the ghostly woman, with her sunken cheeks and round imploring eyes. Did she really want his help? Or did she think Austin had kidnapped her son, hurt him in some way? Harmed him? That's what had been said about him, what the papers printed, so why wouldn't she think it? And if she really was thinking those things then he dreaded to consider what she might do now she'd found him. He never thought he could be such a damn coward but he was hit with an urge to recoil from her.

Because if their roles were reversed he wouldn't be looking for help. He'd be gunning for blood.

Then - Amber

In the weeks that followed, Amber and Ray's relationship flew into a whirlwind, and Amber saw her hopes and dreams playing out in front of her, within touching distance of coming true.

She'd tried to pace herself, even though she was dizzy with excitement. He was the perfect man. Clever and interesting, supportive and kind, confident but not arrogant. Strong, but occasionally shy. She found herself falling in love with his little insecurities, determined to lift him up and away from them.

'I hate my name. It's so...bland.' he told her once.

'I like it,' she'd replied. 'You're my Ray of sunshine!'

He'd smiled his crooked-tooth smile, and it pushed a grin of her own onto her face. Making him feel good made her feel amazing.

Within a month Ray asked Amber to move in with him. She was tempted to let the whirlwind lift her off her feet, but she knew she should remain grounded and be sensible. She didn't want to move too fast, scared she would either ruin her chances of settling down with him, or act with such haste she'd be trapped if it turned out he wasn't right for her. As much as she doubted that would happen, the thought of letting go of her apartment made nervous energy swarm through her veins.

Despite how much she loved her tiny home, turning Ray down was the hardest rejection she had ever made. Because Ray's house was magnificent, a gorgeous manor on the rural outskirts of Manchester, with acres of land and décor that elegantly balanced between modern and homely. She could picture herself living there. Her touch would complete the place, she'd pick out artwork for the blank walls, choosing colours that emphasised the rustic wood-work browns Ray had already chosen for the furnishings.

She could see herself raising a family there too, children chasing each other through the safety of the large private garden. They'd have dogs, Ray had already agreed. They wanted the exact same things. It would be a dream come true.

When Amber rejected Ray's offer, she was terrified the dream would shatter. She was playing it cool, trying to be as mature as he was, maintaining her independence despite a part of her wanting to cling to her new man and never let go. When she'd said no, her stomach folded in on itself, anxiety crawling through her body and immerging as beads of sweat on her forehead. She needn't have worried. Ray bent down and kissed her lips, his hand gently working its way into her hair.

'You're right, he'd murmured. 'It is too soon to move in together. But is it too soon to holiday together?' He reached into his briefcase and brandished two plane tickets to Rome. Amber leapt into his arms with a squeal so loud they both dissolved into laughter.

'I love Rome,' Amber said later that evening, as she and Ray sat in his garden eating carbonara and drinking white wine. The food was rich, creamy, settling in Amber's stomach with a comfortable weight. Combined with the wine, she grew sleepy and content.

'I know you do,' Ray said, his glacier eyes shining. 'You told me the first time we met...twice!'

Amber giggled, her head light and tipsy. On wine, or romance, she wasn't sure.

*

The holiday was dazzling. Ray had never been to Rome, and Amber agreed, more than happily, to re-visit the wonderous sites she'd experienced before. Yet it could not have been more different.

On her first trip she'd slummed with a large group of friends in a hostel. It was cheap but colourful, all eight of them in one room, split out amongst four bunk beds. They took basic self-guided tours of the city and shared slabs of pizza from street vendors, their evenings a buzz of cheap supermarket vodka, which she and the other girls hid in hipflasks.

She'd loved every moment of that holiday with her friends but experiencing Rome with Ray revealed another side to the city, so she could fall in love all over again. He insisted on paying for a private tour of the Colosseum, giving them an attentive guide to answer their questions and even show them areas usually closed off to the public. Amber avoided the envious stares from the other tourists, not used to V.I.P. treatment. But the awkward tension disappeared when she glanced at Ray.

He was transfixed, his eyes misted with wonder, his plump lips parted in awe. When she squeezed his hand, he was too enthralled by the history to notice. He ran his fingers over the rough edges of the stone, traced the engravings with care. He never once took a photograph, as though he could not bear the miniature view through the lens, when the huge, magnificent structure stood before him. It was refreshing, real.

In the evenings they dined in plush restaurants, on balconies with city views. As the sun faded lights sprung on, sprawling below them as though they were looking down at a starry sky. They devoured risottos and pastas, the intense flavours bursting on her tongue like fireworks. Ray ordered champagne with every meal, and the bubbles lifted Amber into a blissful state of delight.

Through it all, Amber's mind whirled with conflict. She loved Ray, of that she had no doubt. And the atmosphere in Rome was only making her fall harder, her heart swelled at his childlike wonder, at his generosity, and the ease of being in his company. Yet, despite it all she had a nagging anxiety that he might propose, and she wouldn't know whether to say yes or no.

And why would she say no? She could not place her finger on any reason other than it being too soon. But then, what was she waiting for? She had scoffed, in her younger years, at girls who said there is no such thing as too soon when you find the one.

When you know, you know.

Was Ray the one? Amber was sure he was. Certain he loved her, and she him. Certain she'd finally found the man she would marry. And she did want to marry him, eventually, she felt certain of that too. But for some reason, she didn't want it yet. She wanted to be a girlfriend for a little while longer, before upgrading to fiancé.

So when Ray took her hand in front of the Trevi Fountain, the water rushing and filling the ancient streets with its romantic song, she was relieved that he pulled out not a ring, but a key to his house.

'This has been the most glorious holiday of my life,' he said, his voice deep and smooth. 'And they say that if you can holiday together, it's a good sign of your strength as a couple. I know we've only been dating for a month but please, Amber. I love you. Move in with me?'

She'd said yes without pausing, flinging her arms around his neck and kissing him, the onlookers cheering as though they'd gotten engaged after all.

And though she fizzed with happiness as they tossed coins over their shoulders and into the cornflower-blue water of the fountain, she was still, for some reason, light with relief that he had not asked for her hand in marriage.

Despite all her certainties, she feared it could all go wrong.

Now - Austin

Every day since, Austin imagined how different his life would be had he not taken the boy to his home. But he'd hoped Jasmine would be there and knew she would be able to work out the best thing to do, without traumatising poor Alfie, who was set on not talking to the police. What had happened to make him so frightened of the people who were supposed to keep him safe? Austin didn't like to think.

'You say you've done your research?' Austin said as Amber gazed at him with her hands clasped, as though he were about to reveal himself as some kind of superhero. 'So surely you know what happened? What I was accused of?'

'You were accused of kidnapping him,' she said, and the word sent a shock of ice down his spine.

Kidnapping.

'Exactly.' Austin folded his arms across his chest. 'You're asking *me* for help? The person who was accused of taking him?'

'You didn't take him. I know it wasn't you. I believe it.'

Her certainty shocked him, and Austin stood and stared, replaying her words to make sure he'd heard her correctly. Had he not dreamed for months of apologising to her? For making the mistakes that meant her son wasn't taken into the care of the police but left vulnerable and at risk? And now she was there, actually there, telling him it wasn't his fault. He should've been relieved, but he wasn't. He deserved her anger, not her understanding. Otherwise what had been the point of torturing himself?

'I did take him,' Austin said, swallowing down the hard lump in his throat. 'I took him back to my home, my girlfriend's house. And he went missing from there. I should never have—'

'No,' Amber cut in. 'No, you shouldn't have. But I trust you didn't do it with bad intentions. I know you were only trying to help. You were trying to do what was right.'

Austin narrowed his eyes at her choice of phrase. 'You read my interview then?'

He'd cursed himself for doing that interview. The press were smart, he had to give the bastards that, and before he knew it he'd agreed to an exclusive interview in an attempt to clear his name. They convinced him that if he told his side of the story, his truth, then people would understand. But most readers deemed he was lying and continued to brand him a kidnapper. Even those who believed his story scolded him, not understanding how a grown man could've done something so stupid.

Trust me, I don't understand it my bloody self.

'Austin, please.' Amber was still wringing her hands, clutching at them as though in prayer. 'I just want to find my son. I need to hear it, in your own words, what happened. When you took him to yours, what happened?'

Austin swallowed again as the memory took to his mind like an amateur actor thrust under their first spotlight.

The bus pulled up outside the house Austin shared with Jasmine and he nudged Alfie's shoulder to encourage him to stand and follow him out to the pavement. It was Jasmine's house really, but Austin had lived with her from the moment he moved to Bath four years ago.

He met Jasmine in London, when he was at the top of his career and performing in Covent Garden. It was the crowning jewel for street artists, a renowned spot where tourists and locals alike rallied around singer-songwriters, fire jugglers, and magicians. She'd been one of the crowd, and when his act was over Jasmine approached him, clutching a twenty pound note between sharp painted nails. She flashed him a dazzling, white-toothed smile, and said, 'I could drop this into your tip bucket, or I could buy you dinner.'

Of course, he had chosen the dinner.

Jasmine had the tanned freckled face of a surfer, the free-flowing fashion sense of a hippy. But as he got to know her, over Thai food that evening, he realised there was no label for her. He fell hard and fast, and after six months of travelling between London and her home in Bath, she asked him to move in with her.

He'd wanted to say yes at once, but performing in Covent Garden was an honour. Not any old wannabe-entertainer could perform there. Otherwise the whole of London and their Granny would show up each morning clutching a worn-out guitar or a box of magic tricks. It was a lengthy application and gruelling audition that earned him his place. Could he really give it all up?

But he soon decided he could, he loved the person he was when he was with Jasmine. He moved his act to Bath, where the streets were still busy and buskers still held in high regard. He was happy, beyond happy, with his new girl and his new home.

That's why he wanted to bring Alfie to her after the *no police* outburst. Jasmine was as natural and as calm as a summer breeze. She had a way of making people feel safe and at ease. She was clever, intuitive, always did what was right. She'd know what to do.

So when he stepped through the door, Alfie at his side, he was devastated to find the place empty. He tried getting her on the phone again, but once more the line rang straight to voicemail. He glanced over his shoulder to see Alfie sat on the edge of the sofa, his little legs dangling, unable to reach the floor.

Austin knew he had to do the right thing, even if it wasn't what the kid wanted. He couldn't keep him at home. What if his mother had reported him missing? She must've done. How would it look if Alfie was found in his house, and Austin had not said a word? He paced to the kitchen and made Alfie a cup of squash, taking it in to him alongside a plate of cookies.

'I've just gotta make a phone call, champ. Can you wait here? I won't be long.'

'You phone my mummy?' Alfie asked through a mouthful of cookie, spraying crumps down his top. He was so innocent it made Austin's heart ache.

'I'm going to call someone who will help us find her.'

'No police!'

'No, champ. No police.' Austin hated lying to him, but what could he do?

I will not be held hostage by a four-year-old. I am the adult, and it'll be my damn decision what happens now.

And so, Austin called the police and stood in the hallway, gazing through the square window with beads of sweat crawling his back, as he waited for them to arrive. He did not go into the living room to sit with Alfie, could not look him in the eye after betraying his trust. It was stupid, he knew that with hindsight. But it hadn't seemed so foolish at the time.

And when the police rapped on the door Austin took them straight through to the living room. But Alfie's cup of squash was empty, and he was gone.

'I'm sorry,' Austin said to Amber, who's wide eyes had filled with tears as he recounted his story. 'I don't know what happened from there. I can't help you.'

'He must've heard you,' Amber whispered, her breath hitching as she raised a hand to her chest. 'He must've heard you on the phone to the police. He was scared. No wonder he ran—'

'Wait, hang on a minute!' He may have spent the best part of a year blaming himself, but now it was someone else pointing the finger it was hard to accept. He'd have been cool with it if she'd yelled at him for taking Alfie back to his house, for losing sight of him. But he would not be scolded for doing what he should've from the start and calling the police.

'Of course I called the police. He was a missing child! What would you have me do? Adopt him and then go on a grand adventure to find you? How the hell would that have worked out? And what is all this *no police* crap anyway?'

'I don't want the police involved.' Amber's voice was low and stern, her words squeezing out through clenched teeth. 'I didn't then, and I certainly don't now.'

'Your son is missing,' Austin said, baffled by the woman's choices. 'Your son has been missing for almost a year and all you can say is *no police?* Don't you think *yes police* would be the more appropriate attitude?'

'Are you going to help me or not?' Amber lifted her chin, resting her hands on her hips.

Austin was reminded of his mother when she was angry at him, and although he hated the way Amber was ignoring his questions and demanding his assistance, he also admired her determination. How was she to know after all? How was she to know how much he'd lost?

Somewhere beneath his fear and uncertainty, his guard was slipping.

And Austin had no idea if it was for the best, or the worst.

Then - Amber

Within hours of the plane touching down in England, Amber had given notice to her landlord. She only had to give a month, but Ray still insisted she paid up and moved out right away.

She didn't mind. She couldn't wait to move into Ray's beautiful house. But it was with some sadness that she said a silent goodbye to every empty room in her tiny apartment. The flat symbolised her ability to rely on herself, to live independently without anyone else's help.

When Amber was only twenty-two, her mother died. Her sudden diagnosis of breast cancer dragged them both into a state of shock, and the three months the doctors gave her stayed true, too cruel to extend her life by even a week or two more. *Three months*. It was a long fight, but not long enough, and her mother had been taken far too soon. Having been brought up an only child, by a single mother, Amber was left orphaned and alone.

When all formalities had been dealt with, and her mother had been laid to rest, Amber received a large sum of money. Not only had her mum left everything to her, but her life insurance payout had been generous. Amber realised, with a stab to the heart, that her mother always planned to leave her daughter financially stable should anything happen.

But Amber had not touched a penny of it in the four years that followed. After university she landed herself a job in marketing and worked her way into a solid position with a modest, but adequate, wage. She rented her flat, she paid her bills, and she lived her life within her means, too guilty to spend any of her mother's money. What use was it when she no longer had her mum? The money was worthless, an insufficient replacement, and spending it felt like a dishonour.

Amber had not mentioned the money to Ray, but she would in time. She intended to keep it back and eventually put it into a trust fund for her future children. Her mum would have loved becoming a grandma, and this way her grandchildren would benefit from the money she left behind. Undoubtedly, had she lived longer, she'd have spent it on them anyway.

The first few weeks living in the manor were like being on a spa break, other than the commute she undertook five days a week for her job. Ray insisted she give it up, at least for a while, but she didn't want to burn bridges when she'd worked so hard to build them. He gave in eventually, and anyway, in the light of her new life even the working day was no hassle. Each evening she raced to get home and soaked in the bath before cooking meals with the exquisite and expensive ingredients that lined the cupboards in the kitchen.

On weekends, when he did not have work and was therefore not back late from the university, Ray cooked for her, and his food was as good as any she'd ever tasted in a restaurant. Her life was a permanent luxury, whether she was lounging on the plush velvet couch in the living room or loading the dishwasher knowing she wouldn't have to clean the dishes by hand.

On the one-month anniversary of her moving in, Amber and Ray sat curled up on the sofa, ignoring the film that was playing on the plasma television, and focusing instead on glasses of expensive wine and cosy conversation.

'I have to go to a conference,' Ray said. He was gazing at his wine glass, his finger tracing the rim in repetitive circular motions.

'Okay,' Amber said, aware of Ray's agitation. He was usually so animated, talking passionately about his work, his love of history. It was unusual to see him so down. 'That'll be good, won't it?'

'Hmm. It will be okay. I don't really want to go, but everyone has been invited from the history department. It'd look bad on the Uni if I didn't show.'

'Well, you'd better show then!' Amber nudged him with her foot, flashing him a warm smile to try and lighten the atmosphere.

'What will you do while I'm away?' Ray asked, his eyebrows pinched.

'When is it?'

'Next weekend. I'll be gone from Friday and be back Sunday evening.'

'Well, I'll be here,' Amber shrugged. *No big deal.*

She didn't mention it, but she loved the idea of some time to herself. She had always enjoyed her me-time and always chosen boyfriends who spent the weekends watching or playing football, before heading to the pub with the lads. Ray wasn't like that, and no matter how much she loved him, it was a little stifling to never have the place to herself. She'd lived alone for so long, it was what she was used to. The constant company was re-assuring but tiring at times.

'But what will you do?' Ray said, setting his glass on the coffee table with such force it nearly toppled over.

'I don't know. Watch a film? Have a long bath? I might meet up with the girls and go shopping, I quite fancy that actually.'

'Right.' There was no light in Ray's shocking blue eyes, it was as though the electric current that usually made them sparkle had been severed.

'Maybe I'll pick out something sexy, just for you,' she giggled, determined to cheer him up. 'It'll give you something to look forward to while you're away.'

'You think I want you parading around a store, picking out lingerie while any dirty old man or love-sick school boy could be ogling you? Jesus, Amber. Don't be crude.'

Amber's skin prickled with cold, despite the roaring fire that was filling the room with warmth. She took a swig of her wine, not worrying about the delicate sips she usually took to appear sophisticated, and emptied her glass before smacking her lips.

'You're obviously stressed, Ray,' she said, swinging her hair over her shoulders and sitting up straight. 'So I'm not going to rise to the argument. But what I will say, is no matter how pissed off you are, don't take it out on me when it isn't my fault. I was trying to cheer you up. And I don't need you speaking to me like I'm beneath you. Got it?'

She wasn't entirely sure where her rage had come from. In arguments she'd had in the past, her boyfriends had said much worse things to her and she'd reacted with less venom. And didn't she love Ray, more than she'd ever loved those boys before? Perhaps that's why she felt comfortable enough to stand her ground. And perhaps that's why she'd been so hurt at his sudden bitterness towards her.

'Oh, Amber. I'm so sorry.' Ray reached his hand to her face, his fingers warm against her cheek. He traced her skin, from the top of her brow to her jaw bone. 'That was so rude of me. I'm going to miss you, that's all.'

Amber shifted on the sofa, not wanting to pull away from him, but unnerved by his rapid mood change all the same. She was overjoyed by how much he loved her, flattered by his attention and affection. But it was only two nights, and she was uncomfortable that the thought of being away from her for a mere weekend was enough to make him so hostile.

What am I thinking? It's obviously not just me, there must be more on his mind. Don't be so vain.

Leaning in, Amber kissed Ray on the lips, nibbling on them before she pulled away, pleased to see the smile her touch left behind.

'Don't worry, my love,' she said. 'I'll miss you too, of course I will. But it's only two nights. It'll fly by.'

'Two nights,' repeated Ray with a slow nod. 'Right.'

*

She hated to admit it, but Amber enjoyed her weekend alone. On the Friday evening she stretched out across the sofa, relieved to be able to fidget without the worry of annoying Ray, who always sat with one hand resting on her leg. He'd never complained before, but she'd noticed the way he frowned when they were enjoying a film and her wriggling disturbed the handsome concentration that took hold of his face as he watched.

But with her own space she tossed and turned, yawning loudly and enjoying the freedom of not needing to make a good impression. Ray called that evening, and he stayed on the phone to her for over two hours. She tried not to be irritated but their conversation didn't flow so naturally on the telephone, and Ray's voice was clipped throughout.

Saturday evening, she laid out like a starfish on the king size bed, wrapped in her dressing gown and ready to start her evening skin care routine. She had spent the day shopping with friends, Sadie and Leanne from Uni, and was looking forward to wiping away her foundation and applying a facemask before getting in the bath. Before she had a chance her phone vibrated on the bedside table and she rolled over to see Ray was calling her on FaceTime.

'Hello, handsome!' She beamed into the camera, relieved at the way her spirits soared when his face appeared on her screen. She'd enjoyed her alone time so much she was worried she wasn't cut out for a serious relationship, but just one look into his eyes made her heart pick up its pace. She missed him.

'What the hell, Amber?' Ray frowned. 'Why have you got so much makeup on?'

Amber returned his scowl, unsure why it mattered. Eager to keep the mood light she twisted her face into a smile. 'I went out shopping, with Sadie and Leanne. I'm useless at shopping though, I didn't come back with a single thing. Sadie bought loads! You should've seen how many bags! It took all three of us to carry them back to her place.'

'Shopping with the girls?' Ray asked, his lips puckered. 'That's true, is it? It's not that you've got another man in my house?'

Amber wasn't sure what stung the most. The accusation, the fact Ray didn't trust her, or the way he said *my* house, even though it was supposed to be hers too.

'Of course not,' she said, no longer bothering to keep her tone light. *If he's going to be a moody arse, then so am I.*

'Show me,' Ray barked.

'Excuse me?'

'Show me the house. Take your phone with you and keep the camera on. I want to see every room. That includes inside the wardrobes and under the bed. And don't mute yourself. I want to be able to hear if you're telling anybody to get out or hide.'

'Ray!' Amber spluttered. 'I presume you're joking?'

'So you've got something to hide then?'

She knew she shouldn't rise to it, that she shouldn't have to prove herself, but she did it anyway. She stomped through the house, into every one of the five bedrooms, right down to the utility room at the side of the kitchen. She made sure to slam every door as she went and pulled back blankets and throws with as much anger as she could muster. All the while her pulse raced, hot and angry, as blood rushed through her veins, throbbing in her ears.

When she'd shown Ray every room, she climbed the stairs to the master bedroom and flopped onto the bed, turning the camera to her face. Her cheeks were red, her brown eyes flared.

'Happy now?'

Ray's face was creased with silent laughter, his expression so relaxed he didn't even bother to raise a hand to hide his teeth like he usually did. 'Oh, Amber. You're so silly. I was only joking!'

She glared down the lens, tempted to end the call so the screen would fade to black and his face would vanish. It hadn't sounded like a joke when he said it. But his smile reached all the way to his eyes, he was shaking his head, and his laughter was loud, a deep chuckle.

'Come on, sweetheart. It was just my little joke. And besides, you're so sexy when you're angry!' He feigned a growl and winked at her, melting her frostiness and making her giggle in return.

'You idiot,' she groaned, embarrassed.

'I'll let you get on with your evening. Goodnight my beautiful girl. I love you.'

They ended the phone call on a high, blowing kisses and laughing again at how Amber had taken Ray's joke so seriously. By the time they hung up the line they'd each said *I love you* five times.

And yet, as Amber took the makeup wipe and slid it across her eyes, leaving a smudged black trail of mascara, she couldn't shake the feeling that something wasn't quite right.

Now - Austin

'No. I can't do this.'

Austin turned his gaze away from Amber, trying not let the guilt flood from his heart and swamp his brain. If he wasn't careful he would agree to getting involved, and that was a hole he needed to keep out of. If he dug himself any deeper, he may as well be digging his grave.

'But I need you,' Amber whispered.

Austin's chest tightened as he shook his head. 'No, Amber. You don't need me. I can't do anything to help. If I thought I could, if I thought I'd make a difference, I would, but I can't. The last time I tried to help somebody it ruined my life.'

Amber's mouth twitched. 'So, you've nothing more to lose then.'

'You think that's funny?' Austin fought to keep himself from raising his voice, aware of the continuous stream of people passing by. 'Your little vanishing act cost me everything!'

She recoiled, taking a step back. Her eyes darted over his face as her mouth fell agape. '*Vanishing act?*' she stammered, her voice weak with the threat of tears. 'You think I just up and left my son on the streets? I didn't walk out on him, and I didn't *vanish*.

I'm not one of your magic tricks! Do you have any idea what I've been through? I was taken! Away from my son, away from here! Away from everything.'

Heat prickled across Austin's face, and he raised a clenched fist to his mouth as he coughed away the pain forming in his throat. He shouldn't have let his rage get the better of him, his mother would be appalled at his lack of compassion. Whatever he'd been through, was it worse than losing a child?

And it's all my bloody fault he's lost.

He had to get off the street. The rumbling of traffic and flow of bodies was making him tense. They were exposed by the side of the road, and as much as he wanted the encounter to be over, they had much more to talk about. He couldn't just push her away.

'Let's get coffee.' Austin waved towards the tiny café across the road.

It wasn't the most ambient of coffee shops. It reeked of bacon, a grease that lingered on the air and made stomachs clench with both hunger and disgust. But it was better than staying where they were, and Amber's skin was so white Austin wasn't sure she had any blood left in her. He thought she might faint if she didn't sit down.

Amber shook her head. 'You want to go for coffee?'

'Tea then, if you prefer.'

She narrowed her eyes. 'That's not what I meant. I have to find my son, I've had to wait long enough! I don't have time to sit down and drink coffee!'

'No disrespect, mate, but you don't look well. How long do you reckon you can go without a drink? Besides, you're asking for my help, I think the least you can do is answer some of my questions.'

He turned and marched across the road, disappearing into the gloom of the café. She would follow, he was sure of it. If she needed him that much, she'd have to. He ordered a coffee for each of them and a pot of tea, just in case. When he turned to carry the tray to a table, Amber was shuffling towards a chair in her ridiculous trainers, fiddling with a strand of her long, mousy hair.

'I don't usually take sugar,' Amber said, spooning a large scoop from the sticky pot in the centre of the table and stirring it into tea as dark as his own black coffee.

'You obviously need it,' Austin said, hoping his sympathy would make up for his earlier hostility. 'Would you like something to eat?'

'Do they do smashed avocado on toast?' Amber asked, her skin souring even more as she glanced at the plastic laminate menus and the egg stain on the checked table cloth.

'Uh...not at this time in the afternoon,' said Austin, pretending to squint at his watch.

'Not ever, you mean?' she queried, and the small smile that crept onto her face transformed her. In that moment she was not a solid imitation of a ghost, haunting and pale, but a real human woman, with warm maple eyes and a dimple in her left cheek. Her smile sagged within seconds, her face dropping as she gazed into her lap, her signature biting of the lower lip falling back into play. Austin was no psychologist, but he suspected she felt guilty for smiling while her son was lost. He knew that feeling. Most days he resigned himself to the fact he did not deserve to ever feel happy again, while wondering if he ever could anyway.

But it wasn't just about him anymore, so he feigned a smile in return. 'Okay, you got me. No smashed avocado. They do a cracking sausage sandwich though.'

Her shoulders twitched, accompanied by a sniff which he hoped was suppressed laughter and not the early onset of tears. He ordered two sausage sandwiches at the counter and returned to the table.

'I know you want my help. And I want to help you if I can. If we're doing this together then I know I'm going to have to answer your questions, but you're going to have to answer mine as well.'

Amber nodded, peering at him from over her mug as she took a long sip of tea.

'What happened?' Austin asked, leaning towards her and lowering his voice. Perhaps it was too big a question to be starting on, but it was undoubtedly the most important. 'Where did you go?'

Amber set her mug on the table, and brought her hands together, twisting and wringing her fingers. 'I...it's hard to explain. It's so...I don't want to talk about it. Not yet. It's too personal, I'm sorry. But I promise you, I would never have left Alfie on those streets and just wandered off. I was watching him. I couldn't take my eyes off him, I *didn't* take my eyes off him! But then...I was taken. Forced to go. That's all I've got right now. I'm sorry.'

Austin stared at her, as though she were a character in an over-the-top television drama. Did that sort of thing happen in real life? Were women snatched from the street, beneath the noses of hundreds of people? She'd been stood, watching his act, shoulder to shoulder with the rest of the crowd. And beyond the onlookers, the streets of Bath were packed that evening, full of tourists and locals enjoying the lingering warmth of the April sun.

'Okay,' Austin conceded. 'I understand it's difficult, and I won't make you tell me about it, not unless it becomes important in our search. Deal?'

'*Our* search?' she asked, and Austin nodded, wondering with each dip of the head if he'd end up regretting it.

'So where do we begin? Do you have any idea where we should start?' It was surely an impossible task, less *finding a needle in a haystack* and more *flailing in the dark for an invisible switch that might not even exist*. He only hoped Amber had knowledge he didn't, a solid starting point.

'The last place you saw Alfie was at your house, right? That's where he disappeared from?'

'Well, yeah, but—'

'We have to go there. Please, Austin, it's the last place my son was seen, and I have to go there to feel close to him. I might be able to work something out, get a sense on where he would've gone. Please?'

Austin wanted to say yes, even though he was failing to see her logic. Being at the house wouldn't give them answers, and her mother's-instinct would be useless if that's all she had. He still wanted to say yes, because it pained him take it away from her, the opportunity to feel close to her boy.

But he didn't live in that house anymore. The house had been, and still was, Jasmine's. And a few months after Alfie's disappearance, she had asked Austin to leave.

When Alfie went missing, Austin and Jasmine's lives rocketed into territories they could never have predicted. Not least because Austin was arrested for kidnap. In those early days he sobbed onto Jasmine's shoulder, hating himself for his stupidity and rash decisions.

'I should've waited until I got hold of you,' he cried. 'I should never have called the police. You'd have known what to. Why didn't I just wait until I'd heard from you?'

'Don't be silly, Aus,' she'd said, running her delicate fingers through his hair. 'You did the right thing. It's what I'd have told you to do, ringing the police. So, it would've happened anyway. You know, the boy running away from them. This isn't on you, babe. It isn't.'

Her support had been as fiery and fierce as her love, and despite everything crashing around him, Jasmine was the one thing Austin thought would remain consistent and positive. Jasmine was the kind of person who breezed through life with an optimism you could easily mistake for naivety. But she was far from oblivious, she was intelligent, tuned into the world around her.

She was too in tune with herself to allow anything to keep her down. She banished negativity with meditation and mindfulness, and little made her sad. If anyone should have been able to cope with Austin and what he was accused of, it was her. But she couldn't. Her demeanour wavered, and nothing could help her deal with the press, who sat on the doorstep to her house and hounded her whenever she tried to leave. The accusations and the attention were too much for a girl who took solace in peace and privacy.

So, she asked Austin to leave, and then she did as she always did, to keep her life sacred. She shut out the negative energy, and refused to let it back in.

'I can't take you to the house, Amber. I'm sorry.'

'Why?'

'Because I don't live there anymore.'

'But whoever does live there might let us in if we explain why. I mean we'll have to be careful not to say anything that might lead them to call the police—'

'You don't understand,' Austin sighed, hating himself for once again extinguishing the light that crept up behind her eyes whenever she spoke of finding her son. 'The house belongs to my ex-girlfriend.'

'Well, isn't that a good thing?' Amber asked. 'She's not a stranger, she must already know what happened? So she should let us in, no questions asked.'

'Are you serious? Mate, she's my ex-girlfriend. She broke up with me, she is not likely to want me snooping around her house, least of all with some strange woman.'

Amber flinched. 'You think I'm strange?'

'This whole situation is strange. Please, don't make me do this.'

But as he looked at her, her tilted head and wide-eyed expression, he knew he'd give in. And it wouldn't have been fair to tell her that while she might feel close to Alfie in that house, he would be forced to confront, once more, the mistakes he made that day.

Then - Amber

A month on and Ray's odd sense of humour had not re-surfaced. Amber was relieved, grateful that he recognised his behaviour had annoyed her, glad he had not made a joke like it since. In fact, since the weekend of the conference, he'd been nothing but charming.

Inspired by her love of art Ray bought her a stunning oak desk, which he put in the master bedroom so that it rested beside the large double window, overlooking the gardens. Amber spent most evenings painting the scenic views, losing herself in the swirl of watercolour as it blotched onto the thick paper and seeped into something beautiful.

'You're so talented,' Ray murmured, nuzzling his lips into her hair and neck. 'This should be your career. Not that ridiculous office job. You shouldn't be staring at a computer screen all day. You should be gazing out of open windows with a paint brush in your hand.'

Amber smiled. She'd never grow tired of hearing him compliment her work. Ray had hung several of her paintings around the house, adding a splash of colour and personality to the rooms.

His favourite was of the Trevi Fountain in Rome, the ripples of blue water glistening beneath white stone.

But Ray's insistence that she gave up her job was becoming more and more frequent, and she tensed every time he suggested it. She didn't like the thought of staying at home all day while her partner brought in the money.

Perhaps she was being unfair. Ray reasoned if she gave up her marketing job she would have more time to paint, and therefore the art would eventually become her career. But it was too naive to assume she could make it in the industry with such ease. And while she tried to remain optimistic, she wanted to keep her job in the meantime. It offered her the stability of her own income, meaning she'd never have to touch the money from her mother, which she still hadn't mentioned to Ray. The card for the account which held her inheritance was hidden at the bottom of her painting case, as though it were a dirty secret.

It wasn't that she didn't want Ray to know. She just wanted to avoid ever discussing it, to dodge the constant reminder that her mum was gone and all that was left of her was her money. And no amount would ever console Amber, nor replace her mother. So what was the point?

No, if she kept her job she could pay her way, and keep the routine that meant she left the house every day. She loved the sense of accomplishment on a Friday afternoon, knowing she had earned her right to relax over the weekend. Would she get the same, bouncy Friday feeling if she didn't have to endure the working week? She doubted it, and so she preferred to continue.

*

Only two weeks after her new desk had been moved into their bedroom Ray insisted on having the en-suite bathroom re-done. It didn't need it in Amber's opinion. She loved the large, deep bathtub, the power shower, and the pristine white that never lost its sparkle. But when Ray said he'd prefer a jacuzzi bath and underfloor heating, she allowed herself to indulge and agree. It was their forever home, after all. Why not pay out for a little luxury?

To Ray's indignation Amber insisted on paying for half the work. Eventually he agreed, and workmen moved in during the day, while Amber and Ray took to one of the guest bedrooms at night, to avoid the clutter.

There was something about the guest bedroom Amber found unnerving. She wasn't sure why at first because the room, like the rest of the house, was beautiful. More like a hotel room than a guest bedroom, it featured a large king-sized bed, white fluffy carpet, a flat screen TV, small desk, and a modest en-suite of its own.

'No window,' Ray said that evening, as Amber eyed the room, her shoulders bunched with tension.

'Huh?'

'The room feels weird because there's no window,' Ray said. 'No natural light. It makes the room seem smaller than it is.'

'You're right,' Amber said, relaxing into the soft sheets and shuffling to Ray's side. 'I've been wondering what it was. It feels almost...claustrophobic, I guess. Not having a window.'

'Well, it's our last night in here, my love,' he whispered. 'The bathroom will be finished tomorrow.'

She wanted to tell him she couldn't wait, but before she could open her mouth his lips were upon hers and she giggled as he rolled on top of her.

*

When Amber awoke the next morning Ray was gone. It was not uncommon for him to be up first, and she rolled over to reach for her mobile and check the time. Her fingers grappled at the bedside table, feeling nothing but the smooth wood surface.

Odd. Where is it?

She was sure she'd taken it to bed with her, could remember setting her alarm before placing it down beside her. She climbed out of the bed and checked on the floor and under the oak frame. But it was gone.

Oh shit. What time is it?

There was no clock in the room. Amber sighed, shrugged on her dressing gown and trudged to the door. But it wouldn't open. The bronze handle twisted and turned, but the door would not budge. Like the others in the house, it was strong and thick, an antique feature that added to the manor's charm. It was heavy and Amber supposed that if something had wedged it shut she would struggle to pull it free.

'Ray! Ray, I'm stuck!'

It was an absurd situation and a giggle escaped her lips as she imagined Ray running up the stairs, pulling the door open and laughing at how Amber had managed to get herself locked in the bedroom.

Locked?

Amber's gaze drifted from the handle to the old-fashioned metal lock underneath. All the bedrooms had locks on them. Amber assumed it was a traditional thing, that people used to value their privacy enough to want to lock their bedroom doors at night. But she had never seen a key in any one of them, and none of them had ever been locked before.

She couldn't really be locked in. Someone would've had to have taken the key and locked it deliberately. The only other person who set foot in their home, other than the builders, was Ray. And he wouldn't do something so cruel. Unless it was another one of his strange jokes?

Amber thumped the door so hard her fists throbbed, pain exploding like firecrackers across her skin.

'Ray! Ray! I can't open the door!'

Nothing. She was greeted with the same silence as before. Was he there? Had he already left for work?

The television!

Amber lunged for the remote control, snatching it from the bedside table and flicking on the screen, comforted as the sound of human voices drifted into the room, killing the unbearable silence. As she'd hoped, the morning television show displayed a clock in the right hand of the screen.

7:24am.

Shit.

Ray always left for work at seven, without fail. He can't have been gone long, but long enough for Amber to miss him, and for her yells of help to go unnoticed. At least the builders would be in. She had no idea what time they'd get there. They were never there before she left for work and gone by the time she returned. She suspected it would be sometime between nine and ten. She'd have to wait until then before she tried shouting for help again. They'd have tools, be able to get her out.

What about work?

She'd never been late for a shift, and only ever called in sick once when she had food poisoning. Even then she'd phoned in to let them know of her absence, her voice weak from a night of vomiting. Would they be angry at her? She thought of her cheerful boss who was always smiling, even when business was bad, and her kind colleagues with their playful sense of humour. No, they wouldn't be angry. They'd probably laugh and use it as ammo for friendly banter for at least the next year. She smiled at the thought, the ridiculousness of it all making her heart rate slow and her anxiety settle.

She padded into the bathroom, poured herself a cup of water, and settled on the bed, waiting for the workmen to arrive and let her out. Although the niggle about not being able to contact work made her uneasy, and the water was no match for her usual morning tea, she relaxed against the pillows as she enjoyed the extra time in bed with the television on.

But as the day ticked on, her eyes constantly drawn from the main focus of the show to the little clock in the corner, her pulse quickened again and knots formed in her stomach. Had anyone come in? She'd kept the volume low, certain she'd hear the workmen arrive, but there had been no sound from outside her room. The master bedroom was only next door, surely if they were working she'd have heard them?

11.37am.

Maybe they had come in, but they'd kept the noise down? Amber hammered at the door, and then at the adjoining wall separating the two rooms. 'Hello? Is anybody here? The door is stuck! Or it might be locked? Can you come and let me out please?'

Still, nothing.

Amber flopped onto the bed, her stomach growling as hunger punched her gut. It was a Friday, she reminded herself. Ray always finished early on a Friday. He would be home by four. It wasn't too long to wait. He would let her out, hold her. He'd stroke her cheek and say he hoped she hadn't been panicking.

Yes, it would all be fine.

*

The second the clock clicked to four o clock, Amber turned off the television and pressed her ear to the door. But there were no footsteps on the stairs, no shout of *hello!* from the entrance hall. She finished early on Friday's too, the office insisting the weekend started at Friday lunch time, and not a moment later. Ray always called out, knowing she'd be home. So why hadn't he? Where was he?

She kept her ear pressed to the wood until her legs ached and the left side of her face was numb. She was weak and tired, but a noise from downstairs sent a bolt of energy firing through her body and she pounded on the door again.

'Ray! I'm in the bedroom, the door is stuck!'

Sure enough, footsteps echoed from the stairs, the footfalls getting closer as they hurried across the landing. She took a step back just in time, the door flew open and Ray appeared, a line of worry etched into his forehead. 'Amber?'

Relief rushed over her in a wave, and she collapsed into his arms, heaving a sob that caught in her throat and made her hiccup. 'The door was stuck! I couldn't get out, Ray! And the builders....they didn't come...I couldn't get out.'

'Oh, Amber. Your poor thing, you must have been so worried,' he soothed, stroking her hair as she rested her head on his chest. She sniffed, stemming the flow of tears, and the heavy scent of Chinese food wafted towards her. She pulled away and looked down to see a large plastic carrier bag in Ray's hand. 'I got all your favourites. A Friday treat! Turns out you need it more than I realised, my poor little love.' He planted a kiss on the top of her head and Amber's stomach roared with hunger, spurred on by the rich scent of Chow Mien.

'I need to call Will,' she said, remembering that her boss would be wondering why she hadn't shown up for work. 'Have you seen my phone? It's not in here, and I need to call him and apologise for missing work.'

Ray frowned. 'I haven't seen your phone.'

'It was in here last night. I set an alarm, like always.'

'Well then it'll still be in here.'

'It isn't. I've had all day to search, remember?' Amber laughed.

'Look, let's just eat, shall we? You must be starving. I don't suppose there was anything to eat in here was there?'

Amber's stomach growled again. She would find her phone and call Will later. He'd understand. The food was more important. She walked towards the hallway.

'I bought chop sticks,' Ray said, stepping in front of the door. 'I thought we could have a real Friday treat. Eat from the trays in bed with the television on. I don't think I've done anything like that since I was a teenager.'

Amber wanted to say no, to scream that she'd had enough of these four-crappy-walls for one day. But Ray's smile was so expectant, and he was never usually the type to endorse the kind of behaviour that included eating food out of trays, with chop-sticks, in any room other than the dining room. Sometimes, though she tried not to think it, their age gap was hard to ignore. It would be nice, for once, to lounge around like college students.

'That sounds good,' she said, softening. 'But in our bed-room? I've had enough of this one.'

'I don't want to stink our room out with this,' Ray said, raising the bag and wafting the smell towards her again. 'I'm sure you've had enough of this room to last you a life time, but come on. I've been excited about doing this all day. I'll do it properly, like a real student. I'll even sit here in only my pants!'

His smile dominated his features, like a goofy child who'd gotten over excited. He wasn't hiding his teeth, a rare confidence settled in his expression, and Amber's heart swelled, making a pact with her hungry belly to sit down, stop whining, and enjoy the food.

When they finished eating Amber was full and content. Her distress from earlier had vanished as she and Ray sat side by side, in only their underwear, the empty food trays stacked on the bedside table and the tangy aroma of the food still lingering on the air.

Ray swung his legs to the side and climbed out of the bed. 'I've been so worried about you, Amber,' he said, a veil on concern shrouding his face.

'Worried about me? Why?'

'You're not well at the moment. I think you're trying to do too much. Working long hours, busying around the house, meeting up with friends. It's wearing you out.'

Amber laughed. 'What are you on about, Ray? I'm only twenty-six, I should have enough energy for all this for years yet! I'm fine, and I wouldn't change anything for the world. I'm happy.'

'Well, no woman of mine is going to run herself into the ground,' Ray said. 'What sort of life is that? You'd leave. You'd have enough of it all, and you'd leave.'

'Of course I wouldn't,' Amber insisted, her heart rate picking up as she tried to work out what had caused Ray's sudden insecurity. 'I'm happy, don't you understand? Really happy!'

'No, Amber,' Ray said, taking a step outside of the room and holding the door close to his chest. 'No, you're not.'

And as he turned to the hallway, he pulled the door shut behind him and before she had time to process what was going on Amber heard the scrape and click of a key in the lock.

There was no hiding from it this time.

He had locked her in.

Now - Austin

Austin's chest tightened, his heartbeat struggling as the taxi pulled up outside Jasmine's house. For a moment his brain tricked him into believing he was coming home, the warmth of it steadying his breathing and soothing his churning stomach.

But it didn't last, replaced in an instant by the ache of the last time he'd been there. Bags packed, waiting for the bus to take him away. He'd made a promise to his pride; he wouldn't look back. But he couldn't help himself snatching one last glance. He never thought he'd come back.

Jasmine came from a loving and wealthy family, and the passing of her father hit her hard. When the inheritance money came through, and Jasmine had waited sometime for the *stars to realign,* she bought the house. Austin hadn't said it at the time, it wasn't his place, but it seemed excessive. The house boasted three enormous bedrooms and stood detached in a quaint village on the outskirts of Bath. The front of the house led onto the quiet country road separated only by a picket fence and tiny path that greeted the front door. Around the back two acres of garden made up for it. It even had a private, moss-covered road that weaved through the trees and towards the city.

It was not like Jasmine, despite her family's wealth, to be extravagant. When Austin moved from London to be with her, she lived in a modest one-bedroom flat. But she claimed the new house *soothed her soul* and would be peaceful and perfect for her business as a designer of home-made jewellery. It had the space and the light she needed, and the post office was just across the road, so she could ship to her customers. It made more sense to him then.

As Austin and Amber climbed out of the taxi, he tried to put those memories behind him, focusing instead on what he'd say to Jasmine today. He had known her so well once, but he could not gauge how she would react when she found him on her doorstep. Nor could he comprehend what she might say when she realised why he'd shown up. All he knew for certain was he might be sick all over her *Everybody is Welcome Here* doormat.

'It's beautiful,' Amber whispered, one hand on her chest, the other pushing her hair behind her shoulder. 'This is where you bought Alfie?'

Austin had not spared a thought for how overwhelming it would be for Amber to see the house. She bought both hands to her face and peeked at it through her fingers, her eyes fixated on the door as though Alfie might emerge and leap into her arms.

Austin swallowed. 'Yes. He should've been safe here...I...'

His words fell short as the red front door peeled open. Jasmine stepped out, wearing a pair of dungarees over a stripy top, her eyes outlined by smudges of silver eyeshadow. The sound of bangles jangling on her wrist filled the warm air as she folded her arms, and it was so familiar, like a song to welcome him home.

'Austin?' Jasmine raised her eyebrows in a way that meant he couldn't tell if she was surprised or annoyed. Perhaps it was both. Her narrowed eyes bore into him before eyeing up Amber from head to toe. Her face seemed to pale a little when she saw her, and Jasmine ran her fingers through her hair so the dark braids framed her face, almost hiding her. 'If you've come to tell me that you've met someone else, that seems a bit much. A text would've been sufficient. Or, you know, no contact at all,' she said.

Was he imagining it or did she sound annoyed? Jealous?

You kicked me out, remember? Why shouldn't I meet someone else?

'Um no,' Austin said. 'But we...I...well—'

"Spit it out, Austin. I'm cooking."

Austin struggled to find his words, but Amber, like Jasmine, obviously didn't want to hang about. She marched toward the fence and reached her hand to the latch for the gate.

'May I?' she asked.

Jasmine shrugged and Amber lifted the latch to let herself in, so they were stood face to face, Amber only the slightest bit shorter.

'My name's Amber,' she said. 'I'm Alfie's mother. And I'm sure you want nothing to do with me, but I'd really like to visit the place my son was last seen. I don't mean to intrude, but could I come in? Just for a minute or two? Please?'

Jasmine's mouth gaped, and it took a moment before she closed it again, her lips pressed into a thin line. She took a deep breath in, and a slow breath out, a mindfulness technique Austin had seen her use many times.

'Wow. I wasn't really expecting this...' Jasmine's voice raised to a high pitch Austin had never heard her use before. He squirmed at how uncomfortable he was making her when he knew how much she hated to have her peace disrupted.

'No,' Amber said. 'I appreciate it's sudden. I ambushed Austin after work today. I hope you don't mind him bringing me here. I was rather insistent.'

Austin felt a spark of respect for Amber's honesty, and a flash of relief that Jasmine would know he hadn't given in too easily. His heart thumped as his eyes rested on his ex-girlfriend, and the ache he had tried to dull since they broke up swelled.

I miss you, Jasmine. I really bloody miss you.

'I don't think it would be appropriate for you to come in. With respect, Amber, you're a stranger to me. And I'm cooking. I can hardly stop right now to give you a guided tour.'

It wasn't like Jasmine to display such a lack of compassion, and Austin wondered if she'd hardened over the months he'd been gone. Had they been the better half of each other? He'd always thought so. Maybe she wasn't half as good without him, as he wasn't without her.

'Alfie was only ever downstairs,' Austin said, addressing Jasmine directly, but finding it hard to look her in the eye. 'We don't need to see the whole house. Just the living room, the hallway, and the back garden. Please, Jasmine? Then we'll leave you to it, I promise.'

Jasmine's expression remained stony, her features angled into a harshness he had never seen on her before. Or perhaps it was the effect of seeing someone without rose-tinted glasses for the first time. They had been separated for seven months, some of his feelings for her must have died, right?

'Please?' Amber begged.

'I don't know what you're hoping to achieve.'

'Will it really do any harm, Jas...Jasmine?' Austin had to catch himself before he used the abbreviated version of her name. It would be too personal, too intimate.

'Oh, alright, fine!' Jasmine sighed, throwing her hands into the air, her bangles slipping to her elbow. 'I need to finish cooking. You have ten minutes, maximum. Austin, you can show her around. I haven't got time. And don't you go filling my house with negative energy.'

She disappeared into the hallway, leaving the door open behind her, and Austin nodded as Amber took a tentative step forward.

Once inside they were greeted with the aroma of black bean sauce, and the loud fizz of vegetables thrown into hot pans. Jasmine was always one to experiment with exotic cuisine, having spent the best part of her twenties exploring Asia. It was so familiar, the smell, the sound, the way the house had the exact same décor, earthy shades with elephant patterned curtains and cushions. Austin was glad Jasmine had only given them ten minutes, he wasn't sure he could stand it for a second longer.

'I sat him here.' Austin gestured towards the sofa. 'I...I gave him some juice and cookies. I was trying to call Jasmine, I thought she'd know what to do. But I couldn't get through to her, so I called the police. I went out to the hallway to do it,' he explained, leading Amber into the hallway so she could see the distance he'd put between himself and Alfie. 'I didn't go back in and check on him. I don't know why. I guess I felt guilty for doing the one thing he'd told me not to. And when the police arrived I let them in, led them into the living room and Alfie was gone. The backdoor was open though.'

Austin pointed at the door, remembering the *what-ifs* and *if-onlys* that had plagued him.

What if the door had been locked?

If only the handle had been out of reach.

'He probably listened to your phonecall through the wall,' Amber said, her voice cracking into a whisper. 'He would've run away, to avoid the police. That's my fault...I should never...'

She shook her head, swiped at her damp cheeks, and positioned herself to stand a little straighter. 'Where would he have gone from here? Why did no-one see him? I read the articles online, apparently there was a van? Or at least a theory...'

Her words sunk into Austin's thoughts, as the horror of his arrest hammered at the wall he had built to block it out. But, standing in the spot of his downfall, the barrier broke and the memories flooded in, powerful and fast.

'So, you say the boy had been left alone? But you bought him here, rather than calling us out to you in the city?' The officer was a tall, thin woman with a stern voice, angular fringe and straight, pointy eyebrows. She glared at Austin with the contempt of an angry headmistress, her mouth downturned, her pen tapping impatiently against her notepad.

'The boy, Alfie, he didn't want me to call the police. He was adamant,' Austin explained, aware of how weak it sounded out loud.

'And how old did you say he was?'

'Four.'

She turned to her companion, a dumpy man with a friendlier face, even though his frown was as deep as hers. 'And you left that decision to him? The four-year-old?'

'Look, I know it was stupid. I know I should've called you right away. But Alfie is gone now, so can we focus on finding him first, and scold me later?'

The woman flushed an alarming red, so deep she was almost purple. Austin was worried she might be about to explode but decided it best not to mention it.

'Mr. Jackson, I do not need you to tell us how to conduct this investigation. Of course, we want to find the boy, but we have a few more questions to ask you first.'

Austin answered their painstakingly in-depth questions about what Alfie looked like, and if Austin knew the boy's full name. His answers were sparse, frustrating for them and for him, and every unhelpful answer wasted time. All that mattered was that Alfie was lost, alone, and it would be dark soon. They had to find him, fast.

'Can you describe the mother? Because it would seem, from what you've told us, that she is missing too.' The policewoman's eyebrows raised as she said it, her mouth quirking into a sarcastic smile that made Austin want to scream in her face. *I am not a liar!*

Instead, he put his mind to the task of picturing the mother, but he couldn't. When he scoured the crowd for his volunteers, his eyes were always on the children. He had no use for adults in his act, he needed people who were old enough to understand his instructions and participate, but young enough to be amazed by his tricks and not expose the secrets.

'Well, I didn't really look at her, to be honest. I was focused on the boy.'

It wasn't until the two officers exchanged an uncomfortable glance that he realised how bad it sounded.

'Austin Jackson....' The way she said his name sent a shock of electric through his body and when it hit his knees, they weakened, causing him to stumble.

It came so fast, so unexpected. He thought they would conduct a search, and he would join them, out in the lanes and the side streets, peering into bushes and behind trees. Instead, she said his name in the tone that meant he knew exactly what would follow.

'I am arresting you on suspicion of child abduction...you do not have to say anything....'

'Can I see the back garden?' Amber asked. 'I might be able to get some idea of where he would've hidden. Because that must have been his plan. To hide from the police.'

'Yeah, yeah, of course.' Austin was glad for the distraction, and even more relieved to step into the evening air, which was starting to cool and helped ease some of the dizzy tension that had built while he was in the house.

The garden was huge, far larger than Jasmine needed, considering she only ever used a small patch close to the house for her morning yoga. The rest of it was overgrown and unmaintained, the concrete road barely visible beneath a tangle of weeds and grass. The sky was darkening, the dim light from the setting sun enough to keep the garden in view. Though with the orange hue and swirl of gathering clouds resting above the trees, it cast the land into an untamed jungle, wild and foreboding.

'So they think somebody drove up here? And took him?' Amber shuddered.

'It seemed the most likely thing at the time,' Austin said with a shrug. 'Because he's so young, the police didn't think he could've made it very far on foot. They searched every hiding spot, in a mile radius far bigger than the ground he could've covered alone. And they found tyre marks in the mud further down the track. No-one uses this road, it's private land, and not exactly well kept. Not even Jasmine uses it.'

'And the tyre tracks were never linked to anyone?'

'They figured out what it was. It would've been a Mercedes Vito. You know, those big vans? They got it from the tyre markings and the suspected weight of the vehicle, apparently. And they picked up a van on a camera in the next village which matched the description. But that was as far as it went. I don't think it was a strong enough lead.'

Amber moved in a circle, taking in every angle of the wide-open space. Was she imagining her son running through the long grass, his little legs urging him away from the police he so desperately feared? Because Austin could picture it, the boy's dark curly hair bouncing, the folds of anxiety on his face.

Who drove up the track and took him? It was the only explanation for him not being found, so it had to have been what happened. Who was it? And why? And how did they know where to find him?

He hated that van, the people in it, for what they had done.

And he hated himself, for being the one who had made the abduction possible in the first place.

Then - Amber

Amber rubbed her fists, taking it in turns, swapping hands to try and relieve the bruised ache growing behind her skin. She had pummelled the door, screeching and shouting, determined that Ray would become so frustrated with the noise he would be forced to let her out.

What the hell is going on? Why has he done this to me?

Ignoring the pain Amber threw herself against the door again, pounding it with knuckles as red as rust. Each thump bounced off the walls in her confined space, causing the mounting discomfort in her head to swell, pulsating with the beat. Through the fog of agony, she tried to work out what had happened.

Ray had obviously locked her in that morning. When he'd shown up after work, with his big smile and the Chinese takeaway, she'd been so sure it was an accident. That something had perhaps gotten wedged beneath the door, making it impossible for her to budge. But he had done it again. Left her trapped between four rigid walls she had no hope of ever breaking down, despite the manic energy that coursed through her limbs, prompting her to stamp and hit and punch.

No window, no telephone...Amber's stomach clenched, the pressure of it squeezing her heart. Her throat was raw from yelling, her mouth so dry she could no longer talk. She trudged to the ensuite and ran the cold tap, lapping at the water like a starved animal, washing away the bitter salt of the Chow Mein that lingered between her teeth and under her tongue.

The water did nothing to sooth her throat, so Amber staggered to the bed and dropped her aching body onto the sheets. How strange to think only a few hours ago she was sat in that exact spot with Ray, in only their underwear, laughing as they slurped noodles out of plastic trays.

She almost wished she had done something wrong, something to anger or annoy him. At least she'd know how to reverse it, to make up for it. But there was nothing she could think of that could've driven Ray to such obscene behaviour. And even if she had upset him, the reaction would be too extreme.

He's locked me in.

Why had he been so easy to trust? Why hadn't she been more careful? She considered all she knew of him, trying to find a clue, a hint of the man he'd become. He was a Professor of History at the University of Manchester. Smart, sharp, interesting. He had no family other than his father, who lived alone in Portsmouth. His mother had walked out on him as a child. And that was that. He wasn't one for friends or socialising either, he preferred his own company.

Was that it? Had he craved alone time as she often did herself? Had he gotten so fed up with her permanent companionship that he'd been driven crazy? No, that was ridiculous. He had asked her to move in, not the other way around. And if he wanted her gone, wouldn't it be logical to end the relationship, rather than acting the mad man and locking her up to keep her out of his way?

He's breaking the law. What if he never lets me go, because he's scared I'll say something?

Amber shot off the bed and launched her fists into the door again, resuming her yelling. 'Ray, I won't ever speak of this, I promise! No-one will ever know! Just let me out, please!'

Her stamina was strong and she kept it up for almost two hours before retreating into the bedsheets and crying until exhaustion stole her consciousness and plummeted her into sleep.

*

When she woke the following morning Amber's throat was ravaged and raw, a headache was pulsing behind her eyes and a sense of deep dread was rooted in her stomach. She forced herself to sit up, trembling as she did, and through blurred vision she set her sight on the closed bedroom door.

She stood, walked to it, and gave a feeble pull against the handle. It didn't budge. She dropped her gaze from the door and on the floor to her left was a plate of food. A croissant spread thick with blood-red jam, a banana, and a cup of orange juice, had been carefully placed on the carpet. Ray must've put it there while she slept.

Amber resisted the urge to hurtle the food across the room in rage. She considered not eating it. She was not his pet, would not lap up what he left out for her like a grateful and obedient dog. He wouldn't let her starve to death. He wouldn't have bought her food if he didn't want to keep her alive. If she refused to eat, he would have to let her out.

She sat on the edge of the bed, arms folded in private defiance. But even as she did, her stomach growled and lurched, and each time it grumbled her eyes were drawn back to the small plate. She decided, at least for the time being, to give in. The plate was light as she lifted it, polystyrene, as was the cup. Odd. Was she no longer good enough for china plates and metal forks? Why hadn't he served her meal on proper crockery?

Because then I'd have a weapon.

The realisation that Ray had thought it all through made Amber's stomach roll, and she dropped the breakfast and rushed to the toilet to be sick. The acidic bile of her vomit scorched her sore throat, sending a wave of tears streaming from her eyes, the droplets plopping into the toilet bowl.

Ray had planned everything, it was more than a mere moment of madness. He wanted to entrap her, he'd made sure she had nothing she could use to escape. Amber squeezed her eyes closed as she vomited again.

*

That evening Amber sat with her ear to the door until the thud of Ray's footsteps on the stairs filled the silence. When she was certain he was approaching the room she stood, took two steps back, and waited.

As soon as the door opened Amber launched at him. Her slender frame hit Ray with a sharp thud, and she yelped as something hot spilt down her front. Ray shoved her backwards and stepped into the room, locking the door behind him and pocketing the key.

Amber fell onto the bed in despair, her failed escape obliterating the last of her energy. She wiped at her t-shirt, which was streaked with gravy, and took in the mess of chicken and vegetables that littered the carpet.

'I'm sorry I pushed you, Amber,' Ray said, stooping to gather the food back onto the plate. 'But what exactly did you think you were doing?'

'What was I doing?' Amber roared, finding some strength beneath her anguish. 'You've had me locked in this room for two days now! What the hell do you think you're doing? This is inhumane, it's illegal, and it's—'

'Oh, Amber.' Ray placed an arm around her with such tenderness she almost believed it had all been a mistake, a misunderstanding. 'What you did just now, it's not normal. You could've hurt us both. That's why I must keep you safe in here. Until you start behaving with some sanity, it's the only way.'

'Excuse me? Sanity? You're the insane one! What the hell are you playing at, locking me in here?'

'It's for your own safety,' he said, giving her a gentle squeeze and shaking his head, his mouth quirked into a sympathetic smile. 'When you're better it won't have to be like this.'

As he spoke a terrifying truth settled over Amber, like a glaze of black ice, a hidden danger lurking, waiting to catch someone unawares. Ray was crazed. Had there been signs, before? What had she missed? She took in his expression, tried to find the madness behind the face she had trusted. She settled on his eyes, the dazzling blue that made them so special. Suddenly, those husky-dog-eyes were no longer endearing, but dangerous. Unpredictable. So sharp, she feared he might snap at any moment.

I can escape this. I just have to be smart. Don't wind him up. Keep him calm.

'Okay,' she said, offering what she hoped looked like a grateful smile. 'I'll behave. And when I'm better, you'll let me out?'

She spoke with the caution of a hostage, every fibre in her body taught, ringing like the wires of a bomb.

'Of course, my love,' he said, kissing her on the head.

He stood and left the room, while Amber sobbed to the sound of the key in the lock.

*

In the days that followed, Amber behaved as though what Ray was doing was perfectly understandable. When he entered the room, she sat away from the door and made no attempt to lunge at him or the gap that would lead to her escape.

She accepted her food, and ate it with plastic cutlery, knowing a hunger strike would only encourage Ray's belief that she needed to be locked away and taken care of. She asked about his day, simpered to him like a good girlfriend, and patiently, painfully, awaited the moment he would say she was free to go.

Now - Austin

'You were arrested,' Amber said, wrapping her arms around her waist with a shiver. 'But they let you go.'

'Yeah. They did.'

'Why? I mean...I'm glad they did, obviously. But what made them drop the case against you? I couldn't find much information about that online.'

Austin cringed, his stomach tightening. The police had hounded him for days, asked him impossible questions, accused him of unthinkable crimes. 'The van couldn't be linked to me,' he explained, his body still fraught with tension.

Not a day had passed when Austin hadn't weakened with relief that the police were able to rule him out, that they could not prove he was guilty of anything more than making stupid decisions. And not a day passed when he didn't heave at how close he'd come to being imprisoned for a crime he did not commit. Though on the darkest days, he often felt it would've been justice, a small mercy. His punishment for being a senseless idiot. Why should he walk free when Alfie was still lost?

'I didn't even have a vehicle of my own,' Austin continued. 'I shared Jasmine's car, and the tracks didn't match. For a while they assumed I was working with whoever owned the van. That I was part of a bigger plan, and whoever was in the van was in on it with me. But they checked my phone records. There were no communications to match their theory, and the only calls I'd made that day were to Jasmine. They had no choice but to let me go.'

'I'm so sorry you went through all that.' Amber shifted on her feet, in the shoes that were so oversized he'd tease her for resembling a clown if the situation weren't so serious.

'Hmm,' Austin mumbled, aware his turmoil was no match for hers. Yet there was no denying it had been the scariest time of his life. The police let him go, but he was still pursued by the press, by the threatening post from people who refused to accept he wasn't guilty and hated him even more for getting away with it.

It's no wonder Jasmine couldn't hack it. I'd have chucked me out as well.

'I really thought I'd feel something here,' Amber sighed, squinting once more through the faded light and taking in the vast garden surrounding her. 'Like, I thought I'd just see some-thing, anything, that the police had missed. Something only a mother could notice.'

'I'm sorry. But remember, this was only ever a starting point. Where do we go from here?' He still couldn't quite believe he'd agreed to help her, and the hopelessness of it all flared brighter as the evening sky grew darker.

'I suppose it makes sense to go to the abbey. That afternoon, everything that happened, I remember it but it's hazy. I...I need to go back, I think. To try and make more sense of it all.'

Austin's heart clenched. When he agreed to help her he'd assumed she had a solid plan, a logical list of places Alfie could be, people he could be with. But instead she seemed intent on revisiting the places that haunted his past, dredging up memories that would hurt more than heal.

But what could he say? This whole situation was on him wasn't it? He was duty-bound to help her, and no matter how indignant he'd been at the start, there was no turning back. He was due to work tomorrow, a phone call would need to be made to his boss to ask for some last-minute leave.

'Listen, Amber.' Austin picked his words with caution, offering them to her with care. 'It's almost dark already. You won't get a proper sense of the place this late. It won't be how you remember it. And I've got things I need to do. I need to call my boss, take some time off work. Why don't we call it a day for now, get some rest and then pick up again tomorrow?'

Amber fidgeted, her jaw clenched, her thin arms pocked with cold as they trembled beneath her thin t-shirt. Austin sensed her desire to say no with such potency it was as though she'd really said it. But she was tired too. He could see it in the dark beneath her eyes, the way her face kept contorting as she stifled yawns.

'I suppose you're right,' she murmured.

'You're welcome to stay at mine,' said Austin. He closed his mouth at once, unsure of why he'd offered without thinking about it first, but he could hardly withdraw the hospitality. He shrugged, as an afterthought. 'If that's not too weird.'

'That's really kind. Thank you.'

It will be weird though, won't it? Because this whole bloody situation is weird.

They walked side by side through the garden and towards Jasmine's home. Austin remembered there was a side path that would lead them out to the front without having to pass through the house again. Jasmine would appreciate that.

Austin called for a taxi, and between tiredness and awkwardness he found no words to fill the silence while he and Amber waited.

'Austin!' Jasmine appeared from the front door and beckoned him, waving her hand. 'A quick word?'

Amber stood back as Austin walked up the path to Jasmine's house for the second time that day. It was as painful as the first.

'I can't believe you're getting involved in all this again, Austin,' she groaned, shaking her head so hard her braids whipped across her shoulders. 'Can't you just leave it?'

'I can hardly leave it. It's my fault it happened. I should never have taken Alfie away from the town like that.'

'It happened. We'd all do things differently if we had the intuition to see how things would turn out. I know you wish you'd foreseen what would happen, but that doesn't make it your fault. Do you really think he's going to be found now, after all these months? By you and the woman who left him on his own in the first place?'

'She didn't leave him. She was taken.'

'What? Taken where? By who?' Jasmine straightened, her hands resting on her hips so her elbows pointed outward, sharp and accusing.

'She hasn't given me all the details yet. But she was taken, she didn't just leave Alfie. She wasn't neglecting him.'

Jasmine squeezed her eyes closed, bringing her fingers to her face and pinching the bridge of her nose. Her fingers were, as always, lined with so many of her hand-made rings it was a wonder she could even bend them, and her long, sharp nails were painted a deep crimson. 'If she hasn't told you all the details,' she said, raising an eyebrow, 'then you are basing her version of events on nothing. She could be lying, have you thought of that? She could be a mad woman. She could be anyone.'

'She's not anyone! She's Alfie's mother.'

Jasmine scanned Austin's face with the glare of a panther, and he stared her out, even though the intimacy of their locked eyes made his pulse race. 'Just be careful, Aus,' she whispered, retreating into the hallway and pushing the door shut in his face.

*

That night Austin lay in bed unable to sleep. He'd offered to take the couch, but Amber insisted she'd be happy there. It felt ungentlemanly to take the bed, but she refused to swap.
Exhaustion rolled over his body in waves, pressing his limbs into the sheets and an itch into his eyes. No matter how hard he tried, he could not shut off his brain, could not distract his thoughts.

It was odd, knowing there was somebody else in his flat, someone asleep just across the hallway. A stranger. Jasmine's words were ringing in his ears, rattling around his brain and shaking it whenever it tried to succumb to sleep.

Be careful, Aus.

Was it the warning keeping him alert? Or the tender way in which she'd said his name, using the abbreviation only she ever used. *Aus.* She always used to shorten it, and he loved that she did, the warmth that could flood that one syllable whenever it rolled from her lips was unreal. She thought she was particularly funny, when they first met, by calling him *The Wizard of Aus.*

'Because you're a magician and you're from Australia...get it?'

Such a beautiful, intelligent woman yet such a dorky sense of humour. Austin smiled in the darkness, remembering the times when her voice had been full of laughter and love, and not the quipped, sharp tones he had encountered earlier. Up until her warning of course, when she'd softened for one tiny, wonderful moment.

Be careful, Aus.

The words played on a loop in his mind, as he finally drifted off.

Then - Amber

Amber no longer turned on the television, and so she lost track of how many weeks had passed. It hurt too much, watching the world carry on as normal while she was confined to the suffocating room that had become her prison.

Why was no-one looking for her? What had happened to her job? She pictured Will calling her, ringing and ringing and wondering why she hadn't shown for work. In her fantasies, Will grew concerned and called the cops. She envisioned the door flying off its hinges as the police bust it down. But it hadn't happened yet.

Ray had taken her phone, she was sure of it. He must've fed Will a story to make him accept Amber's absence without question. Ray was smooth, articulate. Will would never question him. Had Ray done the same to her friends? Loneliness burrowed an ache into her chest when she considered all the people who might miss her. She could count each one of them on her fingers without the need to raise a second hand. If only her mother were still alive. Amber closed her eyes and bit down hard on her lip. She could not think of her mum. It was too painful.

Ray visited her every day and in the early stages it did nothing to abate her solitude. But as the weeks wore on she craved his visits, horrified at the way she longed for his company, a human presence to break her isolation. He treated her as he always had, like she was the only woman in the world and he would do anything to please her. He asked what she wanted to eat and insisted nothing she chose would be too much hassle. She still ordered things that were easy to cook, things she knew he liked too. She was determined to appear compliant, to win his trust in the hope he might finally unlock the door.

During the day, while she awaited Ray's evening visit, Amber's brain sat numb and inactive. Without the television to distract her the days dragged, and her imagination taunted her with daydreams of all the wonderful things she would be doing if she weren't trapped. Some days she did nothing but sleep, too afraid to face the long hours awake. Others, she screamed until her throat was swollen and sore. Sometimes she kicked the door until blood seeped beneath her toenails and her toes swelled like ugly, purple grapes. On the darkest days, she stared at a wall and willed her life to end.

It had to stop. She could not let herself succumb to the bitter and terrifying voices. She needed something to distract her, something to focus on besides her futile escape plans. One evening, she plucked up the courage to ask Ray for her watercolours.

'Of course you can have your paints, my darling,' Ray said, as though he were the most reasonable man in the world. 'What a lovely idea! I'll bring everything in for you tomorrow.'

*

Amber fizzed with anticipation the next day, and the wonderous power of hope thrust everything under a light that killed some of the darkness. Electric currents coursed through her veins, because asking for the watercolours was so much more than an innocent request to paint. It was all part of an escape plan.

The small bedroom in which she was imprisoned was sparse of furniture. All she had was the bed, the heavy bedside cabinets, and the solid oak desk. There was no stool or chair, there had been no need for one before. Ray would have to bring her something to sit on while she painted, and when he did, he would be handing her a weapon. She had no desire to hurt him, despite it all, but if she could throw him off balance for long enough to run it'd give her the head start she needed.

Not only that but, unless the worse had happened, the bank card for her private account was still hidden at the bottom of her paint bag. She could think of no reason why Ray would ever have searched through it and she'd kept the card tucked into the folds of a pallet case. Ray would undoubtedly chase her, when she made a run for it, so she wouldn't have time to search the house for her belongings. But if she had the card, she would at least have something.

It has to work. Please, please, let it work.

*

When Ray bought in her paints she thanked him, planting a kiss on his cheek and beaming as though she'd never been happier. She was determined to make him feel loved, to ensure he had no inclination she would try to escape.

She clutched the bag in her hands, comforted by the rough hessian of the handles and the chalky scent of the paints that drifted up from it.

'Could I have a chair for the desk please?' she asked, trying a small unassuming smile.

'No, Amber,' Ray said, frowning in such a way that deep creases formed across his forehead and under his eyes. 'Don't be ridiculous. I'm trying to keep you safe, and you're doing extremely well. Don't ruin it.'

With that, he left the room and slammed the door.

Amber stood for a moment, shell-shocked, devastated that her plan had not worked. She only hoped that he thought her request innocent and had not been aware of her ulterior motive. She would not cope if all her fake smiles had been for nothing.

With trembling hands Amber rifled through the bag, dis-lodging brushes, until she came across her pallet case. When her searching fingers collided with the smooth plastic of her bank card she heaved a sigh of relief so intense she was almost sick.

*

Ray's visits became more frequent. He joined her for break-fast as well as her evening meal, and she was grateful for the interaction, enamoured by his charm and intellect. After he'd gone, she would shake her head free of his manipulations, furi-ous that she'd been sucked in. Her mind sagged under the weight of confusion, as to why she was not reacting to him with the pungent hate he deserved.

It's because you want to escape. It's all part of the trick. You don't love him anymore, Amber. You don't. You don't.

When several more weeks had passed, Ray made a request that stunned her.

'I want us to start making love again,' he said, his voice deep and solemn. 'But only if you want to. I know you might feel a little trapped against your will in here, even though it's in your best interests. But I will never make you do anything you don't want.'

It took all her strength not to scream at him, hit him, push him away. She still had to play the sweet, compliant girlfriend and so, with bile in her throat she declined with a *sorry* and a self-conscious smile.

True to his word Ray accepted her rejections with patience and understanding. He never once pushed her, keeping several days between each time he asked. She wondered if it was a test. Was saying *yes* the way to win him over, to make him believe she loved him and could be trusted enough to be set free? If so, then he was forcing her whether he felt he was or not. She would not be emotionally blackmailed and so she kept her fierce resolve, her rejections forming a routine.

No, Ray.

I'm sorry, Ray.

Smile.

But to her horror, as time went on, Amber found herself longing to be held, for the feel of human contact, skin to skin. She had loved Ray once, hadn't she? Did she still, despite it all?

And one evening, she relented, and they made passionate love, her body tingling to his touch.

They continued to sleep together. Ray initiated it daily, but Amber only said yes when she wanted to. Some days she was too hollow, the ache of her imprisonment making her too depressed to even sit up in bed or go to the bathroom. Other days she was so afraid of being numb that she craved his touch, craved anything that might make her feel alive. Ray always accepted her rejections, and on the days she did agree, he made love to her with a tenderness that made her wonder if she would ever stop loving him, no matter how long he kept her locked up.

Months passed, and Amber still hoped their passion would ignite Ray's decision to free her. It was only when he bought her a pregnancy test that she realised his motives were about so much more than sexual desire.

'You're trying to get me pregnant!' she wailed, throwing the plastic stick in his face.

She was mortified by the prospect and ashamed that she hadn't considered the possibility. Their unprotected sex was bound to lead there eventually, wasn't it?

'Would that be so bad, my love?' Ray asked, picking up the kit and handing it to her as though she'd not just launched it at his head. 'Imagine, a baby! We'd be a proper family.'

A proper family.

Surely he wouldn't keep her prisoner once she had a baby to raise? Perhaps that was the key after all. He wanted her, wanted them, to be a family. A baby in exchange for her freedom.

But every test, and Ray bought her one weekly, came up negative. It was both a blessing and a curse she thought as she sat holding the stick with shaking hands. One part of her was relieved, because whether Ray let her go or not, it was no normal life. How could she give a child to a father who did such heinous things? It wasn't right. And yet the motherly instinct in her yearned for the baby she couldn't conceive. Why couldn't she? She was only twenty-six. She should be able to fall pregnant with ease, shouldn't she?

After what she estimated to be the twelfth failed test, Ray let out a sigh so heavy it tore from his throat like a scream.

'It's not my fault,' Amber sobbed, still clutching the stick, the single line that indicated a negative result leering up at her, mocking her.

'I know, my darling.' Ray pulled her to him and kissed her on top of her head. 'I know it's not.'

She stared into his crystal eyes, at his soft plump limps, her emotions once again tearing her, pulling her between love and resentment, safety and fear.

'Get some sleep,' Ray insisted, giving her another kiss. 'We're going out tomorrow.'

Now - Austin

The post clattered through the letterbox, landing with a soft thud on the floor. It was such a normal sound, familiar, and as Austin lifted the teabag from his mug it felt, for a moment, like any other morning.

He pictured himself adding a small splash of milk to his tea, burning his tongue on his first eager sip. He imagined the cycle to work, pleasant now Spring had set in, the only enjoyable part of his day before he had to spend eight long hours tapping his fingers against the keyboard. The mundane rattle of keys that had become his routine.

But no, he reasoned, lifting out a second teabag from a second mug. It was not any other morning. Because he was making tea for two, and the small flat was filled with the unfamiliarity of a human presence that wasn't his own.

Had it been a good idea, inviting Amber to stay? All they'd shared was a few hours of awkward discussion, some answered questions, but far more unanswered. Brought together by the tragedy of a situation neither of them could have predicted nor stopped. He supposed Alfie's disappearance linked them in a unique way, one they couldn't escape. Yet they were still alien to one another.

But people opened their doors to strangers all the time, after boozy nights in bars, or enthusiastic first dates. And what was the worst Amber could do? Hurt him? He doubted she was capable of it, her body was skeletal, stripped of any muscle. Would she steal from him? It seemed unlikely, and he owned little of any worth anyway.

Besides, he owed the poor woman far more than a place to sleep. She said she didn't blame him for what happened to Alfie, but Austin still blamed himself, had always blamed himself. It was torture, the sheer number of alternative scenarios his imagination could conjure. The *what ifs* and *if onlys* were endless, with every single option far more rational and sensible than the one he'd chosen.

Kinder minds, like the one belonging to his friend and boss, Sam, shot down Austin's overthinking. 'Hindsight is a wonderful thing, Austin,' he asserted whenever the guilt dragged itself from inside Austin's heart to behind his eyes.

But hindsight was not so bloody wonderful when every single possible outcome would have been a viable thing to do, and the only stupid decision was the one he'd made. He'd always prized himself on being a clever man, a fast thinker, quick witted. All the traits that made him a good magician. But the decision to take Alfie away from the city that day, to not call the police until it was too late, had made those traits disappear. One puff of smoke and that was it, gone. Austin no longer possessed the skills he needed to perform, and he no longer believed in magic, not even the trivial kind in his tricks.

Austin sipped at his tea, glancing at the cup he'd made for Amber. He hovered in the kitchen, not sure if it was appropriate to knock on the living room door and take Amber's in to her. He didn't want to startle her in the vulnerable state of sleep.

Stalling for time, and hoping she'd emerge by herself before long, Austin slouched into the hallway to retrieve the post. It was a modest pile, another nod to the normal day he might've had if he'd not called Sam to ask for last minute leave. He picked up the envelopes and groaned at the common sight of bills and bank statements. He flicked through them all until the very last piece of post, which was not the same as the others.

A scrap of paper, folded in half, with no envelope and no address. Austin peeled it open, the paper stiff, crackling as he prised it apart. Glued to the page were individually sized letters, cut from a newspaper, like an old-fashioned ransom note. Why go to so much effort to hide handwriting, when the digital age meant letters could be typed and printed for anonymity? The time and care that had gone into cutting and sticking the letters was strange. But the words, the sentences the letters formed, were even more bizarre.

Alfred is my son. I am his only living parent. Back off, Amber. He is mine.

'Morning.'

Her voice from behind him made Austin flinch, and he looked away from the note, re-focusing his vision on Amber. Her eyes were red-ringed and puffy, her cheeks flushed pink, her pale brown hair knotted. She looked so beat he considered ripping the note in two and pretending it had never arrived. But he couldn't, of course he couldn't. His palms prickled with sweat, and the tightness growing in his chest wasn't something he'd be able to ignore. He had to know what the note meant, even if he wouldn't like the answer. Could he have really made another stupid mistake? Had inviting someone back to his home been another example of how his naivety manifested in kindness, only to betray him?

'What's this?' he asked, handing her the paper. He had no reason not to show her. It had been meant for her after all, it was little use to him. It made no sense.

She took the note from him, biting her lip. Within seconds Amber shrieked, throwing her hands over her face as the note fluttered to the floor, landing so that the words were still facing up at her, accusing.

'Amber? I don't understand what it means?' Austin pushed. His heart was pounding, the sharp beats pulsing in his neck and ears. Why was she so afraid? The note had been posted through his door, and he wanted, needed, to know who'd posted it.

Amber lowered her hands, revealing ghostly white skin that emphasised the deep darkness beneath her eyes. 'He knows I'm here.'

'Who does? What's going on, Amber? What does it mean?'

She flinched as he yelled, and he stepped away to give her more space, afraid of frightening her further. But it was hard to stay calm because her face was etched with fear, and a sickening dread was invading his own senses.

What the bloody hell have I gotten myself in to?

Amber's eyes lifted to meet his, staring stock still, unlike the trembling that consumed the rest of her body.

'Alfie...' her voice caught as she said his name. 'Alfie isn't my son.'

In the depths of Amber's confession, Austin's mind fixated on the reasons he had taken her in. The tragedy of her loss, of which he felt so accountable. The renewed possibility of finding the boy, which filled him with hope, the chance of a life that was absolved, at least a little, of guilt. And of course, the simple factor of human decency, of honest, humble compassion for a frightened woman who had nowhere to go.

But she'd lied to him. Deceived him.

And if she wasn't Alfie's mother, then who the hell was she?

Then - Amber

Amber hadn't slept, afraid that if she wasn't awake when Ray collected her, he would change his mind and the opportunity would be gone.

Where is he going to take me?

It didn't really matter. She had no intention of being at Ray's side for any longer than she had to be. Out was out. Out was freedom. Because nothing, not a thing in the world, was going to stop her from running from him as soon as she got the chance.

True to this word, Ray entered the room early the next morning. He was wearing smart blue jeans and a white polo top. It was his relaxed look, his weekend style. She had lost track of the days.

Amber was also dressed in comfortable clothes, her t-shirts and leggings somehow baggier than they'd ever been, despite her inactivity. She perched on the edge of the bed, ready to leave. She'd scrubbed at her face, as though the warm water could wash away the darkness resting below her eyes. Her secret bank card was tucked into her sock, creating an uncomfortable rectangle that bit at her skin when she walked, but she didn't care. When she escaped, she would need it.

'I'd like you to hold my hand, please,' Ray said, reaching out to her with long, thin fingers. 'You're still not entirely safe on your own.'

She held herself still, softening her expression to prevent giving away her irritation. If she refused to take his hand he might walk out and lock the door, and she couldn't spend another moment in that room. She reached out to him, lacing her fingers between his, trying not to shudder at his touch. 'Where are we going?'

'It's a surprise. Come.'

They stepped out into the hallway and Amber almost collapsed with the shock of it.

I'm actually leaving!

The air was light, not like the stagnant heavy atmosphere of the spare room. They walked down the stairs, heading towards the front door. Amber had to take small steps to steady her trembling legs.

Ray opened the door with one hand, the other still gripping Amber's with a painful pressure. The wind rushed in, the outside breeze swirling around her. She was sure if it weren't for Ray's grip she would've been whisked away. She squinted into the brightness, lifting her free hand to shield her eyes. Had the sun always been so bright? Her eyes stung as the light lashed at them in sharp scratches.

'Beautiful day for a walk,' Ray beamed at her.

When her eyes adjusted, she saw that he was right. She'd been trapped inside that awful room for so long the seasons had changed from winter to spring. The gentle wind carried the sweet scent of cherry blossom, and the sun was beating down, making the gravelled driveway glitter. She still needed to squint, but what she really wanted was to open her eyes wide and take in every tiny detail. The cornflower blue of the sky, the sunshine yellow of early daffodils. Tears swelled, obscuring her vision even more. She blinked them away.

'It is,' she whispered. 'It's so beautiful.'

She squeezed Ray's hand, determined to show him she was happy and calm. If he trusted her, he might loosen his hold, and she would be able to wriggle free.

As they walked the gravel crunched beneath their feet. Amber's senses were heightened, she could distinguish every bird song, pick out the scent of every flower, see the dancing specs of pollen on the air. All the while her heart raced, causing her breath to come out in short, sharp gasps which she attempted to mute, aware of Ray's tightening grip.

Ray directed her out of the driveway and onto the lane that led from his house to the main road. The only other thing along the way, besides from fields and farmland, was an old stable building, bricked up and presumably empty. They approached it and walked around to the back, where a large wooden door stood proud against the withered brick.

'Why are we here?' Amber asked, a tingling growing in her fingertips. She hoped Ray wouldn't notice the sweat that had gathered in her palms.

'I own this building,' Ray said. 'I had it converted.'

Converted it into what? A prison?

That was it. She would not be locked away again. Amber writhed, yanking her hand, trying to prise it from Ray's fingers. She pulled her body, legs poised to run, and launched herself away from him.

She didn't budge.

Ray's grip tightened, and he bought his other hand up to snatch hold of her arm, his fingers pinching the skin beneath her thin jacket.

'Let me go,' she whispered, tears flooding her cheeks. 'Please. This is wrong. You can't lock me in there. Please!'

'Lock you in there?' Ray raised an eyebrow. 'I told you that you weren't well, Amber, and you're only proving my point. Why would I lock you in there? Someone lives here. We're visiting.'

'Visiting?' Amber panted, her body weak and warm from her attempt to escape. 'Visiting who? What is this? Ray, please, take me back. Take me back!'

She never thought she'd beg to go back to the spare room but as the outbuilding loomed over her, pocked grey stone towering into the cloudless sky, it seemed the better option. Less isolated, somehow.

'Quit making a fuss, for goodness sake,' Ray snapped. He knocked on the door and it flew open within seconds.

In the doorway, her face flushed, stood a young woman. She had sheets of dark hair that fell to her waist and a pixie-like face, smooth skin, and a pointed chin. She was so young, Amber suspected she was no more than twenty.

Who is she? Why is she here?

'Ray! Is this her?' The girl wrinkled her face at Amber, losing some of her beauty as her features squashed together.

'This is her,' Ray said. 'Get in, Amber.'

She couldn't tell if he pushed her, or if she simply obeyed, but she found herself stepping into the brick building as Ray followed and closed the door behind them.

Inside, Amber was stunned to find the converted stable was in fact a beautiful little home. It had the style of an old cosy farmhouse, though it was all open plan. The kitchen floor was tiled with slate the colour of marmalade, the appliances were rustic in image but clearly modern and expensive. The room was framed by thick wooden beams and though there were no windows, a skylight flooded the open space with natural light. Amber gazed at it, her heart clenching in jealousy when she considered her windowless existence. If she lived in the stable, she'd sit in that square patch of light all day, letting the sun soak into her skin. What was such a home doing out there? She could only assume Ray had converted it and then rented it out to the girl.

But why does he want me to meet her?

'Amber, this is Sarah. It might be best if you do the more in-depth introduction, Sarah. I need to go out.'

'Okay, Ray. See you when you get back!' Sarah blew a kiss, her green eyes peering up beneath dark lashes.

Amber stared at Ray as he headed to the door. He said nothing to her, and she had just dared to hope again when she heard the familiar click of a key in the lock. The metallic clunk sent a weight dropping into her stomach. Ray was gone and she was still trapped. At least this time, she wasn't alone.

'What's going on?' Amber rounded on the young woman. 'He's locked us in!'

'No, Amber,' the girl said, her whole demeanour stiffened in Ray's absence. She folded her arms across her body and lifted her chin into the air. 'He's locked *you* in.'

They stared at each other for a while, Amber too shocked to speak, Sarah with bitter eyes and a smug smile. She wore a dress as tight as her expression, it clung to her tiny frame, outlining the subtle curve of her breasts and hips. Who was she? Amber was so deprived of company the girl's beauty overwhelmed her, as though she were a mirage. She resisted reaching out and touching the tip of her finger to the girl's smooth cheek.

'You need to help me,' Amber pleaded, shattering the silence between them. 'He's been keeping me locked up in his house. I've got to escape him. I've been trapped!'

'You're not trapped, woman. Fuck, don't be so over dramatic.'

Amber's head snapped back as though she'd been slapped. 'I've been locked in a single room of his house for months! *Locked in.* Do you have a phone? We need to call the police!'

'No, we don't.' Sarah shook her head. 'Ray is looking after us. That's what he does. He's a good man.'

'What do you mean looking after us?' Amber shuddered as a bead of sweat trickled down her back.

'I'm his girlfriend.'

What the hell is going on?

'No,' Amber said. 'You're not.'

'I am. We both are. People were made with enough love in them for more than one person, you know. I know that know. Ray loves us both, and he's looking after us both.'

Amber clasped a hand to her stomach as jealousy burned green in her heart. But as she took in Sarah's home, a prettier prison, but a prison all the same, she knew she was wrong to feel it. She didn't *want* to be Ray's one and only, the man was a monster. And if Amber wasn't his only victim, then she had even more reason to act. If she wanted to save herself, she had to save Sarah too. They had to work together, not against one another.

'Sarah, I know you understand what I'm going through. Because you're trapped too, aren't you? You're trapped in here.'

'I'm not trapped,' Sarah said, unfolding her arms and placing them on her hips. 'Ray only locked the door because *you're* here. Usually, he leaves me a key.'

'What?' Hope raised in Amber like a rocket blasting into the sky, making her head spin and her vision fill with sparks of light. 'But then you need to leave, Sarah! Why would you stay?'

'Because Ray loves me, and I love him. I'm not safe out there, but I am here. It's so kind of him, to offer me this home. I don't pay for a thing, he takes care of it all. He used to keep it locked, when we first met. But he trusts me now, he knows I'm not going anywhere.'

Her lips pucker into a smile and Amber wouldn't have been surprised if she'd stuck out her tongue, like a child. *He loves me more that you,* she pictured Sarah saying. *He trusts me!*

'Sarah, listen to me. This isn't normal, what he's doing to you. You are safe, you'd be safe in the outside world. Can't you see that what he's doing is wrong? How long have you been here?'

'Two years.'

Amber's skin prickled, plunged ice cold. Sarah had been there, in the stable, the evening Amber met Ray in the bar. Sarah had been there while Amber and Ray jetted off to Rome, while

Amber moved into the house up the lane. And if she'd been there for two years, was it likely Amber would ever be set free?

But Sarah's not locked in anymore. She has a key.

'Do you ever leave though, even for a little while? Surely there's other places you want to go?'

Sarah wriggled her shoulders, her age showing in the teenage way she shrugged off the question. Her dark eyebrows lowered into a moody scowl. 'I don't need to leave. I have everything I want. I mean, it'd be nice to live in Ray's house with him. But whatever. He comes here most nights now anyway.'

Amber's stomach clenched. All those hours she'd spent hammering on the door, battering the floorboards, trying to stir a reaction in him, to annoy him enough he let her go. And most of the time he hadn't even been in, had popped down the lane for a cosy night in with a girl who looked half his age. She forced herself not to show her bitterness. She had to convince Sarah there was more to her life, a reason to leave.

'Come on, Sarah. You can't tell me there's nowhere you'd rather be! What about a beach in Spain? Or a showering under a waterfall in Bali? Or...I don't know...Disney World!' Amber tried to inject her voice with friendly laughter, but it sounded more like she was about to cry.

'Bath,' Sarah said, her expression suddenly softer, her green eyes warming to the colour of a summer meadow.

Amber was surprised by the answer. 'Bath?'

'Yeah. I went once, with my dad. I was only twelve, but my sister was at university there, so we went to visit her. I loved it. The Roman streets, the pretty clothes in the shop windows. Dad let me buy some gorgeous dresses while we there. And earrings.

That was before his memory went. Before he became distant and weird and...anyway. Whatever.'

'But if you leave, you could go back there! Wouldn't that be amazing?'

'No. I know what you're trying to do, and it won't work. You want me out of the picture, so you can have Ray all to yourself. But it's not going to happen.'

Amber spluttered, failing to find the words to express how little she wanted Ray at all.

'Do you know why he bought you here?' Sarah asked, tilting her head so her black hair rippled over her shoulders in waves.

Amber shook her head.

'Because I needed a friend. I've been excited to meet you. But now I'm not sure. You're being so horrid about Ray, and I don't want to be friends with someone so ungrateful and negative.'

'Sarah...' Amber was about to interrupt, to insist again on how wrong Ray was, and how Sarah was delusional. But she stopped herself. Sarah's glassy green eyes shone when she spoke about Ray, her love and admiration for him emitted from her every movement, every word. Two years was a long time to be confined to one small building, and Ray had obviously done a good job of convincing Sarah she needed him. That delusion would not break so easily, with a few hurried words from Ray's other-lover.

Other-lover.

Amber bit back the bile that rose to her mouth. She had to be smarter, smarter than Ray. And she knew how to do it. 'I'm sorry, Sarah,' she said, taking a tentative step forward. 'It would be lovely to have a friend. I get lonely too. Would I get to see you often?'

'Yes, I think so. Do you really want to be friends?'

'Yes, I really do. I was rude about Ray, you're right. He's taking care of us, and that's all that matters, isn't it?'

Sarah nodded hard, flashing Amber a dazzling smile. Her beauty was devastating, and it made Amber wince to think of Ray having such a hold over someone so delicate.

'So, that's that then?' Amber asked, holding out her pinkie finger like she used to as a child. 'Friends?'

'Friends.' Sarah grinned, hooking Amber's finger with her own and giving it a shake.

Amber returned her smile. She had a purpose now, not only to save herself, but to save Sarah too. And if Ray trusted Sarah enough to leave her with a key then it would all be okay. Amber would build Sarah's trust and gently she would help her to see the true horror behind Ray's actions, help her realise it was wrong.

And once she managed that, Sarah would find the confidence to leave one evening and run to the police, setting herself, and Amber, free.

Now - Austin

'What do you mean, Alfie isn't your son? What the hell is this, some kind of sick prank?'

Austin could've screamed with frustration, but he held it in, clenching his fists as his jaw tightened. What was he thinking, inviting a stranger into his home? He'd let himself down again with his poor bloody hindsight, and crappy decisions. What if she was a journalist after all? The thought alone made his mouth dry. She could even be a detective, trying to trick him, to find the truth they thought they knew, that they'd never managed to prove before.

'He's not biologically my son,' Amber said, speaking so fast and low Austin had to lean closer to hear her. 'He...his mother died. When he was very, very young. A baby. I bought him up after that. He's not biologically mine, but I love him every bit the same as if he was. I raised him. That makes him my son.'

Amber sniffed, raising a hand to wipe at her nose before curling her arms around her body and leaning forward, eyes squeezed shut. Austin considered calming the atmosphere, putting an arm across her shoulders. But it wasn't the time for hugs and words of comfort. He had to find out exactly what was going on and why she'd lied to him.

'What's the note about, Amber?' Austin bent down, picked it up, and let his vision crawl over the page again. '*I am his only living parent.* Who sent this?'

'He's found me.'

Amber's skin was the colour of sour milk, her eyes still shut, her body held so tight it was almost as though she were folding in on herself. As if the *he* she was talking about could appear at any moment and she wanted to tuck herself into hiding.

'I suppose *he* is Alfie's father?' Austin pushed, resisting the urge to take Amber by the shoulders and shake her until the answers spilled out.

'He's a monster,' Amber said, her lids flying open, a flash of light igniting in the pale brown. 'We had to escape from him. We had to...'

Austin stared as Amber trembled, a slick of sweat glazing her forehead. The previous day, when he'd looked at her, he'd seen somebody head-strong, independent. Someone who wouldn't take no for an answer, who knew what she wanted. But that morning, as she stood shaking in the dingy hallway of his flat, he saw another level to her strength and bravery. She was terrified of that man, of the *he* who had written the note. But she was still fighting to find the boy she raised, against the odds. He admired that.

But if the man had tracked her down then he must've been watching her, and it had led him to Austin's home. Somebody dangerous, somebody who sent Amber into a quivering wreck, was watching his house. He lifted his gaze to the front door, relieved to see the chain pulled across. He wondered if it was enough, but then he shook his head. The man wasn't going to kick down his door, was he? Otherwise he'd have already done it, rather than leaving the note. Austin paused in the silence, listening for any sign of life outside the apartment. But there was nothing, just the ticking of the clock on the wall as time pushed on and he and Amber stood still.

For one moment, one awful moment that he hated himself for, he considered asking Amber to leave. He wanted no part in it. No angry, deranged madman waiting on his doorstep. No drama, no disaster. Not anymore. Not ever again.

What sort of a bloody coward are you?

Austin swallowed, digging his fingers into his palm until it hurt. It wasn't about him, it was about Alfie. And Amber too.

I can't leave her to face him alone. We have to find Alfie, and then find somewhere they can both be safe.

'So, today's plan?' Austin tried to keep his voice steady. 'Go take a look at the abbey, yeah?'

Amber's body lifted as she peered up at Austin with eyes like treacle. 'You still want to help me?'

'That man is clearly dangerous. You need to find Alfie, before he does...' Austin paused before voicing his next thought. 'Are you certain Alfie isn't already with him?'

Amber nodded. 'Yes. I'm certain. I...he wouldn't have posted this note otherwise.'

'Right. Look, Amber, I'm going to help you, like I promised. But I can't pretend I'm not a little freaked out about this nutter that's been watching us. Are you sure we shouldn't speak to the police? We could use the help.' He refrained from adding *and the protection.*

'No, Austin! No police.'

He hated those words, the insistence of the demand that made no sense. He decided not to push it, but he wouldn't make the mistake of obeying bizarre orders again. If she came to any harm he'd never forgive himself, and he didn't need another failure to torture his mind. If it came to it he'd dial those three nines and yell for help.

'I'm going to have a wash, and then we'll go,' Amber said, skirting around Austin and into the bathroom.

He stared at the closed door for a while, wondering about Amber and the strange secrets of her life that she hadn't yet divulged. It hadn't been until he'd bought her to his flat last night that he realised she had nothing with her. No bag, no belongings. He had given her a spare toothbrush, and a t-shirt of his that was far too big for her but fine for sleeping in. He supposed today Amber would have to wear the same outfit she'd been wearing the day before, including the massive trainers which clearly did not belong to her.

Where were all her things? It made sense to him that wherever she'd come from to find him, she'd left in a hurry. Had she been with that man, the note sender, all that time? Was it Alfie's father who had taken her from the streets while his boy played magic tricks with Austin? But if he took her, then who took Alfie? And Amber was so certain he did not have their son, so who did?

He hated all the questions, laid bare in the open while the answers remained hidden in the shadows. He longed for a script, some stage directions, anything to point him the right way so he didn't have to think for himself. Acting, performing, magic...it was all about routine, carefully rehearsed down to every word, every movement. Timing was key, planned and perfected.

But in that moment, Austin was clueless, alone on a darkened stage, unsure if he could live up to the part he was supposed to play.

Then - Amber

The hardest thing about getting to know Sarah was her adoration of the man who had stolen her from the world and locked her away. She still glowed when she spoke about Ray, refusing to believe his intent was anything other than pure. He was her hero. Amber picked her way lightly around the subject, careful not to turn Sarah against her.

And it was working. Over the past three months, Amber and Sarah had formed a tight bond. It wasn't surprising, given they were each other's only human interaction, excluding Ray. Amber was both surprised and relieved to find the friendship was genuine. She liked the girl. Beneath her naivety, Sarah was interesting and kind.

They had things in common. They both lost their mother's young. And although Sarah had a sister, unlike Amber's only child status, she had often felt like a lone ranger in the world. She had always been different, more intense than her sister who, in Sarah's words, *never had a care in the world.* They fell out years ago, and Sarah had distanced herself, kept herself isolated. That was until she met Ray.

Ray still locked Sarah's home when Amber visited, and he still did not trust her enough to leave the door to the spare room unlocked when they returned to the manor. It was her own fault. Twice she had tried to wriggle away from him and escape, and both times she had failed. She shouldn't have done it, could see the damage she'd caused in the icy blaze that shone from Ray's angry eyes. But her survival instinct was strong, and nothing could diminish her desire for freedom.

It was another *visit Sarah* day. They met once a week, always at the weekend. On Saturday mornings Ray would walk Amber to the stable and lock her inside with Sarah. Then, for a blissful eight hours of companionship, the two of them would watch television, talk about their childhoods, and laugh at silly jokes.

Getting ready, Amber splashed water over her face, avoiding glancing in the mirror when she lifted her head. She didn't recognise herself anymore and couldn't cope with the physical evidence that she was deteriorating. Hollow cheeks, white skin decorated with dark blemishes and angry pimples. Eyes sunken in desperation. The only thing keeping her sane was Sarah, the friendship they shared, but also the underlying hope that she would be the one to save Amber in the end.

Please.

Amber knew there was still a long way to go before she finally convinced Sarah to break free. She wasn't ready to turn her back on Ray, and though Amber was growing impatient, she was still looking forward to her visit. Spending the day with a friend was a blessed relief from the loneliness that consumed her throughout the week. Even Ray had stopped his visits, no longer interested in sex, he only visited to deliver her meals. After handing her the paper plate of food, Ray would turn and march from the room as though he were a soldier, doing no more than his duty. Silent and strong.

It wasn't just seeing Sarah that made those days special. It was stepping outside, breathing in the fresh air on the short walk to and from the stable. Winter had rolled around both too fast, and in months that had been long and slow. Frostbitten grass crunched beneath Amber's footsteps as she walked at Ray's side. She savoured the sound and squinted in the low winter sun that made the spiders webs in the bushes glisten like camera flashes. But the early January weather brought with it a stark reality. It had been nearly a year since she met Ray.

A year. How the hell did I let this happen?

Christmas had been a sad event. Ray bought a Christmas dinner to Amber's room, and she ate alone, watching the festive joy on the television and wishing she were somewhere, anywhere else. A month before, her twenty-seventh birthday had gone a miss, with not even a comment from Ray, nor a gift. Though what could he gift her that'd matter, if not her freedom? She'd screamed at herself for the birthdays she wasted, resenting each step closer to thirty. Such a mundane worry. She'd be grateful for any age, if only she could live it with the sun on her skin every day.

The air was bitter and crisp as Ray bundled Amber to the stable, his grip tightening every time he sensed she had moved in a way she shouldn't have. But she was too cold to try and escape, her legs stiff and tender in a pair of worn leggings. Once inside, she relaxed into the warmth, slumping with relief when Ray let himself out, leaving Amber and Sarah alone. She unravelled her scarf with numb fingers, setting it aside.

'Hi, Sarah.' Amber lifted her gaze to find her friend sat on the sofa, curled up like a child. 'Sarah? What's the matter?

Sarah sniffed as Amber sat beside her, draping an arm around her petite shoulders.

'Amber?' Sarah's eyes glistened with tears, but a small smile elevated her expression. 'I'm...I'm pregnant!'

Amber lurched, her head filling with pressure until her vision blurred and she blinked, swallowing the urge to be sick.

Sarah's pregnant.

All those months Ray had tried with her, and nothing had happened. And then he'd given up, abandoned all affection, no longer offering hugs or planting a kiss on her hair before he left the room. He obviously hadn't given up on Sarah though.

'We're not sure how far gone I am, but I've done the test. It's really happening!'

'He has to take you to hospital,' Amber said, her compassion outweighing the bitter jealousy that curled in her baby-less belly. 'You need proper scans, proper advice, proper care.'

'Ray says we can all handle it together.' Sarah grinned, her beauty breaking free across her face, dimpling at the cheeks. 'We're going to be parents! And you'll help won't you Amber? Maybe you'll get pregnant too? And the babies will be best friends, like us!'

'Oh, wake *up*, Sarah!' Amber snapped. It was too much, to listen to her spin their horror story into a fairy-tale. 'You think this is some kind of dream come true? This is sick! He locked you up in here, he brainwashed you into thinking it's for your own safety, and now you worship him, even though he's a monster. Having sex with you is manipulating and against your will whether you think otherwise or not! I'm not going to be having a baby too. You can't bring a baby up like this. You think your child could live its whole life here? You need to do the right thing. Get out, once I'm gone. Get out tonight and tell the police what's happened. They'll keep you safe. They'll come and get me out too, and I'll look after you and the baby. Ray will never find you, and we can raise your baby in safety. We'll be free, Sarah.'

Battered by Amber's words Sarah doubled over, clutching at her belly. Amber's own stomach clenched, wishing she'd delivered her thoughts with less venom. Sarah was vulnerable, she needed to be handled with the delicacy and care of painting a portrait. Instead, Amber had thrown paints at the page so they smudged and blended into an ugly mess.

'How could you?' Sarah sobbed, tears glazing her eyes, shading them the colour of river water. 'I thought you'd be happy for me.'

'I can't be happy, Sarah. Not while you live like this.'

'I'm happy! You might be ungrateful for what you've got, but I'm not. I love Ray, I love my home, and having this baby completes it. This is the best thing that has ever happened to me.'

Amber couldn't find the energy to push anymore words from her brain to her lips. They spent the rest of their day in silence, sat on opposite ends of the room, waiting for the click in the lock that meant Ray had come to collect her. Amber could not look at him when he arrived, feared she would be sick if she even dared. She walked home with her head down, glad of the darkness, frustrated at the lack of strength that meant she couldn't prise away Ray's grip on her arm.

What the hell am I going to do?

*

The weekly visits to Sarah continued, and for months they sat in stony silence. Their friendship was shattered, and Amber had nothing more to lose, so eventually she worked on reasoning with Sarah once more. She had to get her and the baby out, protect them from Ray.

But Sarah wouldn't listen. She zoned out from Amber's rants, stroking her growing belly, which bulged against soft sweaters. Her face had become puffy, her hair no longer draped in sheets but sat in a messy bun, like a crow's nest.

Amber feared for her, for the birth that would take place without a midwife, without drugs or birthing pools. Sarah was tiny, petite, and Amber doubted the birth was going to be easy. She feared it would all end in disaster, the anxiety of it forcing her awake at night, as she stared into the darkness with no idea how to help.

And then, against the odds, Amber was there when it happened. A sweltering morning in August, when Ray had opened the door to the stables and the heat inside was stifling, the air stale and unmoving. Amber stepped inside and, as though she'd been holding on until she had company, Sarah stared up at the two of them, as a rush of water cascaded from between her legs and splattered the floor.

'Oh my...*Ray!* She's going into labour! Call an ambulance!'

Despite the panic that rushed into the humid air, Ray still managed to throw her a look of contempt. 'Don't be ridiculous,' he hissed. 'Go to her, keep her calm.'

Amber loathed to do Ray's bidding, but it wasn't about him. She ran to Sarah's side, helped her lay on the floor, while she intermittently clenched her body and yelped in pain.

'I need to go to hospital!' Sarah gasped, her face slick with sweat, her dark hair plastered to her forehead. 'Please!'

'It's going to be okay,' Amber soothed, stroking her flushed cheek. 'Just breathe. Okay? Breathe!'

Hours passed. Sarah drifted between wailing in agony and a sleepy state of panic. Amber continued to comfort her, dabbing cold flannels on her face, and reassuring her it would all be okay. It was strange, having Ray with them when he usually left them alone. He remained silent, a vein pulsing at his temple, his jaw taut. Sarah reached out to him, wriggling her fingers, groaning his name. But he didn't take her hand, nor respond to her words. He just sat and waited and stared.

By the time evening dawned, the sky visible through the skylight burning scarlet, Sarah was in hysterics. She thrashed and screamed and gritted her teeth, her sweaty hand crushing Amber's fingers. The first time Ray spoke, all other noise in the room came to a halt.

'I can see the head,' he murmured.

'This is it,' Amber said. 'You're nearly there Sarah. Come on push, push!'

The final moments happened as though in slow motion. Sarah's rhythmic squeezing of Amber's hand, Ray positioning himself on the floor, the final scream of pain followed by Sarah's body relaxing. And then the sharp, piercing cry as Ray scooped up a pink, bloodied bundle from between Sarah's legs and lifted it up towards the light, as though checking it were real.

'A boy!' Ray grinned. 'Amber, he's a boy!'

Amber turned away from him, stunned that he was sharing the news with her, rather than Sarah. But Sarah didn't notice, her face was a violent red, her eyes blood shot, her body trembling.

'My baby,' she whispered, reaching out.

Ray placed their child in Sarah's arms, kissing the baby tenderly on the head. And there it was, Amber thought, looking on. A family.

This is so wrong. What are we going to do?

*

There was nothing she could do. And so, she did the only decent thing possible. Amber spent long days helping Sarah look after Ray's baby. He took her to the stables almost daily, dropping her off before he went to work and collecting her again in the evening.

Amber fell in love with the child as instantly as if he were her own. She supposed her part in delivering him had created a unique bond. Sarah and Ray named him Alfred Tallon, after Ray's father. He was strict on that, insisting no-one abbreviate it. Sarah respected his wishes, but when Ray wasn't around, Amber referred to him as Alfie, a cuter name that suited his chubby cheeks, round eyes, and tufty dark hair. Sarah was always tired, the nighttime crying was not something Amber had to deal with in the quiet solitude of her room at the house.

So, while Sarah caught up on sleep, Amber cared for Alfie as though he were her own son. She bathed him, fed him from the bottle, which he always took without fuss. She breathed in his warm, powdery smell and kissed him on top of his soft head. Her pulse quickened whenever he looked up at her through his thick lashes, his dark blue eyes peering at her with adoration.

Is this how it feels to be a real mother?

She thought it must be. She couldn't imagine a stronger love, felt certain her feelings for Alfie were as real as Sarah's. They would raise him together, Amber promised herself, as she cradled a sleeping Alfie in her arms. He was heavy when he slept, but she loved the weight of him, the sound of his small snores and the flutter of his breath tickling her skin.

It was awful and beautiful. The horrific reality of existing entirely in locked rooms, lit by the overwhelming joy of a newborn child. The only thing tainting Amber's time with Sarah and Alfie was Ray's involvement. He loved Alfie too, for all his flaws, he doted on his son. And Amber knew he would never be the type of father who walked away.

But still, she longed for it. For him to disappear, and leave her, Sarah and Alfie to experience a real life, and not live as caged animals.

Now - Austin

Austin waited in the kitchen while Amber got washed and ready for their trip into the centre of Bath. He sipped on a strong sugary cup of tea as he recapped her story. So much of it still made no sense to him. She had explained it in a rush, her cheeks pink, her eyes glassy, and her words whispered.

If he'd understood her correctly, she had been locked away by her partner. And he had another girlfriend, Sarah, and Sarah had given birth to Alfie. She was the biological parent. Amber helped with his birth and then subsequently helped to raise him too. Naturally, when Sarah died, Amber stepped in as the child's mother. But when Austin asked how Sarah had died, Amber turned away and shook her head until strands of hair fell loose from her ponytail.

What the hell did I just hear? What am I getting myself into?

Jasmine's warning from the previous evening flared in his mind as Amber divulged some of the horrors she'd survived. And yet, despite his apprehension, his desire not to get involved, Austin felt it would be too cruel to step away. She had nothing and no-one to turn to. And Alfie still needed to be found. No amount of fear would override the sharp, cold dread that plunged

Austin into despair every day, plagued his dreams at night. The dark, unanswered questions that taunted him, reminding him Alfie could be dead, and it'd be all his fault.

When Amber stepped out from the bathroom her hair was brushed free, falling over her shoulders. She had tucked another borrowed t-shirt into her jeans, stretching the fabric tight so it almost looked as though it fit her. She smelt of Austin's deodorant, earthy and sweet. He wasn't sure why, but he found himself smiling.

'Let's go,' Amber said, and he was relieved to see she wore a tiny smile of her own.

*

The centre of Bath flowed like a river, a constant current of bodies being pulled and pushed in the direction of carefully placed sale signs and advertisements. It was always busy. Austin had avoided it since Alfie's disappearance, sensing no need to return once he'd hung up his magician's jacket and started work at the office. He had no desire to shop in expensive stores or visit the over-priced cinema. He preferred to confine himself to his flat, the office, and the short distance between the two that he cycled. After learning of Amber's imprisonment, and considering how close he'd come to jail himself, Austin's stomach knotted in shame at how little he'd done with his freedom over the past eleven months.

Amber remained silent as they walked through the bustling High Street towards the court outside the abbey. It had always been Austin's favourite place to perform. The large stone slabs were his stage, the gothic abbey his backdrop, the hordes of passing tourists his audience. On sunny days, beams would illuminate the old buildings, casting a sandy yellow glow over him, like a spotlight. It was the perfect theatre.

Austin was proud to have earnt that spot. And yet, if he hadn't, perhaps Amber and Alfie would not have passed him that day, and he would still be a performer. In a different part of the city, with less passing traffic and fewer onlookers, but with the life he had loved still in-tact.

'Oh,' Amber's voice rose at his side. 'Here. He was right here.'

She shuddered to a halt, exactly where the crowd would've stood, eyes fixed on the last place she ever saw her son. Her eyebrows were creased, twisting her face into such an expression of pain that Austin felt like he was intruding just by looking at her. Her jaw trembled as her teeth nipped at her lower lip, and her shoulders slumped as though she were struggling to hold herself upright. She reached a hand forward, towards where Austin had performed, her thin fingers shaking as she clasped at nothing but air.

'Alfie,' she whispered, her eyes snapping shut. 'Where are you?'

Austin had expected a similar sense of despair to cloak him upon returning to the abbey. But while Amber clenched in anguish, Austin was jabbed with a shot of adrenaline, a spark that lit his mind into action. He scanned the surrounding buildings, noting a small CCTV camera a short distance away. Why hadn't he returned sooner? Surely there were answers to be found there, in the place it had all gone wrong?

He wasn't entirely sure the positioning of the camera would've covered the area he needed. But if it did, it was bound to have caught what happened. Would the police have checked it at the time? They must have. But then, what would they have seen? If they'd watched it, they'd have been focused on Austin, on Alfie. They'd have seen the two of them talking and they'd have sat back, arms folded, expressions grim as they watched Austin lead Alfie away. He cringed at the thought, his body flaring with a pungent heat.

They'd have seen no more than that. At the time of the disappearance, Amber was a mystery. Austin was unable to describe her to the police and no-one had come forward to say their son was missing. But she had come back. Austin was sure the police could help them if they knew what she looked like. They could find her on the footage and find out once and for all what had happened.

She claimed to have been taken. It still struck Austin as odd that someone could be snatched away beneath the noses of all those people, without anybody noticing a commotion. Watching the CCTV footage would confirm or deny her story.

She could be lying. She's lied already.

Austin returned his focus to Amber, who had opened her eyes and was staring at the exact spot where Alfie had taken centre stage, silent tears streaking her cheeks. He knew what she would say, if he were to suggest his plan to her, and it made him want to bang his head against the rough stone of the abbey walls in frustration.

No police.

Then - Amber

She should never have picked up the knife.

That afternoon, Ray entered the bedroom earlier than usual. Amber peered up from her painting, stooped over the desk because he had still not allowed her a chair. She stretched out the ache in her spine, massaging her lower back with her fingers.

'I need you to help me prepare dinner,' Ray said. 'I've got too much to do.'

Amber frowned. He'd never once asked for her help, and it had been almost two years. She swallowed the bile that curled in her throat as she made the calculation. What was it that had made him so busy for the first time? And why did the dinner matter so much?

'I can help,' Amber shrugged. 'But don't worry about dinner if you haven't got time. I'm not hungry.'

A pulse flickered in Ray's jaw as a purple haze crawled from his neck and into his cheeks. 'It's Sunday. We have to have a Sunday dinner.'

It never ceased to amaze Amber how Ray could not bear to break traditions. He couldn't stand it if his routines were interrupted, as though he were a conventional man, with a conventional life. A man who did not have two women locked up. That was how monsters slipped through life unnoticed, Amber had grown to realise. They blended in, hidden behind a canvas of high standards and family traditions.

'Fine. What do you want me to do?' Amber's heart rate sped up as she considered the possibility of him letting her go to the kitchen. Was that what had changed? Did he finally trust her enough to let her out of the room without his fingers clamped around her arm?

'You can prepare the vegetables,' Ray said, retreating from the room. 'I'll bring it up to you.'

She nearly cried, shaking her head at her own stupidity. Of course he wasn't going to let her out. Yet, despite the mundanity of chopping vegetables, Amber was looking forward to having something different to do. She was never taken to visit Alfie and Sarah on a Sunday, and so the day would otherwise stretch into mind-numbing boredom and too much thinking time. Sundays were reminiscent of the days before Sarah, long and empty, until Amber's mind was as blank as the four beige walls that were her daily, and only, view.

Ray returned almost instantly, holding a thin plastic chopping board with a bag of vegetables and a large knife resting on top. Amber tried not to look at it, fighting to keep her eyes on Ray's face, forcing a small nonchalant smile to mask her thoughts. But she couldn't stop her gaze wandering towards the glinted silver edge, the sharp pointed tip. She snapped her eyes away. She could never hurt anybody, not like that.

Not even Ray?

She stamped down the idea, squashing it into the corner of her brain reserved for disturbing thoughts. Ray was Alfie's father. And despite all he had done, all he was still doing, she could never use the knife as a weapon.

But you could use it as a threat.

The idea turned her cold, even while a small spark of hope ignited in the darkest depths of her heart. Ray followed her line of sight, his own eyes lingering on the knife before darting back to her face.

'Don't do anything stupid now, will you?' he said, placing the chopping board upon the desk.

'Of course not.'

He left the room without another word, and Amber stared for a while, not daring to believe he had actually left her alone with the knife. She set to work, the handle cold against the warm flesh of her palm.

When everything was peeled, cut, and portioned, Amber lay flat on the bed, her muscles tender from hunching over the desk as she'd pushed the knife through the vegetables. The air in the room was ripe with the stench of raw broccoli, and her hand hurt from gripping the knife handle. Her body had grown weak after so many months of inactivity, but it had given her some release to slice through the carrots, watching pieces chip away. It gave her a shimmer of power.

How pathetic. Cutting up carrots does not make you powerful.

There was a sharp rap at the door and Amber leapt to attention, her body sore. Without conscious thought her eyes moved to the knife again, resting on the desk with the handle pointing towards her. She could pick it up. She could threaten Ray, force him to let her leave. She had no phone, would she get to one in time to call the police? Would they find Alfie and Sarah in time, or would Ray cut his losses with Amber and rush to move Sarah and his son to a safe place where no-one would find them?

'Amber?' Ray's voice was deep and serious. 'I'm going to collect everything now. Make sure the knife is resting on the chopping board. And remember what I said...don't do anything stupid.'

Her fingers twitched at her side as she battled her options. Comply, and keep them all safe, together. Rebel, and bid for a chance of freedom. The vegetables were already stacked in neat piles on one side of the chopping board. She should place the knife on the other side, hand it to Ray without a fuss. Maybe he'd grow to trust her, like he did Sarah, and start leaving her door unlocked. She could escape without the threat of violence.

And there was still the hope that eventually Sarah would take Amber's word against Ray and escape herself, taking Alfie with her and sending the police to rescue Amber. She couldn't stand to consider a drawn-out future, the uncertainty of freedom, but it seemed like her only option. She sighed as she lay the knife on the chopping board and walked towards the door.

'Okay, ready.'

The door inched open, Ray peered round, eyes narrowed into sharp slits. He noted the knife and stepped inside, taking the board from her.

'Good girl!' he beamed, and Amber's stomach curled. She was not his pet.

Turning away from him, Amber flopped onto the bed once more, and as the door clicked into place behind her she wondered if, just once, violence would have been the answer.

*

The room was dark, the only light was the little red circle that meant the television was on stand-by. Not enough to illuminate the room. Amber leapt out of bed, flicked the light switch, and winced as the room was plunged into a brightness that stung her eyes. She stood still, listening for the noise that had woken her. It pierced the silence in an instant, the cry of a baby.

Alfie.

'Ray!' Amber called, pounding the door. The ache that flooded her hands reminded her of those early days of entrapment, the hours she spent hitting the solid oak in a futile bid to escape. 'Ray! What's going on? Is everything okay?'

She stepped aside as Ray's footsteps approached, Alfie's cries getting louder. The door flew open and Ray stepped in, placing the baby in her arms.

'He's yours now,' Ray said, a manic smile on his face that forced Amber to step back, pulling Alfie tight against her chest. 'You're a mum. We're parents, Amber. Just like we always wanted.' There were tears in his eyes, swimming amongst the sharp blue, more dangerous than sharks in the ocean.

'What do you mean?' Amber croaked, her throat dry from sleep, her mind whirling with confusion. 'What do you mean, Ray?'

'It's Sarah. She's gone. Alfred is ours now, mine and yours. We always wanted a baby together, didn't we? And now we have one.'

'Sarah's gone?'

Amber's pulse quickened. Hope and fear blended into an acidic bile that coursed through her stomach and sent heat into the back of her throat. Had Sarah run away? Had she fled to the police at last, told them what had been going on? The bile hit her tongue as Alfie's cries quietened, and he nestled his warm head against her arm. No, she can't have. She would've taken her son with her.

'Yes, Sarah's gone,' Ray said. 'And you're going to stay. You're going to stay with me forever.'

'But this isn't right,' Amber whispered. 'You can't keep us like this. It's not fair, it's certainly not fair on Alf...Alfred.'

'If you ever try to leave,' Ray snarled, towering over her as she curled a hand around Alfie's head, 'I will see that you are locked away properly. Do you hear me?'

'Locked away properly? As if I'm not already? It's illegal what you're doing. It'll be you who gets locked up, not me!'

She wasn't sure where her rage was coming from. She had been good for months at playing calm and compliant. But she was scared, scared for her friend, for Alfie, for herself. She no longer possessed the willpower to hold back.

"'Oh really, Amber?' Ray spat.

He lifted the carrier bag that was balancing on his arm and reached his hand inside. It was only then Amber realised he was wearing tight latex gloves. Her vision blurred, as though she were being held beneath murky water, as he removed his hand from the bag, his glove-clad fingers curled around a knife that was covered in blood.

At first, all Amber could register was the crimson stain that was drying to a dark brown. But as she stared she realised, with a jolt that nearly toppled her over, it was the knife she had used earlier to cut the vegetables. She steadied herself, determined not to fall while she still held Alfie in her arms. Ray chuckled.

'You go anywhere, Amber, and believe me, I will make sure this knife is found by the right people. It's covered in your finger-prints. And I think it's the perfect story, don't you? Pathetic, jealous girlfriend finds out her partner is seeing someone else. When she finds out the other woman has had a baby, she is tipped over the edge. Because the poor pathetic girlfriend couldn't get pregnant herself. It won't be so hard for the police to believe you stabbed her, Amber. I'll make sure they find the knife. And the body. So you stay put. You're mine. Got that?'

A bitter coldness rushed through Amber's body. Her head was light, as though it had been pumped with air, and the flash of flickering lights that sparked through her vision made it feel like she was hurtling through space. The world she had known was gone, miles beneath her, growing more and more distant until the life she once loved was more than two years away, but lightyears in the past, impossible to get back.

Her limbs were so numb she may as well have been floating. The only real thing she could feel was the weight of the baby in her arms, and that weight anchored her to the earth, keeping her solid and still and stopping her from keeling over and giving into the oblivion threatening to overcome her.

The baby. Keep him safe, Amber. Don't you give up now.

As Ray pulled the door closed, Amber sank onto the bed, the jarring movement setting Alfie into hysterics again. She held him close and sobbed in tune to his crying, her tears falling down her cheeks and gathering in Alfie's hair.

Now - Austin

Austin wasn't surprised when Amber refused to go to the police even though he pointed out the CCTV camera. He was sure they'd find something but she shook her head, her skin blanching with every refusal, until he gave up trying to convince her. But she did agree there was nothing else to be figured out by staring at the large stone slab where Alfie once stood.

Crowds were swarming into the city centre, and Austin's scalp prickled beneath his matted hair as he longed to get away from the masses. Amber couldn't hack it either, he could tell. She flinched whenever somebody passed too close to her, clutching at her hands and whipping her head around whenever a male voice carried over the drone of city noise.

'Shall we go back to mine?' Austin suggested. 'We can plan our next step there, get away from all this?'

Amber nodded and Austin let out a sigh before leading her to the bus stop. She was still peering over her shoulder every five seconds, her twitchiness putting him on edge until he almost yelled at her to stop. But he remembered the note she'd received that morning, the threat that Alfie's father was lurking, watching her every move. Perhaps he was still following them. Perhaps not.

Either way, the thought of home had lost some of its appeal, the safety of it uncertain.

They were silent on the bus, stood gripping the handrail due to a lack of seats. Austin unbuttoned his jacket, straining toward the open window for some air. It was impossible to imagine how different his day would've been if he were at work, like he should be.

Of course, Sam had allowed him time off. He was decent, the only person who supported Austin after Alfie went missing. He would've had no chance of finding a job at that time, what with his arrest, the constant police interrogation, and the stream of sensationalised news stories. The press followed him everywhere, questioning everything he'd ever done. He was accused of using his magic act to lure children to him, and he knew he'd never take to the streets to perform again. How could he? No-one was going to give their time, attention, or loose change to a suspected paedophile. If Sam hadn't set him up with a place in the office, he would have been broke. Financially, mentally, emotionally.

Austin wondered, as they got off the bus and walked back to his flat, quite how long he could get away with helping Amber. He couldn't stay off work for too long. He was taking a week of holiday, approved at the last minute thanks to Sam's generosity and understanding. But how long could it go on? Even if he tried to claim a second week, his holiday entitlement wouldn't last forever.

It didn't seem possible they would find Alfie in the space of a few weeks. He'd been missing for almost a year, and nobody had found him so far. But then, the whole situation had been strange. No-one other than Austin reported the boy missing. Other than the police's initial weak investigation, had anyone been looking for him at all? Perhaps, now he and Amber were searching, Alfie would be discovered in no time.

If he's alive.

Austin hadn't mastered the art of keeping his darkest fears from manifesting as bitter voices hissing in his ear. He couldn't ask Amber what she thought, if she genuinely believed Alfie was still alive. How could he suggest that to her? It was too horrible to even consider. They had to find him alive. Austin crossed his fingers at his side, a meaningless practice, but another habit he couldn't break.

'After you.' Austin opened the door to his flat and gestured at Amber to go through.

She smiled at him, and he was struck, as always, at how she managed to muster those little acts of kindness and gratitude despite her pain. He almost felt good, until Amber's scream pierced the moment.

'Oh! No!'

Austin darted into the flat behind her, following her line of sight to a piece of paper resting on the floor. It was decorated with cut out words, exactly like the one from earlier that morning.

He slammed the door, worried the sender might be skulking outside planning to sneak up on them. There was no denying Amber had, unintentionally, bought danger to his door. Austin picked up the paper, whatever it said they would face it together. But he was not expecting the words that screamed up at him from the page. The blood drained from his face, leaving his skin cold, and his mind dizzy.

She's a murderer. Watch your back.

'Amber...what the hell...' Austin handed her the paper, staring at her soft brown eyes, her gentle features, trying to decide if there could be any truth behind the words. The note from that morning had been true. Amber admitted she wasn't Alfie's biological mother. The sender-of-notes had not lied about that.

How did Alfie's real mother die? Amber had neglected to share that with him. Perhaps Amber hadn't led danger to his door after all. Rather, she was the danger, and he'd held the door right open and let her in.

'I....' Amber's voice wavered, her teeth sinking into her lip as she breathed in and wiped a tear from her cheek. 'I'm not a murderer. It was Ray. Alfie's father. He...he killed Sarah. He said that Alfie was ours now because we always wanted to be parents, but I hadn't fallen pregnant. It was all part of his plan to keep me, to stop me from running away. He said he'd frame me for her murder if I ever left. This note is his reminder. It's a threat.'

Austin pinched at the skin on the palm of his hand, the sharp sting telling him it was real life, and he hadn't been plunged into a crappy television drama. He had tried to roll with it, the weirdness of Amber's arrival, the secrets she kept hidden. Not all lives were straight forward, after all, and he acknowledged his role in Amber and Alfie's story. He'd put up and shut up, following Amber like a guilty puppy who had to behave to make up for what he'd done.

But that word....

Murderer.

It was too much. Was she a killer, or was she telling the truth? And if she was being honest then the man posting these notes, these threats, he was a murderer. Either way, Austin had surrounded himself in a darkness of which he had once been blissfully ignorant. He knew that people killed, that evil existed, of course he did. But he never thought those kinds of people would be drawn into his life. Once again, his naivety let him down.

'You have to believe me, Austin!' Amber pleaded. 'Sarah was my friend, my only friend at that point. I loved her. I loved Alfie. I didn't want to be his mother, not instead of her. I wanted to bring him up alongside her, as a friend. I'd have been like an aunty to Alfie. I was in shock for months after what happened, terrified and distraught with grief. But I had to stay strong because I needed to raise Alfie, and I needed to protect him. Not a day went by when I didn't plan to get him away from the monster who'd killed his mum.'

Austin steadied his breathing. How many things could he brush off and ignore? He didn't want to give up on Alfie, but he didn't want to dig himself into deeper and darker places either. He wanted his life back on track. But then, after all he'd done, he didn't deserve things to be that easy.

'It's why I always say *no police*,' Amber whispered. 'It's why I installed it in Alfie too. *No police,* I used to tell him. Because if the police get involved then Ray will save himself by putting the blame on me. I'll be locked away for Sarah's murder, and he will take custody of Alfie. I can't let that happen. I can't let my son, Sarah's son, be handed over to Ray.'

Austin took in her words, considering both options. Truth or lies? Fact or fiction? From what she'd told him Ray had kept her, and Sarah for that matter, locked up against their will. Was it so unbelievable he was capable of murder? It was more likely to be him than Amber.

'Why don't you just tell the police everything?' Austin asked. 'Tell them what he did to you, to Sarah. Tell them that he's threatening to frame you. There is so much they can do, they'll prove your innocence. They'll prove his guilt.'

'Ray's too smart,' Amber said, shaking her head. 'And he has money, a good job, a reputation. He'll get away with it, trust me.'

When Austin didn't reply she matched his silence, fixing him with a stare, her expression a mixture of desperation and determination. 'If you don't want to be a part of this anymore, just say.'

'No...I do...' The words escaped before he'd even considered his answer. But they were out, impossible to reverse. Amber's shoulders relaxed.

'What do we do though?' Austin rubbed a hand over his chin, grazing the stubble. 'I hate that Ray knows you're here.'

'I want to go and speak to his Dad,' Amber said. 'We went to visit him once...he's a nice man. Ray loves him, if love is even possible for someone like him. He respects him at the very least. His name's Alfred, Alfie's namesake. That's got to mean something, right? Maybe Alfie is with him?'

'Where does his Dad live?'

'Portsmouth.'

Austin had never been, but he knew it wasn't too far away and that it was near the ocean. As he pictured it, the thought of getting out Bath, away from the flat and out from Ray's watchful eye, was a great idea.

'I don't have a car. Shall I check the train times?'

Amber smiled, colour returning to her cheeks. 'Thank you, Austin. For sticking by me.'

'No probs,' he shrugged, hiding the ripple of nausea coursing through him.

They agreed to leave the following morning, to avoid turning up on the old man's doorstep too late for him to answer. That night, Austin lay in his bed, flinching at every sound, hoping he'd made the right decision to ignore the note and believe Amber's side of the story.

The voice that often plagued his thoughts crawled its way in again.

Sleep with one eye open, mate.

It was good advice, and Austin considered it.

But he didn't sleep with one eye open, didn't know how. Instead, he didn't sleep at all.

Then - Amber

Amazing, how the time passes when bringing up a child.

Amber sat against the pillows on her bed, two-year-old Alfie resting against her as she read him a story. His thumb was stuck between his lips, slick with spittle. Ray would hate it if he saw, but Amber couldn't bring herself to tell Alfie not to. She gazed down at him, and he stared back at her, eyes startling blue, his dark hair cut into a neat, straight fringe above his tiny eyebrows.

'Mumma,' he said, with a seriousness that made her giggle. 'Story!'

'Yes, of course, Alfie,' she smiled. 'Story.'

He loved books, became absorbed in the pictures, tracing them with his fingers as Amber read the words. She doubted Ray ever let him watch television, he'd taken hers out of the room when Alfie came to live with them, not trusting that she wouldn't sit him in front of it during the day. Alfie was only allowed to stay with her in the daytime. At night, Ray took Alfie into his own bedroom and settled him there. It pained her that she had never tucked him into bed, never wandered in to check on him during the night. On Saturdays, Ray would take Alfie on day trips, and those days were long and agonising for Amber, who waited in lonely silence for their return.

But most days, it was just her and Alfie. The lack of television didn't bother her. They had books and educational toys and games. She helped him learn, determined he would count, read, and write under her guidance. She wasn't much of a mother, bound to the confines of the spare room, but she would do her best by Alfie no matter what. For him, and for Sarah.

Her heart glowed every time Alfie called her *Mumma*. But it also throbbed with guilt, knowing that he did not know the truth, and his real mother would never know the boy he'd become.

It was a Friday and Amber was making the most of her time with Alfie before his day out with his father the following morning. She had allowed him to demand the same story be read to him several times over and was enjoying the way his head lulled against her arm, heavy with tiredness. His little lids had just pulled shut when the key rattled in the lock and the door opened with a thud. Alfie's eyes shot open, and so did his mouth, causing his thumb to drop from between his lips.

'Dadda?' he babbled, rubbing his eyes with pudgy fists.

'Hello, son!' Ray grinned, striding towards the bed and ruffling Alfie's hair. 'We're going on an adventure this weekend, Alfred! We all are.'

'Me as well?' Amber couldn't help herself. She had never stepped outside with Alfie, never been beyond the bedroom since her last visit to Sarah. She convulsed as she thought of her friend but pulled her focus back to how wonderful it'd be to watch Alfie toddle and play in the open air.

'Yes, you as well. We are going to stay with my father for the night. He lives in Portsmouth.'

Amber stayed silent, unsure how to respond. She had never met Ray's father, but in the early stages of their relationship, when she could never have imagined how things would turn out, he had spoken about him a lot. It was hard to tell how he felt about him. Sometimes he seemed to deeply respect the man who raised him, other times he spoke as though he were ashamed of him. Amber had no idea what to expect. Was he like Ray? Was he a monster too? And above all, there was the trip to Portsmouth. The drive would take hours. She had never been one for long car journeys, but the thought of living free from the spare room for a whole weekend was a pull she wouldn't pass up on for anything. Portsmouth was on the coast. Would they be able to see the sea? When was the last time she'd seen the sea?

'Early nights all round.' Ray lifted Alfie from the bed so that he flopped against his chest. 'We're leaving first thing in the morning.'

*

The next morning Amber sat, strapped into the front seat of the car with Ray beside her, programming the sat nav. She wanted to sit in the back seats with Alfie, but Ray wouldn't allow it. 'We're a family. I'm not a taxi service, Amber.'

As the tyres crunched on the gravelled driveway and the car slipped down the lane, Amber marvelled at the beauty surrounding her. It was a crisp early October morning, and there was a haze of fog lifting as the sun rose, painting the sky with streaks of orange and yellow. As sun beams tried to peak through the mist, the whole world was plunged into a fiery hue, and Amber clasped her hands in her lap, wishing she could clasp the moment instead, and keep it forever.

Within an hour they were on the motorway, and the view was bleak and grey. Amber stopped focusing on the sky, which she'd previously been unable to tear her eyes from, and allowed her mind to wander into the dangerous territory of hope. Could she finally be in a strong enough position to escape? If they stopped at a service station she could say she needed to take Alfie for a wee. All she'd need to do was speak to another woman, tell her what was happening, ask her to call the police.

No. No police!

She balked as she recalled Ray's threat, the horrific end to Sarah's life, and what Amber would be accused of. If she called the police she would be playing right into Ray's hands, and there'd be no place to hide from them, or him. Could she convince someone to drive her and Alfie away instead? Would it be possible without Ray spotting them?

Amber turned her gaze to Ray, lingering on the way his hands gripped the steering wheel so tight his knuckles strained against his skin. He threw a glance at her, and his blue eyes were so knowing, she was sure he could read her thoughts. It was useless. If she wanted to stay with Alfie and keep him safe, she had to behave. And though she had not abandoned all hope of escape, she knew she needed a better plan.

*

Four and a half hours after they left Manchester, Ray pulled up outside a red bricked town house in Portsmouth. They had not seen the sea on the drive, but Amber still enjoyed watching the world pass, pretended she was a bird flying free as the contrast of countryside and cities flashed by in a blur.

The house was narrow, sandwiched between two others, with a cracked tile path leading to a neat blue door. As Ray rapped on the wood, Amber stood beside him, Alfie's tiny hand in hers. She would have to keep up a pretence in front of Ray's father and didn't know how convincing she would be. Ray had warned her how important it was for this trip to go well, and for his father to believe Alfie was her son. She had no intention of letting him think otherwise. He *was* her son.

The door creaked open to reveal an elderly man, with fluffy white hair and a warm, gap-toothed grin. His skin was loose around his cheeks, his nose red and bumpy. Amber couldn't help but smile at him.

'Ray!' he beamed, embracing his son into a hug and patting him hard on the back. 'And this must be…'

'This is my partner, Amber.'

'And what a beautiful young lady she is,' Alfred smiled. 'Lovely to meet you, Amber.'

'Lovely to meet you too, Mr. Tallon.'

'And our little boy. Alfred the second!' Ray laughed, but it was a tight sound, as though it had caught in his throat. Amber wished he's choke on it.

'Hello there, little one. From one Alfred to another!' He reached forward to ruffle his grandson's hair, but Alfie stepped towards Amber and buried his head against her leg.

'No need to be shy,' she said, bending down and encouraging him to take a step towards Alfred. 'This is your granddad. His name is Alfred too! Isn't that great?'

Alfie nodded, his head bowed as he managed a chubby handed wave, fingers curling.

'Come on in, come on in!' Alfred enthused.

They were ushered inside to a comfortable living room, that was too warm even for the cold October day. The carpet was dark with a floral design, an ugly clash to the opposing pattern of the sofas and curtains. There was little else, but a television, a coffee table, and stacks of old newspapers. It lacked any care or attention, dust mites swirled, caught in the act by the light shining through the window, and the air smelt musky and stale. Amber bit her lip, as hot tears rose behind her lids.

'What are you doing Amber?' Ray hissed, as Alfred hobbled into the living room carrying a tray of tea and cakes.

Amber shook her head and smiled at Alfred, who didn't seem at all fazed by his home, and its striking absence of a woman's touch. She took comfort in that. If he was happy, what did it matter?

With the lure of Bakewell tarts, it wasn't long before Alfie was himself again, chatting and smiling and smearing his sticky fingers on the furniture. Ray apologised, pulling Alfie's hands away and wiping them with a napkin, but Alfred laughed and said *boys will be boys.*

Later that evening, when Alfie was asleep upstairs, the adults sat together at the dining room table with glasses of red wine.

'Tell me some more about yourself, Amber,' Alfred said, his eyes twinkling over his wine glass.

'Well, I...I used to work in marketing until...' she swallowed, noting the way Ray's body stiffened in the seat beside her. 'Until I had Alfie. *Alfred*. Now I stay home and look after him. Which is a joy, of course.'

'Yes, he's a lovely little boy. Do you think you'll go back to work? When Alfred goes to school?'

Amber took another sip of wine, enjoying the way it coursed through her, making her feel confident and alive. She hadn't drunk alcohol in years. 'Yes, I'd love to. I really would.'

Ray tensed at her words, but he twisted his scowl into a smile as he turned to his father. 'Amber's an artist,' he said. 'Like mother was.'

'Oh, well that's wonderful! What's your style?'

'Watercolour,' Amber nodded, facing away from Ray so she would not be tempted to glare at him. He'd never told her his mother had been an artist. He'd made it clear he did not want to talk about her. 'I paint buildings I've visited and loved. Many of my favourites are in Rome.'

'Wonderful!' Alfred's eyes were shining, the colour of pinecones, far warmer than the icy hue of his son's. 'You've found yourself someone special here, Ray.'

The conversation was interrupted by a whimper from upstairs, Alfie's voice drifted down the hallway, calling out. Instinctively Amber stood, but Ray pushed his chair from the table and ushered her to sit down.

'I'll see to him. You stay with dad and enjoy your conversation.' He kissed Amber on the cheek before leaving the room, and the wetness of it lingered. She forced her hand to remain on her wine glass to stop herself from reaching up to wipe it away.

'I'm so glad he found you,' Alfred said. 'He seems happy. And to have little Alfred too. He's always wanted his own family. It was tough on him as a child, you know? When his mother left.'

'Why did she leave, if you don't mind me asking?'

'She had always been a bit of a free spirit,' Alfred sighed, swirling his wine in the glass and peering into it as though it were a vessel of memories. 'She was independent, had her own mind. It's one of the reasons I fell in love with her, really. She never wanted children, she wanted to travel the world instead. She wanted us to be one of those couples that always had money to spend on trips, because they didn't have to spend it on children. That sounds so cold, doesn't it? She wasn't though. She just wasn't maternal. Not every woman is.'

'No, that's true.'

Amber thought of how she had always wanted to marry, have a family with at least two children and a large, docile dog. She'd never considered settling down to be a compromise of freedom, and it shouldn't have been. But of course, her life with Ray was just that. She longed to tell Alfred, to beg him to help her, but it was futile. He loved his son, who was she to turn them against each other?

'She fell pregnant by accident and tried to be happy about it. She altered her life plans, started looking at trips that we could take with children in tow. But Ray wasn't an easy child, bless him. He cried a lot, got sick often. It wouldn't have been fair to drag him around the world on grand adventures. And two years later she fell pregnant again. Dean was born, and she became very depressed. She loved him, she loved them both. But pregnancy can do that can't it? And love isn't always enough to conquer depression.'

'No,' Amber agreed, amazed at the new insight into Ray's life. She did not know he had a brother.

'When Dean was three, Ray five, she left. Marie. She didn't even tell me, not face to face. She called me, and told me she loved us all, but she belonged in a different life, in another part of the world. I thought it was a blip, that she needed some space and time, but she didn't come back. We lived up in Cheadle Hulme then, in the house Ray still lives in. I stayed until the boys had grown up and when Marie still hadn't returned, I moved down here to be by the sea. The ocean is a short walk away, you know? The station too, which I don't get to use much now, but when I did it was only around the corner. Suited me wonderfully. Anyway, Ray bought the house from me, didn't want it out of the family. I think, privately, he still hopes she might come back.'

Amber took a long sip of wine to hide the tears filling her eyes. She could not imagine the betrayal Ray must have felt. She'd grown up with only one parent too, but her father walked out before she was born. It hadn't impacted her, she hadn't known a life with him, so it was no bother without him. But she thought of her connection to her own mother, the love, the impossibility of being apart from her. It had torn her in two when her mother died, but at least she only left Amber because she physically couldn't fight anymore. She would never have walked away, healthy, into a new life.

This is why he won't let you leave.

The voice penetrated Amber's thoughts, her own internal voice speaking a truth that made her gasp. She coughed as the acidic wine hit the back of her throat. She was right though, wasn't she? His mother had left him, and now he was making sure Amber didn't leave him too. Should she tell Alfred the truth? Maybe he'd help Ray consider the horror of what he was doing, what he had done.

'Have you met Dean?' Alfred asked.

Amber shook her head, answering his question and snapping herself back into the conversation. She couldn't tell Alfred about Ray's issues. His son was beyond help. 'No. I...I didn't even know Ray had a brother.'

'Ah. Those boys. They fell out years ago, over a woman no less! I was sure they'd be over it by now.'

'What're you two whispering about?' Ray asked, re-entering the room.

'Oh, nothing much, son,' sighed Alfred. 'How's the boy?'

'Asleep again. And it might be time for us to do the same. It was a long drive down, dad. I'm exhausted.'

*

Amber and Ray lay side by side. She had not considered that they'd be sharing a bed, but she should've assumed it. How would they explain it to Alfred if they were to sleep separately? She also suspected, by the way Ray's arm was curled around her waist, that he did not trust her not to get up in the night and run. He couldn't lock her up, not without his father noticing.

She positioned her body as far away from his possible, trying to ignore his raspy breathing and the weight of his arm against her. She felt for him, for what he'd been through, but she would never accept it as an excuse for what he had done to her. In over three years she had not managed to convince him she would stay, had not earned the trust Sarah had, that would allow her to live in a life of unlocked doors.

But she would have to make it happen. Because after hearing about Ray's mother, she was even more certain that, unless she did something drastic, Ray would never let her go.

Now - Austin

The train snaked out of Bath Spa station and Austin gulped a large mouthful of coffee. He'd ordered it strong, an extra shot of espresso, to make up for his lack of sleep. He'd spent the night turning over Amber's story in his head, re-reading the words from the note in his mind. He'd writhed against the bed sheets, unable to settle. At one point he even stared towards the bedroom window, considering if he'd be able to run at it and clamber out, should Amber attempt anything in the night.

In the morning light, when he'd padded into the kitchen to find Amber leant against the counter with a cup of tea and a bleary smile, he felt an idiot. She was petite, too skinny, gentle, and calm to be a threat. He had spent the night with his eyes forced open for nothing. He hid his red-faced shame by claiming he was too hot, and darted past her into the bathroom, plunging himself into a cold shower.

Now, sat opposite her on the train, Austin was still ashamed of his cowardice the night before. But there was no use dwelling on his stupidity. It was time to move forward.

'So, how come you think Ray's father has Alfie anyway? You think he was the person who drove up to Jasmine's house and took him?' Austin may have grown certain that Amber was telling the truth about Ray and Sarah, but he had less confidence in her plan.

'No. I...' Amber stopped, her skin milkier than her latte. 'When I was taken back to Ray, the day you met Alfie, he always insisted I'd lost his son. He blamed me, scolded me for it. But I was certain he was lying about Alfie not being home with him, to torture me. I was sure Ray had found him, that he was living in the house. But on Monday, when I escaped, I searched every room. And there was no sign of Alfie, no toys or books out, nothing. I can't believe Ray would just sit by while Alfie was missing. He'd have found him. The only thing that makes sense to me is that he found Alfie then sent him to live with somebody else. He has a busy job. I can't imagine him bringing up a child alone.'

'And do you really believe that?' Austin's stomach was knotted and tight, an acidic burn flaring in his chest. 'Do you believe Ray found him?'

'Somebody did.' Amber shuddered. 'I can only hope, can't I? And if Ray did find him, but wanted to keep him out of his house for some reason, he'd have given him to somebody he trusts. I don't think there are many people to choose from. I'm sure his father would be one of them.'

'So are we just going to march up to the old guy's front door? Demand to know if he has Alfie?'

'Alfred isn't like Ray,' Amber insisted. 'He's kind. If Ray had given him a good reason, he wouldn't have hesitated to take Alfie in. And Ray is a good liar. I'm sure he could've convinced him.'

'And how do you expect to get Alfie back from him? He's not likely to hand him over without checking with Ray first, is he?'

'He doesn't know about Sarah. He thinks I'm Alfie's real mum. We have to hope he doesn't question why I've turned up.'

'You've no idea what Ray could've told him, to explain why he was leaving Alfie in his care. It's pretty likely he would've made sure to turn his father against you, isn't it?' In Austin's mind, Amber's logic was becoming more and more flawed. He wanted her to be right, but he couldn't see the fairy-tale ending for the monsters and darkness. Amber shrugged, but her eyes betrayed her true feelings. They were pinched with uncertainty.

'I have to try, Austin.'

He tried to summon a fraction of her optimism. If Amber was right, and Alfie was with his grandfather, would everything be okay? For Austin, it would be the positive turn he'd dreamt of. Even if they didn't retrieve Alfie into Amber's care, at least they'd know he was okay, that he was alive. And if he'd been with his grandfather the whole time, then he would've been happy, loved, well looked after. Austin didn't dare hope too much, because if Amber had got it all wrong, he wasn't sure he could cope with another dead end.

Don't be selfish. How do you think she feels? What if she doesn't get him back?

Amber's body was tense, from the grip on her cardboard coffee cup, which was denting the sides, to the thin line of her lips. How must it feel for her, the not knowing?

But he's not really her son.

Austin shook his head. Sleep deprived thoughts were often dangerous. Nasty, niggling things that made him irrational and grumpy. She didn't need that. She needed support.

Alfie's real mum was murdered. Maybe by her.

Austin shook his head again.

'Are you okay?' Amber asked, tilting her own head, as she watched him through narrowed eyes.

'I'm fine.'

The proximity of their bodies in the cramped train put him on edge. They were still strangers, their lives entwined only by tragedies and mistakes. He longed for some time on his own, so he could be quiet and not feel bound to partake in conversation. He'd even take a shift at the office if it meant he could sit in silence, and think of nothing but the mundane, nothing that mattered. The roar of the train reminded him of the persistent rattling of the carriages that passed by the office window, shaking the glass. How he had longed to jump onboard one of those trains, and now he was, he longed to jump off.

'Alfie really loved magic,' Amber said, the softness of her voice breaking through Austin's thoughts. 'He always did.'

Austin smiled. He thought of his own love of magic, of circus acts and illusions. For most people, it wasn't their first choice of entertainment anymore, but he had still drawn in the crowds. Still made them laugh with classic jokes and tricks that were simple but clever. Alfie had been a willing volunteer, wowed and amazed at every moment.

'That's why you stopped to watch my act?'

'Yes. We watched a lot of street acts. We were heading towards a café at the time though, I wasn't planning on stopping to watch anything. And then we heard a lady's voice from the crowd. She said *oh wow, this guy is amazing!* And that was that. As soon as I saw you were a magician I knew I'd never pull Alfie away.'

'Magic does that to a person.'

A shimmer of excitement sparked in Austin's veins as he pictured the shows he had loved the most, the thrill of trying more daring acts, which he'd gotten to experience for a time in London. How alive it made him, to play at magic, to make it. An energy so strong he could be sure magic was real, not in the tricks themselves, but in the way people responded to them. In the way they made him feel.

'You were good.' Amber smiled. 'You were really, really good.'

Her words set Austin's mind racing, sent him flying back to happier times. He remembered his training, his failed years trying to make it as an actor, and the magic that had lifted him out of despair and into a world of applause, of joy, of happiness. He thought of the moment he passed his Covent Garden audition, the celebrities he sometimes spotted in his crowds, their kids in tow. He thought of Jasmine, of her unashamed enthusiasm, the only adult that whooped and cheered with all the abandon of a child. He thought of the effortless bliss of their early relationship, the willingness to pack up his box of tricks and move it from London to Bath.

'Yes,' Austin agreed. 'Yes, I was good.'

'Why don't you do it anymore?' Amber asked, but he could tell from the way she avoided making eye contact that she already knew the answer. Did she blame herself? Were they both guiltily aware that their actions, in one way or another, had ruined the other's life?

'Oh, look!' Austin pointed out of the window, desperate to pull the conversation away. 'I see the sea!'

Amber twisted in her seat until her face was almost pressed against the glass, taking in the sprawling, glittering blue that had come into view as the train thundered on. Austin was relieved when she carried on staring, grateful the conversation was over.

But beneath his awkwardness, buried under his discomfort, there was a slither of something heating his veins, so potent his blood rushed and his heart came close to bursting.

Then - Amber

By lunch time the following day they were already hauling their bags into the car, ready for the long drive back to Manchester. Amber didn't want to go. She liked Alfred, his presence was warm and welcoming. She'd had such little interaction with adults over the last few years, it was refreshing to spend time with somebody kind and genuine. Alfred's expression was as stooped as his posture as he waited to wave them goodbye. She wished she could stay, with Alfie too, and look after him. A life by the sea, the station just around the corner for days out and adventures, and a male influence that would be positive in her son's life. It would be perfect. But she knew it could never happen.

In the car the seatbelt pinned Amber to the chair, and she tugged at it, pulling it away from her chest as she squirmed in her seat.

'Will you sit still?' Ray hissed, fastening his own seat belt without a fuss.

Amber did as she was told, if only to avoid an argument. As the car rolled to a start, they all waved from the windows, Alfie included, fingers wiggling, smiles on their faces. Through the glass the whole world could be convinced they were a normal, happy family.

The journey took even longer than the trip down, piles of traffic slowing the pace. Ray drummed his fingers against the steering wheel, muttering profanities under his breath. When the cars finally fell into a steady flow, he leaned back into his seat, his shoulders lowering as he let out a long sigh.

'Dad liked you,' he said, throwing a quick glance in Amber's direction. 'Well done.'

She cringed at his words. *Well done.* As though it had been some great achievement, as though she'd needed to trick Alfred into finding her likeable. She'd been herself around Ray's father, that was all. Or at least as much herself as she could remember to be.

As the car slid down the motorway, Amber sunk beneath the heavy weight in her stomach. A fluttering sickness motioned like waves and forced her to clench her jaw to keep anything that rose to her mouth inside. Could she cope going back to the spare room? How many more years would it be?

Years? No, no, no, not years. Not even days, please!

The helplessness tormented her, and as she dug her fingers into her palms she believed she might go crazy. Ray's plan had worked. Having a child had put an end to Amber's escape plans. Any opportunity requiring speed or spontaneity would be abandoned, hindered by the need to carry a two-year-old.

Amber looked at Ray, studying his face, as she often did, for signs of madness. His features were soft; plump lips, round nose, a thin graze of light hair. It was only his eyes that were sharp, the dangerous husky-blue she once found so alluring. Noticing her attention, Ray's brow furrowed while he kept his sight on the road ahead.

'What are you looking at me like that for, Amber?'

'Why do you do it?' The question was out before she'd even decided she was going to ask it.

'Do what?'

'This. Me. Keeping me locked away. Everything you did to Sarah.'

Did she imagine it or did he flinch when she said Sarah's name? Was that his weak point? The murder? Perhaps even he never thought he was capable of such senseless evil.

'It's no life, Ray. You can't keep me locked up forever. And what will it do to little Alfred? He needs more of a life than this.'

'I take Alfred out, every Saturday! We're out *now* aren't we?'

'But it's not enough! He needs more, he needs to make friends, he needs to spend more time outside. It's not good for him, cooped up in the house all day. And what about me, Ray? Didn't we love each other once? Can't you find enough respect for me to at least leave the door unlocked?'

'Respect? I still love you, you stupid woman! I told you before, I am keeping you safe. I'm doing it because I love you. I can't believe your lack of gratitude.'

'Are you sure you're not just doing this because your mum left you? You're scared I'm going to do the same, aren't you? You were scared back then, when you first locked me up, and you're scared now. Because you did the same to Sarah, and you're doing it to your own son as well. You can't just lock away everybody you love, like exhibits in a fucking museum!'

'Shut up, Amber,' Ray snarled, his fingers tightening on the steering wheel, his body stiffening.

They were still on the motorway, thundering over the asphalt, and Amber knew she shouldn't distract him. But the words were spilling from her lips like cascading water, and she couldn't stem the flood.

'You can't lock women up just because your mum left your dad, abandoned you and your brother! It may not have been kind, but people have a right to freedom, to make their own choices. It's not for you to make choices for me, Ray!'

With a dizzying lurch, Ray swerved the car to the left, dragging it onto the hard shoulder. The tyres squealed as he slammed his foot onto the break, and once the car was still he punched the hazard light button with such force, Amber was amazed it didn't shatter. Without hesitation Amber spun in her seat to check on Alfie. He was fast asleep, his breathing soft and steady, his black lashes fluttering as he remained in the blissful state of dreaming. By contrast, Ray's face was a deep, blood red, his jaw so taut he looked manic.

'Get out then,' he said, his voice soft and calm, despite the curl of his lip, the tension in his bunched shoulders. 'If that's what you want, get out.'

'What?' Amber's mouth was dry, her fingers itched to grab the handle but her arm was too heavy to lift them there.

'The door's unlocked. Go, if you want to. See if I care. But you don't get to take Alfred. He's my son, remember? It's my blood he shares, not a drop of yours. If you want to leave, leave. But I won't let you have my boy. And even if you tried to take him, how would that look? I'd report you for kidnap. Kidnapped by the woman who stabbed his real mother. That's got quite a ring to it, hasn't it? That would really cement my story, Amber. You would go to prison and you would never, ever see Alfred again.'

Dread and horror crawled over Amber's skin, scurrying spider's legs that made her want to scream. Two years ago, before Alfie was born, nothing in the world would've stopped her from throwing the car door open. She'd have scrambled out onto the grassy bank without a moment's hesitation, undeterred by the flash of passing traffic and the lack of anything but countryside for miles. It wouldn't have mattered. She'd have been free.

But that all changed when Alfie was born. Because she wasn't one person anymore, she was two. Whether Ray believed it or not, despite the difference in blood, she was a mother, and her priorities had shifted. Ray had exactly what he wanted. She would never leave Alfie behind.

Understanding her silence, Ray smirked and revved the engine with a roar that made Amber flinch. He merged onto the motorway with ease, and drove them onwards, back towards her prison.

Now - Austin

They exited the station and though there was no sign of the ocean, sea salt lingered on the air, mingling with the cry of seagulls.

'This way.' Amber waved to the left and strode with confidence as Austin followed.

It had been years since she visited Ray's father and Austin was amazed at her memory, even though she shrugged off his appraisal.

'Alfred lives near the station. He said as much when I met him. I recognise the streets. I hadn't been out for a long, long time when I came down here. Alfred took us for a walk, the morning before we left. I took in every little detail. You don't forget after that.'

Guilt smouldered in Austin's chest as he recalled once more the freedom he had taken for granted. The madness of Amber's world plunged his own into a light he'd been too stubborn to switch on. She had been locked away, forced to live in a darkness far greater than his. It frightened him to accept somebody could do such a thing to another human, that such wickedness lay undetected, ready to lure in innocent bystanders and blow their worlds apart.

He could think of nothing to say to convey his empathy, nor his admiration, so he followed Amber's lead in silence until they reached a narrow row of town houses. When they were halfway down the street Amber placed her hand on one the gates, reaching down for the latch without a moment to pause. Austin took a step back, away from the house. He didn't have a part in the story Amber would spin to Ray's father, and he wished he could wait around the corner.

Bloody coward.

'Do I really need to come in with you? He'll ask who I am, won't he? What are we going to say?'

They'd already established Alfred did not know of Ray's true nature, and Amber intended to keep it that way. She was to tell him Ray left her after a row and ask for ideas on where he might have gone, hoping he would admit he'd been looking after Alfie. If he had, and Alfie was there, Amber planned to improvise stage two of the plan, making it up on the spot. Even after his years of training, the notion of putting on such an act made Austin queasy.

'I'd like you to come in with me. We'll just say you're a friend. I'd go with brother, but the Australian accent might give it away.' She managed a smile.

'I am a qualified actor,' Austin said, indignant. 'I can do an English accent.'

He much preferred the idea of being introduced as her brother, worried Ray's father would otherwise think he was the cause of the fictional row between Amber and Ray. If Alfred thought Amber had another man in her life, he could be less willing to help.

'Brother it is then,' Amber agreed, letting herself in through the gate and knocking hard on the door.

The silence as they waited dragged, and it could've been two hours rather than minutes. Austin didn't know what would be worse, the door opening or the door remaining closed. Eventually, it creaked open and an old man peered into the sunlight. He had pocked skin, his hand trembled as he lifted it to his brow and cast shadow over his eyes. His back was bent, distorting his posture, but he still managed to stand tall as he studied the two of them.

'Can I help?' he croaked. 'Am...Amber? Is that you, love?'

'Hello Alfred,' she said, with a tearful smile. 'How are you?'

'Oh, I'm fine, love, I'm fine. I wasn't expecting to see you! Is Ray here? Who's this gentleman?'

'This is my brother, Austin,' Amber explained, as Austin held up a hand in hello. 'Ray's not here. He...we had an argument, Alfred, if I'm honest. Quite a while back. He...he took little Alfred, and I've not seen him since. I wondered if he might be here? Or if he's left Alfred with you?'

'Slow down, Amber. Why don't you come on in, and I'll make us all a cup of tea?'

They followed him into his house, down a tight hallway and into a living room that was messy, though not unclean. The curtains were closed, and the pale orange from a lamp in the corner wasn't enough to light the room. When Alfred gestured at them to sit down, Austin put his hand out first to make sure he sank into the sofa instead of falling flat on his arse.

*How is anyone meant to see anything in this crappy light?
No wonder he had to squint like a lost mole when he answered
the door.*

As soon as Alfred hobbled into the kitchen to make tea,
Amber leant forward and peered through the dark, taking in
the piles of newspaper and ugly ornaments. Austin followed her
lead, searching for any sign a child might be living there.

There were no toys, no crayons or books or tiny pairs of
sneakers. Amber twisted her fingers in her lap and Austin didn't
dare admit, even to himself, that it wasn't looking likely. Alfred
returned in time to save Austin from having to find some words
of comfort, placing mugs of tea in their hands before dropping
into the armchair opposite with a wheezy sigh.

'I've not heard from Ray in a while, love,' he said. 'I'm sorry.
But I'm sure it's all going to be okay. This row, whatever it was
about, it doesn't have to mean the end. You'll figure it out.'

'I thought that maybe...maybe he might've bought little
Alfred to stay with you for a bit? Because Ray still has to go
to work, doesn't he?' The desperation in her voice was painful.
Austin stared into his tea, hoping without confidence.

'I've not seen little Alfred, or Ray for that matter, since your
last visit. When was that now?'

'Almost three years ago,' Amber whispered, her lip trembling.

'Don't cry, love. You'll all be back together soon, you're his
family. He can get in nasty strops, our Ray. Remember his falling
out with his brother? Terrible those boys are, I could knock their
heads together.'

Austin snapped his attention to Amber, expecting her to look surprised, but she didn't. Ray had a brother. If she knew that, why hadn't she said?

'Are they still not talking?' she asked.

'I don't think so. I spoke to Dean just last night, on the phone. I asked about Ray, if they'd seen each other, but he said no, and he didn't want to talk about him. Those boys.'

Austin groaned inwardly, bringing his hand to his mouth to stifle the sound. It seemed obvious now that Amber hadn't mentioned Ray's brother because she hadn't considered Dean an option in her search for Alfie. If the brothers had fallen out then Ray wouldn't have placed his son into Dean's care. It was another dead end. Unless...

Austin thought hard, hope stirring his mind into a frenzy. What if Ray and Dean had made up? What if Ray had kept that from Amber, so she would never assume Dean was the person she needed to find? She always said Ray was clever, so of course he'd be the type to play games. They couldn't let him win.

He wanted to leave, to explain his theory to Amber. But it felt rude to get up and ditch the old man within minutes of arriving. His frail features lifted in Amber's presence, it'd be cruel to walk out so soon. Even if the house did smell a little like sour milk.

'Where does Dean live?' Austin asked, hoping his English accent was convincing. It was a little strained, he was out of practice, but he doubted old Alfred had the strongest ear for listening.

Alfred's heavy eyebrows dipped at his question, and Austin regretted asking it so bluntly. It wasn't the sort of thing Amber's *brother* would ask, but he wasn't sure if she knew the details of

Ray's brother's life, and he was damned if they were going to leave without them.

'I just mean, does he live near Amber and Ray?'

'Not far off,' Alfred nodded. 'Still the Manchester area. He lives in Hazel Grove. He runs his own business there.'

'Manchester?' Amber asked, her spine straightening as though something had lifted inside her.

Austin felt it too, a sense of progress. He dared to hope. Funny, how he had trained in walking through fire, and not once had that been as daunting as allowing himself to believe he and Amber were on to something.

*

After two hours of small talk they finally made their way out of the house and into the salty sea air. Austin knew Amber had dragged out the conversation to be kind, not wanting to show up on Alfred's door only to leave again moments later. But Austin was still glad to be out, where he could stretch his legs and take away the pretence of being Amber's quiet, English brother.

'So, Dean?' he asked her once they'd rounded the corner.

'He lives near Manchester' Amber said, nodding with an enthusiasm he'd not seen in her before. They were clearly thinking along the same lines. 'I suppose it makes more sense than Alfie living all the way down here. Ray was living with me in his house, but Alfie wasn't. If Dean lived nearby then he'd have been the perfect choice for looking after Alfie. Because Ray would've been able to visit him whenever he wanted.'

Austin battled to keep his hopes as high as hers, but logic was starting to seep through the cracks in his optimism. Alfred had said the brothers had not made up. And even if they had, why would Ray not have Alfie live in the same house as him? Was it purely to torture Amber, as she suggested?

'Amber, I know you've told me a lot now, about Ray and what you've been through. But tell me more about the last eleven months. What happened after you were taken from Bath?'

Amber sighed, but for once she did not resist.

'I was taken back to Ray, to his house in Cheadle Hulme. Whenever he came to see me, to give me food, I begged to see Alfie. But Ray kept saying Alfie wasn't there, that I should've looked after him better. He was just punishing me though, I'm sure of it. Trying to drive me to insanity from the guilt. It wasn't until I escaped from my room on Monday morning that I realised Ray had been telling the truth about Alfie not being there. But I'm sure he found him the same day he found me. He must be keeping him safe somewhere else. I honestly think Dean might be our best bet now.'

Austin scratched at the itch that told him Ray hadn't lied and Alfie was still lost somewhere, after all this time. But Ray would've called the police, wouldn't he? To report his son missing?

He's an abuser and a murderer. You think he wants to speak to the police?

Austin couldn't make sense of any of it, but he knew one thing. Amber would not rest until she had found her son, and if that meant travelling to Manchester to hunt down Ray's brother, then she would do it. And he would too.

Then - Amber

Amber sat cross legged on the bed, gnawing at the skin around her thumb. It was sore and sensitive but she couldn't stop nibbling, nor find any other way to distract herself. She had the resources to paint but no energy or drive to pick up a brush. What was the point?

In her university days she had painted between lectures, proud of her creative enthusiasm and productivity. Things shifted when she tumbled into the real world and landed her first full time job. During her time in marketing she missed those care-free painting days. Designing logos was art, she'd supposed, but it was static and still. Blocks of colour, clear cut fonts, sharp angles, and a professional finish. She had longed for the lucid freedom of paint, the pastels leaking into one another, chaotic but beautiful.

And yet, with more spare time than she had ever thought possible, painting wasn't enough. It did not free her as it used to, nor fill her with a blaze of passion. Even when she stared into the mirror at the thinner, paler version of her former self, she took no comfort in the smudge of sky blue across her cheek, or hazy pink flecks in her hair. She used to think the clumsy splashes dried to her skin made her look like an artist. But they didn't, not anymore. She just looked a mess.

Saturdays were the hardest days. Ray and Alfie's day, father and son bonding time. She couldn't make the most of her free time, without Alfie at her side she was rendered incapable of even the simplest functions. She curled herself onto the bed like a cat, waiting, vision pinned to the windowless wall, chewing away the skin from her fingers.

It was so much more than loneliness. Every Saturday, a fiery itch prickled beneath the surface of her skin, a fear she couldn't reach to scratch. What if, one day, they didn't come back? One day, Ray might take Alfie and start a new life. It wasn't her inevitable perishing that worried her, but the prospect of never seeing her son again. She couldn't cope without him.

So far, they had always returned. She reminded herself by saying it in her head and sometimes out loud.

They always come back. They always have.

Alfie would bound into the room with flushed cheeks, babbling as he recounted his adventures to Amber with such excitement, he often shouted it. A hurricane of jealousy tore through her, knowing Ray was able to spend time with Alfie at zoos and parks and museums. She could picture his round blue eyes, his mouth agape as he took in his surroundings and learnt new and amazing things. At three years old he was mesmerised by everything and anything, and Amber longed to experience his discovery of the world.

Unfurling her stiff limbs, Amber leant over the side of the bed and dragged her paint bag from underneath. Inside was no longer just her paints and her secret bank card, but so much more. A collection that grew by the week. Unbeknown to Ray, whenever he took Alfie out for the day, he bought a treasure back for her. It was always something simple, something small, but he never returned with empty pockets. Every time, it was a tiny link the outside world that she craved.

She emptied the gifts onto the bed in front of her, wiping away a tear as her heart raced for her compassionate, intelligent son. She brushed a finger over an autumn leaf, careful not to let it crumble beneath her touch. The day Alfie bought it back, several months after the trip to Portsmouth, she had bought the leaf to her face and breathed in its tangy scent. She cried at his choice of gift, pulling him into a tight hug and thanking him with kisses until his cheeks were pink and he couldn't stop giggling.

Amber continued her ritual, picking up the treasures one by one. She clasped a smooth, round stone in her palm, rubbing it until the surface was warm. She touched her tongue to a shell that tasted of salt water, brushed a feather across her cheek. She studied a tiny, purple flower, amazed by its intricacy, and knotted a piece of string around her finger before unknotting it again and laying it flat on the mattress.

Alfie never came back empty handed, and it comforted Amber to know she was not alone in the world, not entirely cut off. If she had Alfie, she would be okay.

And that was why she sat so rigid, her body sore and tired, waiting for his return.

Now - Austin

They agreed they would go back to Bath before heading to Manchester. Get some rest, do some research on Dean Tallon and his business. Hopefully he would be easy to find. Austin called Sam and asked if he could borrow his car for the journey, so they could leave early in the morning without having to wait for the train. Ever the supportive friend, who rarely asked questions and was as generous as he was kind, he said yes.

'Let's go to the beach before we go back to yours,' Amber suggested.

Austin raised his eyebrows, surprised, but was more than happy to oblige. The sun was still high in the sky, the evening darkness at bay for a few more hours. And he was starving, eager to find somewhere that sold fish and chips.

It wasn't hard to find a chippy, and before long Austin and Amber each held a steaming paper bag filled with salty chips, the rich vinegar seeping through and making their hands greasy. Austin shoved fistfuls into his mouth, burning his tongue, while Amber picked at hers as they made their way to the seafront, the air ringing with the jingle of an ice cream van and the screech of gulls.

They walked off the promenade, over the stony surface of the pebble beach and right up to the water's edge. Amber slid off her shoes and stood where the lapping waves could tickle her toes. Austin moved his gaze from her and stared out across the sparkling blue of the ocean, a weight settling in his chest. He'd not realised it, but he longed for home. Not Bath, but Melbourne, the home that was so, so far away.

He'd always loved the beach and Australia made that love effortless and impossible to diminish. He could picture it, the miles of golden sand, the glittering waves that lifted the surfers as they rode into the shore. The crystal clean views and meaty aroma of BBQ smoke. It was nothing like that in Portsmouth.

Sharp shards of rock littered the shore where the sand should be, shingle and shells greeting the sea instead. The surroundings were moody and grey. Old navy bases and ugly brick buildings that Austin guessed were apartments, even though they looked like prisons.

And yet there was something charming about it. He loved the way the pebbles crackled as the waves swept back to the sea, the quaint sailboats dotting the horizon with white peaks. The way Amber stared at her bare feet as the ocean lapped against her white skin, and her toes wriggling against the shells.

'I never want to forget how this feels,' she sighed, smiling up at him, the sun catching her eyes and turning them the colour of honey.

'Forget how what feels?'

'The sea. The shells. The sun. All of it.' She laughed, but only for an instant. She snatched the sound away, burying her smile and facing the floor with her face screwed up.

'You're allowed to laugh, Amber. You don't need to feel guilty about it.'

Amber shook her head, initiating a silence that grew between them, water spilling through the cracks. After a few deep breaths Amber bent down and lifted a pebble, bringing it to her lips as she straightened to stand. She stuck her tongue out in a neat point and grazed it along the surface of the stone.

'Uh...you okay, Amber?' Austin didn't know whether to laugh or cry, but tears gathered in the corners of his eyes and he blinked hard to dull the stinging and keep them from falling.

'Yeah. My mum used to take me on beach holidays as a child. I'd spend every day splashing in the sea until my hair was caked in sand and my mouth was full of sea salt. The taste, it takes me right back.'

'Did you used to lick pebbles back then too?'

Amber smirked, raising an eyebrow. Austin was relieved to have defused some of the tension, glad she hadn't taken him the wrong way and been annoyed by his comment. She shook her head.

'You're from Australia,' she said.

'Yeah. Haven't lived there since I was a kid though. My parents are back out there now. I've not been over myself for a while.'

'I bet the beaches there are incredible.'

'Oh yeah. Nothing like this. Stunning, absolute beauty! And the pebbles?' Austin kissed his fingertips. 'To die for!'

Amber launched the stone at Austin so that it hit him on the arm.

'Ow!' he cried, even though it hadn't hurt.

She laughed again but shut it off at the same speed as before, wrapping her arms around her waist and letting her lips droop to a grimace. Austin plunged into an ice-cold wave of empathy, a sensation so strong it could've forced him to his knees. What must it be like to be locked away, never knowing if you'll ever feel the sun on your skin again? Never knowing if you'll ever hear the roar of the ocean or the cackle of gulls? He was stunned Amber hadn't descended into madness. Away from her prison, her freedom was tainted by her missing son, the grief, the need to find him, so strong that it spared no room for moments of happiness or laughter. The weight of her reality crushed the air from Austin's lungs, and he leant forward, resting his hands on his legs.

'Are you okay, Austin?'

When he looked up, Amber's eyes were on his, her hair tangled as the wind whipped it around her face. She kept bringing a hand up to push the gold-brown strands away.

'You're so brave,' he told her, aware of how lame the words sounded out loud. 'You really are. You've been through so much and...well, I just...'

'It's not really bravery,' Amber said, but her cheeks reddened. 'It's coping. I got caught up in a nightmare, I made some awful mistakes. But I'm coping with it because I can't give up now. I've got to make it right.'

'Tell me more about when you were taken from my act. Who took you? How?'

Amber's face paled, any trace of her blush erased as her haunting memories took centre stage in the theatre of her mind. 'I really don't know who it was. I don't know of any women in

Ray's life. His mother left the family when he was young. And she'd have been too old anyway. Not that I saw the woman, but I heard her voice, saw her arm. That was the most I saw of her.'

'But why didn't you see her? I don't get it. How did it all play out, without you getting to look at her?'

'She threatened me. Told me I'd never see Alfie again, that he wouldn't be safe. When she spoke, I thought it was Sarah at first, I nearly passed out from the shock. But my mind must've been playing tricks on me. Willing her to be alive, you know? I realised pretty soon it wasn't her. Whoever it was, she told me not to look at her. And I didn't because I was scared. Then she made me climb into the back of a van and I was in darkness until I arrived at Ray's house. It was him all along, the one driving. But the woman who led me there? I have no idea. I saw her arm as she was helping me into the van. She had a slight tan, a couple of freckles. No tattoos, no jewellery, nothing identifiable. That's all I've got.'

'Maybe Ray paid somebody?' Austin suggested, though he found it unlikely. Amber's story was difficult to believe. Why did he keep doubting her? They'd been through so much in the space of only two days, and yet he found it unnatural to trust her.

'Maybe. I don't know, Austin.'

He couldn't piece it together. Why, in a plan so elaborate, was no-one placed in the crowd, waiting to snatch Alfie when the act was finished? Perhaps they were...

So why didn't they just bloody take him, instead of leaving me to deal with it?

Austin shook his head, ashamed at the thought and glad it remained trapped in his conscious, and not out in the open.

They must've been watching him, whoever it was. They could've followed him, and then crept the van up the track at the back of Jasmine's house. They got lucky when Alfie fled from the living room and ran out, unwatched as Austin called the police. Even as he considered it, Austin knew it didn't add up. There were too many coincidences.

Cutting through all his thoughts and theories, Austin couldn't silence the nagging voice whispering in his ear, telling him that Amber knew a lot more than she was letting on.

Then - Amber

Amber sat with her legs drawn to her chest, eyes fixed to a blank section of wall. She often stared at that spot, pretending there was a window in its place. Beyond the crystal-clear glass, she could see the sprawling countryside, the greens morphing to orange as the leaves stiffened and fell. She could see birds with their wings spread wide as they dipped and dived through the sky, and Alfie playing in the garden, his mouth wide open in laughter.

In reality, there was nothing but beige, painted to perfection, no streaks or lines to find patterns in. Empty nothingness, like the hollow weight in her heart whenever Alfie wasn't with her. The only thing keeping her from flying at the wall and banging her head against it was knowing her little boy would be home before long, with his gift from the outside at the ready. She occupied herself by wondering what it might be.

It was October, early Autumn. She hoped for another leaf, so she could take comfort in the warm auburn hue and crisp texture. It had always been her favourite time of year, wearing boots with soft lining as her footsteps crushed the fallen leaves, making them creak and crunch. She loved the earthy scent on the air, and the sweet sips of hot chocolate from takeaway cups full of frothy cream and fat marshmallows.

What else might Alfie bring for her? Sometimes it was twigs or berries, their colours catching her imagination and sparking the motivation to pull out her paint sets and lean over the desk as she dabbed watery browns and reds onto the page.

She still hated the waiting, the wondering what time they'd be back. But as time passed she had come to trust that they would always return, and her old fear of Ray disappearing with Alfie had somewhat calmed. Alife had been sleeping in her room recently, Ray apparently fed up of his night terrors and the need to wake up and console his son. So, Alfie spent the days and the nights with Amber, curled at her side while he fell into dreamless sleep. He never so much as twitched or groaned, and Amber smouldered with pride, knowing she was able to comfort him. She knew it was wrong, the life Ray forced upon them, but when Alfie was asleep at her side it felt so right she couldn't imagine living any other way.

When they returned, Amber heard their footsteps before their voices. Ray insisted they use quiet voices inside, something Alfie was still getting used to. As they drew closer, Alfie's voice grew louder, his high tones full of excitement. Amber crouched as the door opened, arms outstretched, welcoming Alfie as he bounded into the room and nearly knocked her over with the force of his embrace.

'Did you have a lovely day, sweetheart?' she asked, planting a kiss on his cold, rosy cheeks.

'Yes, mummy. We played in the garden.'

'In the garden? Did you not go out somewhere?'

'We don't always have to go somewhere else, Amber. The garden is more than adequate. He was perfectly happy.' Ray's voice was clipped and Amber turned her attention to him. Deep frown lines were etched into his skin, he flexed his fingers, balling his hand into a fist before opening it again.

'I'm sure he was' Amber said. 'I was only asking. I'm so glad you had a lovely day!' She changed her pitch for Alfie's sake, shielding him from the tension.

' We played in the garden 'cause daddy lost a key.'

'Quiet, Alfred,' Ray snapped.

'A key?' Amber asked.

'Yes! Daddy found a key. Took ages!"

'Yes, son. Daddy found a key. Now enough about that. I'm going to make our dinner.'

He stormed out, the door slamming into the frame with a bang that made Amber flinch.

'Daddy found a key, mummy,' Alfie repeated, unfazed by his father's stress. 'He was sad, he looked like this.' Alfie scrunched his face, frowning and puffing out his cheeks. 'When he found the key, his face was like this!' Alfie's face transformed into a huge smile.

'Well, it's good that daddy found his key. What was it for?'

She already had a suspicion, but she wanted to know for sure. It had to be the key for her room. Had he dropped it, misplaced it? Her throat tightened as she imagined what would happen if he'd not found it. Would he have removed the whole door to get to her? He couldn't leave her without food. Or would he have left her? Better to let her rot, than to make it too easy for her to escape. She relaxed into the knowledge that he'd found it, but her body stiffened when she considered his carelessness. How could he risk losing something so important? She was a human being, not an old box of unwanted possessions.

'Don't know. Guess what, mummy?' Alfie hopped from one foot to the other, and Amber could tell he was desperate to tell her something.

'What's that, little Alf?'

'I found a key like daddy. It's for you, mummy.'

He plunged his hand into his coat pocket and pulled out a long, silver key. Amber's heart galloped, pounding the walls of her chest. Did she dare believe it was the key Ray had lost? Her key? It couldn't be, he had found it. He used it only five minutes ago. A sharpness punctured her heart so all the hope leaked out, deflating it.

'Oh, it's beautiful, darling. Thank you.'

She pulled Alfie into a hug, grateful for his gift, as she always was. She tried to ignore the nagging optimism, stamping it down. The disappointment would break her. It was probably a random key. Every door in the house had similar locks to the one on her room. It could be for any one of them.

'Don't tell daddy about the key,' Amber whispered, tucking it into her pillow case. She wanted to believe, at least for a little while. 'It will be a mummy and Alfie secret.'

'Okay, mummy,' Alfie whispered, bringing a finger to his lips with a hushed giggle.

While they waited for dinner, Alfie told Amber about his games in the garden. He played wizard, using a long stick as a wand and babbling funny words like spells. She stroked her fingers through his thick, black hair as he told her, amazed at how inventive he was, even at three years old, with nobody to play with.

Dinner was chicken breast with rice and vegetables served, as always, on paper plates with plastic cutlery. Alfie didn't seem to mind, he didn't know any different. But for Amber, she could never shake off the semblance to being in jail.

When they'd finished eating, and Ray had taken away their plates and said goodnight, Amber settled Alfie into the bed for sleep. As soon as his breathing deepened, and his body relaxed, Amber removed the key from the pillowcase and paced the room.

Please let this be it. Please let it be the key.

She thought of Ray's behaviour when he and Alfie came in from their day together, the haggard skin and sunken eyes. Why would he have spent the whole day searching for a key? It had to be an important one, and she considered that gave her three options. It was either the main house key, his car key, or the key to her room. She doubted he'd have been so frantic about the first two, he had spares for them both.

Spares.

Did he have a spare key for the bedroom too? Maybe he gave up looking for the key, resorted to using the spare instead. What if the reason he'd never found the original was because Alfie had already picked it up and tucked it away, pleased at his choice of gift for his mummy.

Amber needed to be careful, be clever, bide her time. She would wait, and she would wait for hours, until Ray was almost certainly asleep. She sat on the bed, determined not to fall asleep herself, the key warm and heavy in her clammy palm. There was a fission of energy coursing through her, spurred on by images of the door pulling open at her will.

But there was another image too, dulling the current. They key sliding into the lock but refusing to twist. No turning, no motion at all. It could be the wrong key, was most likely the wrong key. But she couldn't *not* give it a go.

Long, agonising minutes passed, and she wished she had a way of knowing the time. When she was certain she'd left it late enough, she pulled on her jacket and a pair of daps. She longed for more comfortable shoes, but knew her trainers, if Ray had kept them, would be on the shoe rack in the hallway. She did not want to dither. She would have to make do. She pulled her debit card from its hiding place and slipped it into her pocket.

Without a sound she woke Alfie by rubbing his back, rousing him from sleep so he grumbled, rubbing his eyes. 'Mummy? What you doing?'

'Shhh, Alfie. I've got a game to play, but you have to be really quiet, alright? Promise me you'll be super quiet.'

'Promise,' he yawned.

He was quiet and compliant as she removed his pyjamas and wrapped him up warm in the clothes he'd worn earlier that day; a jumper, a large puffy coat, and his tiny walking boots. Alfie remained silent throughout, either because he was tired, or because he was doing as Amber had asked. She wondered what she would say to him if the key didn't work and she had to undress him and tuck him back into bed. She supposed she would tell him it was all part of the game and hope he didn't tell Ray about it in the morning.

When they were both dressed, Amber looked at Alfie and bought her finger to her lips. He copied her, grinning. Amber pulled the key from her pocket and slid it into the lock. She held it still for a moment, scared to twist. Terrified it wouldn't work and the searing hope would plummet and send her spiralling into dark and dangerous despair. Through her tension she forced her wrist to take action, to move, her fingers clasped around the key as she did.

It clicked.

Oh my god, it clicked!

She pulled the handle, holding her breath until her chest ached. The door inched open and Amber guided it until the exit was fully exposed. She stared into the empty hallway, lit only by the moonlight pouring through the glass double doors that led to the balcony.

She turned to Alfie, placed her finger to her lips again, and then reached out for his hand. They tiptoed through the hall, Alfie's body shaking in a way that meant he was suppressing giggles. To him it was all a game, and Amber was happy to keep it that way. They crept down the stairs. Amber's pulse halted as one of the boards creaked. It was no use stopping to listen for any sign that Ray had woken. Blood rushed in her ears, drowning out any other noise. All they could do was press on.

From the staircase they shuffled to the front door. Amber pulled the bolt across, grateful that it slid into place without a clunk. She reached for the latch, pulled it down, and the door opened with a creak so low it was a whisper of its own. Even through the tension Amber couldn't suppress a smile. It was like the house was co-operating with her, willing her freedom.

'Cold, mummy!' Alfie groaned as the air filtered in.

'Shh, Alfie. It'll be okay,' Amber whispered back, stepping forward and letting the cool air embrace her. She didn't bother to close the door, it would've meant turning around, looking behind her. The only way was forward. 'Want to run, Alfie? It'll warm us up. And the winner, whoever runs the fastest, can have a hot chocolate.'

Alfie stopped shivering and grinned, breaking into a run. Amber ran to match his pace, though her legs longed to push harder, faster, carrying her far, far away. She grabbed Alfie's hand once they reached the lane outside of the driveway, and with a stab to her heart, ignored his confusion as they continued to run down the track towards the distant lights of the town. When they reached the lit streets of Cheadle Hulme, Amber's muscles were screaming in pain. She slowed her pace.

'We can walk for a bit now, Alf. Not far to go.'

'Where we going, mummy?'

'For hot chocolate, remember?' Amber forced a smile. Further ahead she could see the glowing blue sign of a convenience store, the ATM logo silhouetted against its hue. All she needed was the cashpoint and then a taxi. They were so close.

Though her muscles ached, Amber's body was light, her fingers and toes tingling in a way that was not unpleasant, but still odd. It was like she was dreaming.

After all those months, all those years, of planning elaborate escapes, it was so easy.

They just walked away.

Now - Austin

As they rounded the corner, heading towards his flat, Austin scanned their surroundings as though Ray might be perched on a rooftop, watching like a sniper. He had even prepared himself to find his window smashed, a rock on the carpet surrounded by a sprinkling of glass. He'd used ransom-note style cut outs before, a brick through the window didn't seem like a stretch.

All appeared normal as he and Amber entered the hallway. There wasn't even a folded note on the floor or tucked into the slit of the letterbox. Amber sighed, her shoulders loosening as she checked. She was relieved, but Austin couldn't force his own taut muscles to relax. Was it likely that Ray had given up, left them alone? The absence of contact was almost worse, the silence as intimidating as words and accusations and threats.

'I don't want to wash the salt from my hair,' Amber said, lifting a strand to her nose and breathing in. 'I'm sure I can still smell it, the sand. But if we're going to get Alfie back tomorrow I should probably make sure I'm presentable.'

Austin couldn't tell her not to get her hopes up, but he suspected, from the way her smile didn't meet her eyes, that her own doubts were in place anyway. She was hiding them from him, or at least trying to. He didn't need to voice his own thoughts.

'You're very welcome to,' he said, gesturing toward the bathroom. 'Use whatever you need.'

'Thanks, Austin.' Amber stepped forward, lifting his hand and holding it between her thin fingers. 'And thank you for everything else too. Yesterday, today. Tomorrow. Hopefully it's not much longer now, and this will all be over.'

She squeezed, and Austin squeezed back, offering a reassurance he didn't fully believe in. She let his hand drop and slipped into the bathroom, the warmth of her touch lingering on his skin.

He flinched as his phone bleeped, the vibration shuddering against the worktop in the kitchen. Austin reached for it, a solid lump forming in his throat. He expected to see an unknown number. Ray making contact, voice to voice, no more cryptic letters. But it wasn't. Jasmine's name flashed on the screen, a once familiar sight, only without the little red heart that used to follow her name.

Austin answered, forcing his '*hello*' to sound like a question. There was a pause, and he allowed himself the satisfaction of letting Jasmine believe he had deleted her number.

'Austin? It's Jasmine.'

'Oh. Hi.'

Play it cool.

'I popped over earlier. After work,' she said, her voice full of false cheeriness. She must've known he'd notice it, the faux-happy that raised her usual, husky tone to something high pitched and stilted. He remained silent until she pressed on. 'You weren't in though.'

'Sorry I missed you.' He didn't inject any enthusiasm into his own voice, kept it flat. Was he sorry? He had texted her his address when he first moved, sure that before long she would want him back, and he needed her to know where to find him. He'd pictured opening the door to find her standing there so many times, but it had never happened. Ten months later she'd finally made a move and he hadn't been there to receive it.

'Where were you?' She wasn't hiding her emotions anymore, her voice was hard, the edges softened only by a flicker of anxiety.

'That's not really any of your business, Jasmine.'

'Please don't tell me you're still with that woman? Please, Austin. Don't get yourself involved in that mess again.'

'You chucked me because of this mess. You don't have any right to tell me how to deal with it. When I needed your advice and support, you turned your back. You don't get to come back now and push your opinions on me!'

Austin had never argued with Jasmine. Even when she ended their relationship, he'd not put up a fight. He loved her and was prepared to give her the time and the space to come to terms with what he'd done, what he'd been accused of, and the storm that came with it. If he'd known she'd never take him back maybe he'd have tried harder, fought his case. But as he snapped at her his stomach knotted, making him glad their row was happening over the phone. He didn't think he could stand to see any hurt in her great green eyes.

'I know I let you down, and I'm sorry. But you know me. I can't have negativity in my life. It blocks the—'

'Energy from the stars,' Austin interrupted. "Yeah, yeah. I know. I remember.'

'You might mock me, Austin, but you could do with some celestial energy yourself. At the very least, you could do with not letting in any more negativity. I'm worried about you. If you don't find the kid, how are you going to cope?'

'That's not your problem anymore.'

'I still care about you, Aus.'

His mind lingered on the way she emphasised the word *care*.

I still care about you.

It meant something, a small something, but not enough. She cared about him, but caring wasn't the same as love. If she'd said that instead, *I still love you, Aus*, he might have considered what he was doing, and what would happen if he dug himself further into the grave he made the day he took Alfie back to their home.

'Sorry, Jasmine.' Austin swallowed. 'But like I said, it's none of your business.'

'Maybe I could come over tomorrow? It'll be easier to talk face to face.'

'I'm not going to be here tomorrow.'

'Where are you going? Austin, please...'

'Don't worry yourself, Jasmine. The stars won't like it. Take care.'

He had to add the sentiment before hanging up, couldn't muster enough anger to cut the line on a negative. He still cared about her too. But he cared about finding Alfie more, and nothing was going to stop him heading to Manchester. It was the last possibility. And whether the answers were up north with Ray's brother, or not, he at least needed to know.

Then - Amber

The town was quiet, desolate, but light and sound filtered into the air. Amber's breaths were ragged, Alfie beginning to stumble as his tired legs struggle to carry him. But she couldn't stop, because if Ray caught up with them they were doomed.

Sirens blared in the distance and for a minute Amber considered running straight to the police, telling them what had happened, so they could help her to hide. But then she imagined them showing up at Ray's house, their reaction to his accusation that she had killed Sarah. She looked down at Alfie, stroking a finger over the smooth skin of the hand that was clasped in her own. Her stomach clenched as she realised that going to the police put her and Alfie in danger. She'd be taken away, Alfie sent back to his father.

'Alfie, listen,' she whispered, bending down and placing a hand against his cheek. 'I know you're tired but listen. If we see any police, we're not going to talk to them, okay? Even if they ask how we are. You mustn't say a word.'

'Why, mummy?' Alfie mumbled, his lids drooping, his mouth twisting into a yawn.

'I just need you to promise me, Alfie. No police, okay? Not ever.'

''kay.'

Amber straightened, ruffling his hair and hoping he wouldn't notice the trembling in her fingers. With a shaky hand she waved towards a taxi in the rank near the hole-in-the-wall where she'd withdrawn some cash. Amber climbed into the back, leaning over to Alfie and strapping on his seatbelt. He was tired, confused, his head lolling to the side as he was pulled back into sleep.

'Piccadilly station please,' Amber said to the driver.

He was a bald man with a gruff face squashed into a grimace. If she wasn't so desperate to get away from Cheadle Hulme she might've waited for somebody else.

'You know there ain't gonna be no trains til morning, don't ya?' huffed the driver.

Amber had no idea what the time was. She peered at the dashboard, squinting at the red blinking lights that told her it was almost an hour past midnight.

'Of course.' Amber forced herself to sound calm and confident, but the pitch of her voice was unnatural, too high. She just wanted the taxi to pull away. 'We're staying at a hotel tonight.'

'Weird time to be checkin' into a hotel. With no bags either?' The driver glanced at her as the car shuddered to a start.

Amber wanted to tell him to mind his own business, but she giggled instead, desperate for her situation to appear normal. He didn't look convinced, his frown deepening as he tutted. But her silence was enough to end the conversation.

It was half an hour before the station loomed into view, and Amber tore her eyes away from the wing mirror she was using to check for Ray's car creeping behind them. She took in the movement of the night instead, wincing at the flurry of bodies and sound of voices, present even in the middle of the night. It had been a long time since she'd seen so many people in one place. The streets looked too full, as though everybody was in danger of getting crushed. Even though she was still in the car, her body clenched with fear.

'Which hotel you stayin' at then?'

Amber swallowed, scanning the neon signs. The budget hotel had changed brand since she'd last seen it, years ago. But The Hampton was still there, beaming its golden lights, elegance flooding from the large, grand windows. Ray assumed she had no money. If he did come to the station to find her and Alfie, he would not even consider looking there.

'The Hampton, please,' she said, ignoring the way he raised his bushy eyebrows in disbelief. They didn't even have any luggage, after all. At least he hadn't mentioned it again.

It was a relief to step out of the taxi, away from the driver's judgement. But Amber hated the vulnerability of being out on the street and so she dragged Alfie into The Hampton's bronze doorway. He grumbled that he was tired, begging to go home to bed.

'Don't you want to stay here instead, Alfie?' Amber probed, leading him into an entrance hall with its glittering marble floor and extravagant chandelier hanging from the ceiling.

'Wow!' Alfie rubbed his eyes, blinking against the glitz and brightness. 'Cool!'

Amber smiled, his approval giving her the confidence to stride over to the reception desk.

'A twin room please,' she said. 'Oh, and can we have two hot chocolates bought straight up?' She winked at Alfie who squealed in delight, and the lady behind the counter laughed.

She didn't ask for proof of ID when Amber gave a fake name for the booking, and within a matter of minutes she was handed the card key to a room on the first floor. With the door locked behind them, and a hot chocolate in hand, Amber allowed herself to relax into the safety of their private space.

Alfie fell asleep the instant he finished his hot chocolate, and Amber sat up in the bed next to his, wondering where they would go in the morning. She was dazed, the last couple of hours burned fresh in her mind, yet at the same time it was as though they hadn't happened. She pinched at her skin, relieved with the sharp sting that followed. She wasn't dreaming. Her life with Ray was over. She and Alfie were safe.

Would Ray go the police, as he had always threatened? She wondered how he would explain it, what stories he would spin. Would he really tell them about Sarah, frame Amber for what happened? Or would he be scared they'd unravel the truth, resulting in his own arrest instead of hers?

Amber bit her lip, forcing the rising bile down, burning from her throat to her stomach. She didn't care what Ray did. She would escape with Alfie, and nobody would know where to find them, not even the police. She had her mother's money, and though guilt had stopped her from ever spending any, she had little choice. She'd been saving the money for her future children, and this escape, the new start, was for Alfie as much as her. It had to be okay.

But where should we go?

After spending most of the past four years within the four beige walls of Ray's spare room, the world seemed too big. She wished she had her passport so she could fly Alife away. But she didn't, and she had no way of getting one for Alfie either. Still, she allowed herself to indulge in a fantasy where the two of them strolled hand in and hand in Rome, eating gelato and exploring the ancient, Roman streets.

Roman streets.

They could go to Bath, couldn't they? Sarah had visited with her dad, that's what she'd said. She loved the place. Wouldn't it be perfect to take Alfie there in her memory? Amber had never been to the city herself, had only ever seen its gorgeous, glorious streets and buildings on the television. Had she ever mentioned wanting to visit? She was certain she hadn't. Ray would never think to look for her there...

Was it far enough way? She knew it was south. Not as far south as Ray's father in Portsmouth, but it was still an escape from northern England. She didn't want to stay near Manchester, no matter how many large cities there were to hide in. It was too close.

Bath would be perfect. And if it wasn't, then they would move on again. Amber longed for a phone, a laptop, anything she could use to check the train times. Instead, she would have to sleep, wake Alfie for an early breakfast, and then bundle him to the station to catch the very first train. It calmed her a little, to have a plan, but she couldn't stop her legs from twitching as she climbed under the duvet.

The bed was soft, the linen crisp and cool. Amber tossed and turned, writhing against the sheets, her skin burning and glazed with sweat. Her mind was electric, full of thoughts she couldn't shut off despite her fatigue. A new start, a new life, the ancient streets of Bath she'd only glimpsed through a screen, and the train that would lead her and Alfie away from her hell and into the light of something so much better.

But there were also images of terror, of Ray banging on the hotel door, or waiting at the station, catching them before they could board the train.

She tried blocking it all out and eventually her aching body won out over her active mind, and she succumbed to a deep sleep.

Now - Austin

It'd been years since Austin had driven anywhere, but as soon as he settled behind the wheel his nervous anticipation calmed. His body slipped into old habits, reacting with ease to the controls, until it was as though he'd been driving Sam's car every day.

He wondered if it would be as easy to get back into magic. He'd practiced daily during his training, and even once he was accomplished, he didn't let a day pass without spending at least an hour on his craft. Until Alfie. It'd been eleven months since Austin last attempted a trick, and he couldn't be sure it'd all slide into place as effortlessly as driving. Or perhaps it would be even more natural, his fingers curling around a deck of cards, his swift movements causing deception and intrigue. Did he still have the required balance, the speed, the charm? Magic required a front, an enthusiasm. His had vanished at the same time as Alfie.

He never considered he'd get back the spark. But over the past couple of days something had ignited in Austin and, when he allowed himself, he could imagine one day picking up his bag of tricks again. If they found Alfie alive, it would change everything.

To Austin's left Amber scrolled through his phone, her task for the four-hour journey was to find out exactly where Dean Tallon worked so that when they arrived they would not waste any time looking for him.

'His business is called Solution Capital. He has an office building on Union Street. When we get closer to Manchester I'll put the postcode into the sat-nav so that it takes us straight there.'

'Sounds like a plan,' Austin murmured, stifling a yawn. 'We will be stopping for coffee though. I'm knackered.'

'Have you been sleeping?'

'Last night, I did.'

'Not the night before?'

'No, not really,' Austin admitted, glad he was responsible for watching the road, an excuse not to make eye contact.

'Is it because of me? The stranger in the living room?' She laughed, but it wasn't enough to hide the strain in her voice. She was obviously worried her presence was the cause of Austin's unease at night.

'Not you directly,' Austin lied. 'It's the whole situation. There's a lot to take in, and a lot to think about.'

'Yeah, you're right.'

The conversation died, and Austin flicked on the radio, tuning into the inane conversations and up-beat pop songs that filtered into the car and kept the awkwardness of their silence stifled, right until they pulled up on Union Street.

*

They paid to park and walked straight to Solution Capitol, which was easy to spot amongst the other businesses on Union Street. It had a large black sign with silver writing, and great glass windows flashing a glimpse into the glossy reception area.

'This reminds me of Monday,' Amber said, as they hovered at the door. 'Waiting for you, outside of your office. I was so nervous.'

'Are you nervous now?'

'I am actually. I'm scared Dean will be like Ray. Manipulative. Evil. Alfred is so different, so kind. I hope Dean takes after his father.'

'And do you really think he's the one who's been looking after Alfie?'

'It would make sense,' Amber nodded. 'Ray wouldn't expect me to go looking for Dean. I'm sure of it.'

'Should we go in? Ask to see him?'

It was just past midday, and they were banking on Dean leaving the office for a lunch break. But there was every chance he wouldn't. They didn't even know if he was on site. According to the website, Solution Capital offered business and financial advice. There was every chance Dean didn't operate from the main offices or that he visited clients.

'Okay,' Amber agreed. Her skin was waxy-white, her bitten lip bright red in contrast. Austin took the lead, striding into the plush reception and approaching the desk.

'We're here to see Dean Tallon,' Austin said, keeping his tone casual and confident in the hope the receptionist would assume Dean was expecting them. But she frowned, eyes flicking to her computer screen, her manicured nails tapping against the desk.

'Do you have an appointment with Mr. Tallon?'

'Well, we—'

'If you don't have an appointment, I can take your details and arrange one for you. Mr. Tallon is busy and will not be seeing anyone today.'

'The thing is—'

'I'm his sister-in-law,' Amber interrupted. 'And I need to speak to him about his nephew. It's urgent.'

The receptionist raised an eyebrow, her fingernails still clacking as she thrummed them against the silver desktop. But they stopped as she assessed Amber's face, the tears in her eyes. It would've taken somebody super cold-hearted to say no.

'I'll ring up to him,' she sighed. 'But I'm making no promises. What did you say your name was?'

*

Five minutes later a tall man emerged from the lift and strode towards them. His light hair was cropped neat, held in place by a slick of gel. His shoulders were broad, framed by a dark blue suit that Austin reckoned was more expensive than every item of clothing he owned put together.

'Amber?' The man held open his arms. 'About time we met, wouldn't you say?' He embraced her, planting a kiss on her cheek before facing Austin. 'And who's this rugged fellow?'

'This is my friend, Austin.'

Austin held out a hand. 'Good to meet you. Dean isn't it?'

'Yep.' Dean returned his handshake but let go before he'd applied any pressure. 'You stopped by at a good time. Lunch hour! We'll go for a coffee, shall we? My favourite coffee shop is only next door.'

They followed him out of the reception and into the adjacent building, a sleek, too-bright coffee shop with prices that made Austin's eyes bulge.

Can they really charge that much for a coffee? What's it made of, holy water?

'It's on me,' Dean smiled, and Austin wasn't sure whether to be relieved or offended. 'Have what you like, something to eat too. But I will say, I recommend the Queen's Gold Latte, and the steak sandwich. Absolutely divine!'

Must really be made with the Queen's Gold, the bloody price of it.

'That'll do me.' Austin was too anxious to focus on the menu and pick something for himself. His leg bounced beneath the table, and he pushed his palm onto it, hoping to maintain some composure.

'Me too,' said Amber, her skin even paler, her hands bunched into fists and pressing against her stomach.

Dean clicked his fingers and within seconds a young waitress appeared at their side.

'Dean!' she simpered. 'So good to see you. Same as usual?'

'Yes please, Amy. Three of the same actually.'

'Of course!' She scuttled away, beaming. Austin wasn't sure what it was about Dean, but he oozed charm. It was not just that he was handsome, but he reeked of charisma and confidence. Was this what Ray was like too? Is that how he'd lured Amber in? He eyed up Dean, trying to spot sinister intentions behind the sharp suit and sparkling teeth.

'So, what brings you here, Amber?' Dean asked, resting his chin against his fist as he leaned forward, his face close to hers.

'Well I...' Amber straightened in her chair. 'I don't know if you've spoken to Ray recently?'

He wasn't sure if he was imagining it, but Austin thought Dean's perfectly plastered smile faltered for a moment. 'I...yes, I have. We talk now, from time to time. I spoke to him just last night actually.'

'You fell out over a girl, we've heard,' Austin said.

Dean's jaw clenched so hard, a muscle twitched beneath his eye. 'That's right. Ray didn't win though, she chose me eventually. It wasn't this one by the way,' he nodded towards Amber with a wink. 'Although, I'm sure we would've fought over her too, had I ever met her. Perhaps that's why he kept her well away!'

Amber flinched, and Austin fought against the urge to swing a punch. Did Dean know what Ray had done to Amber, that he had imprisoned her in their own home? Or was it a throw away comment, an innocent joke to make light of the fact they'd never been introduced? Either way, Austin knew violence wasn't going to get them the answers they needed. And he'd hold back his anger if it meant they found out the truth about Alfie.

'I was just wondering if you knew that...well...Ray and I...'

'You left him didn't you? That's what he told me. At the end of last week?'

'Um, yes, that's right.'

So, Ray hadn't told Dean the truth. Austin still didn't know how Amber escaped, but given it had taken her eleven months between the disappearance of her son, and her reappearance outside Austin's office, he suspected she'd had to break free, in one way or another.

'It's just, Alfie hadn't been living with us...' Amber's words came out slowly, as though she were figuring them out before setting them free. 'I guess it was because things were rocky and Ray thought it was for the best to hide Alfie from the tension. But I don't know who was looking after him, or if they still are. I thought it might be you.'

'Oh.' Dean's smile collapsed into a frown. Amy the waitress set down their coffees, but Dean pushed his to the side, ignoring the froth that tumbled over the edge. 'I do know some things, Amber. I know that a couple of years ago you left and took Alfie with you. That you didn't tell Ray where you'd gone.'

A rush of crimson flooded Amber's cheeks. 'Yes, but...I had my reasons, Dean. You must know, I wasn't...I wouldn't—'

'It's none of my business,' Dean said, waving his hands. 'But it's clear you and Ray had an odd relationship. It's too much for me to catch up with to be honest. Ray and I don't talk about it. And Alfie doesn't live with me, he never has.'

Austin slumped in his chair, his body ravished by a heaviness that shrouded him like a red curtain shielding a stage. The smell of the coffee sent a ripple of nausea into the hard pit of his stomach. He stared into it, the foamy substance in the tall glass. He couldn't stand to look at Amber.

'But you've met him?' Her voice was thin, stilted by rasps, as though she'd just been punched in the stomach.

'Of course I've met him. He's my nephew.'

'And you don't know where he's living now?'

'I don't know, Amber. I haven't actually seen Ray in a while, you know. We stay in touch. I spoke to him on the phone last night, like I said. He's fine, in case you were wondering. Well and good. He didn't say anything about Alfie. But you can be sure that he's keeping his son safe. Maybe it's best to just leave it.'

'Leave it?' Amber's voice had found its strength and Austin drew from it, forcing himself to look up. Amber was trembling, her eyes blazing as she glared at Dean. 'Leave it?' she said again. 'He's my son!'

'Is he though?' Dean leant back, folding his arms.

Amber paled. She pushed out her chair, the legs screeching as they scraped against the floor.

'Look, mate,' Austin said, pushing out his own seat so he could stand. 'Do you know where Alfie is, or not?'

'No, I don't. But I would agree it's time for you to go now. Amy! Can you have the sandwiches wrapped up, please?' he called to the waitress before turning back to Amber. 'I have to get back to the office anyway. Nice to meet you.'

Amber yelped, no longer able to hold back the tears which flooded her cheeks. She twisted away, fleeing the coffee shop and running out into the street. Austin turned to follow her, but Dean reached out and grabbed his arm.

'Be careful, buddy,' he said. 'Have you known Amber long?'

Austin's silence betrayed him, and he cursed himself for not acting quicker.

'Look,' Dean continued. 'Ray told me about her. She's an angry, jealous woman. She flares up, and she is completely unpredictable. You should watch yourself.'

'Thanks, mate. But I know what I'm doing,' Austin said, yanking his arm from Dean's grip.

'You trust her, do you? Funny how pretty girls can suck men like you in.'

'Men like me?' Austin clenched his fist at his side.

'Just an observation, buddy. I'm only offering you some brotherly advice. Man to man. She's dangerous, and you don't know what you're letting yourself in for.'

'It's your brother who's dangerous!' Austin snapped. 'Do you know what he did to her? He locked her up! Kept her caged like an animal, for years!'

'And what proof do you have? That's her story, and I'm telling you now, you can't trust it. She's a vicious liar, and she will use you. Why do you think Ray is keeping his son away from her?'

Austin stormed after Amber, refusing to hear anymore, leaving Dean stood alone at the table with three mugs of coffee and three steak sandwiches wrapped in clingfilm. He didn't want to spend another moment in his presence.

But as he scoured the street for Amber, he couldn't help thinking that Dean was now the second person, after Jasmine, who had warned him to be careful.

Then - Amber

The train to Bath took longer than Amber expected. They changed onto a different train when they reached Birmingham, and it was almost four hours before the city slid into view. There were houses on hills, like rows of beige dominoes.

The length of the journey didn't bother her though. If anything, every passing minute put her more at ease, the distance between her and Ray growing and growing as the country whizzed by, changing from fields to cities and back again.

'Do you remember what mummy told you last night, Alfie?' Amber asked, nuzzling her cheek against his and whispering the words into his ear. 'About talking to the police?'

She felt Alfie's head nod, his hair tickling her chin. 'No police,' he said, clear and unquestioning.

'That's right, little Alf. I'll keep you safe. We don't need anybody else.'

Alfie nodded again. For the rest of the journey he remained on his best behaviour. He gazed out of the window, giggling as the blurry carousel of scenery made him dizzy. He babbled about trains to the man checking their tickets, and eventually he lulled his head against Amber's arm, his excitement dissolved into tiredness.

Amber woke him when they arrived, and they stood in the aisle with the other disembarking passengers. She and Alfie were the only ones who didn't have luggage. When the doors opened, bodies heaved into the open and she clutched at Alfie's hand so hard she feared it would hurt. But sore fingers were a smaller worry than losing him, jostled and squashed amongst the forest of legs. Once they filed onto the platform, she didn't know where to go, so she drifted with the tide of bodies down steep stairs until they squeezed through the ticket barriers. Finally, they stepped out of the flurry and into the street.

It wasn't much of a relief. People swarmed in all directions with no co-ordination, the motion of it made Amber queasy. Buses heaved fume-filled sighs, so the air smelt of burnt rubber. She was sure the city dirt was settling on her clammy skin, a gritty sheen prickled against her face and crawled beneath her fingernails.

'You 'kay, mummy?'

Amber looked down at Alfie, his hand still in hers, his face contorted with confusion and kindness. He was so brave. She had to be brave too. But for the first time since their escape, Amber's elation had faltered. They had nothing to their name, not even a change of clothes or one of Alfie's favourite books. She traced the outline of the debit card in her pocket.

Thank god Ray didn't get his hands on this as well.

Ignoring the crowds as best she could, Amber glanced behind her. The station loomed over her but beyond it, dwarfing it, were great plumes of green. The bushy leaves of thousands of trees clumped together, as round and as perfect as broccoli heads. It was as if the city, with all its life and noise, was shrouded by the calm of nature. Nestled way down below hills of emerald ripples and jade layers. It comforted her. She forced herself to turn away and look ahead at the grand buildings. They looked new, but with a façade that matched the age of the city. Sand brown brick and great stone pillars.

She tried to feel soothed by the resemblance to Rome, but people were still moving around her without order, the chaos of it made Amber sway, nausea creeping up from her stomach and burning her throat. Clouds parted and suddenly it was sunny, too sunny. With one hand on Alfie's, she lifted the other to shield her eyes. She longed to bring both her hands up and press them against her ears. The contrast of noise made her giddy, the roar of traffic, the hum of voices, the deep thrum of music. What had she been thinking? She couldn't handle it.

'Why are we here, mummy?' Alfie asked, his soft voice helping Amber to steady herself as they hesitated on the pavement. 'Is it a 'venutre?'

'It is an adventure, darling,' Amber tried to sound excited. 'But we're going to live here now, too.'

Alfie frowned, lifting one leg and stamping his foot down. 'Don't want to!'

'It'll be wonderful, Alfie! This city, it's called Bath. The Romans lived here once. This city is very old.'

'Oh. Cool!' Alfie's eyes widened.

Their conversation soothed her, she no longer had the urge to give into the swelling haziness in her head, nor to hide in the dark with her fingers stuffed into her ears. She was responsible for Alfie, for making sure the horrors of their life were erased by their fresh start. She steadied her breathing, putting her thoughts in order so she could figure out the priorities.

We need a place to live.

She scanned the new city, eyes drifting over shops and restaurants until she caught sight of a large Wi-Fi logo plastered across the window of a café on the other side of the road. She crossed with caution, encouraging Alfie to look left, right, left again. To her relief, the internet café offered more than Wi-Fi, but public computers too. While Alfie busied himself with a hot chocolate and a croissant, Amber sat at the computer and searched for a place to live.

Her stomach clenched at the prices, but she couldn't give up just because they were extortionate. The thought of taking the train to another new place sent tears to her eyes. She blinked them away, but they swelled again when she thought of the amount of money she would have to part with.

She'd not thought anything through, and though Alfie was oblivious to it, she hated herself for putting him through such an unpredictable situation. The Estate Agent sites listed requirements, including references and proof of identification. She didn't want anybody knowing who she was, and even if she did, she had nothing bearing her name but her bank card. She doubted it'd be enough.

She continued browsing, scrolling, and staring at the screen until her eyes ached. Eventually, she found a man on a forum who was advertising a fully furnished, one bedroom flat, under a private rental agreement. The lady serving in the café let Amber borrow their telephone, and she thanked her by buying another cake for Alfie. She nearly cried with relief when the man from the forum said the property was still available and agreed to meet her at the café.

*

'I'm looking for something really quick,' Amber explained to a short, round man with a toothless grin. He smelt of tobacco and his once-white t-shirt was grey and dappled in coffee stains. Alfie scrunched up his nose as he stared at him, but Amber kept a forced smile pasted on her face.

'I mean, we could stay in a hotel for a couple of nights if we needed to,' she continued, wincing at the thought of the extra expense. 'But ideally, we're looking for something kind of...instant.'

'The flat's available, love,' the man shrugged. 'I 'aint gonna ask many questions, okay? But I still gotta do this proper. It 'aint worth taking risks.'

'"I'll be no hassle,' Amber insisted. 'It's just me and my son. Please? I'll pay the deposit and six months' rent up front.'

The man furrowed his brow, fat fingers scratching at the speckled grey stubble that grazed his chin. The silence dragged, and Amber sunk her teeth into her lip as she stared at him, hoping her wide eyes would win him over.

'Deposit, and six months' rent,' he said, pulling out a creased receipt and scribbling the amount and his bank details on the back. 'Transfer that to me, and I can give you the keys right now.'

He turned away respectfully as Amber logged into her online banking and transferred the money. She balked at the amount but knew her mother would understand. She would have to find work once she and Alfie were settled, but she couldn't think about that yet. She'd secured them a home for the next six months. It was a start.

'Okay. You can look now.' Amber pointed the man towards the screen, showing him proof of her transaction.

'It might not land in my account right away, seeing as it's Sunday,' he huffed. 'But it all looks cushty to me. And if it doesn't land, well...I'll know where you live!' He chuckled at his joke and Amber tried to see the innocence in it, but she didn't like the thought of him showing up at the door.

'I'm only joking, love,' he said, noting her expression.

'Yes, I know. It's fine.' Amber smiled again, but her skin prickled cold, a strange sensation compared to her hot, sweaty hands.

'Here are the keys, and a copy of the address,' he said, dropping them into her hand. 'Want me to come and show you the place? I feel a bit guilty you've paid all that money when you haven't even seen it yet. But I can assure you, it's all good.'

'No, it's fine. We'll find it. And I'm sure it'll be okay.'

She accepted his directions but did not want him coming with her and Alfie to the flat.

They walked there themselves, arriving outside a small boutique shop with a little black door to the left of the store entrance.

'Are we going to live in a shop, mummy?' Alfie asked.

'No, sweetheart. Above the shop, I think.'

'Cool!'

Amber sighed, relieved. Considering Alfie grew up in a manor, she was glad he was able to appreciate even the tiniest of things. She so hoped he would be happy there, with her.

They let themselves into the foot of a narrow staircase. They climbed the steps, far too steep to be safe, with a lingering odour of onion on the air. The carpet was threadbare and stained.

What have I done? We can't live here. What was I thinking?

When they reached the top, Amber pushed a second key into a second lock, and shouldered the stiff door to open it. Following Alfie inside, they stepped into a bright, airy space, where the sour smell from the staircase disappeared. True to the man's word, the flat was immaculate. It was bare and basic, a two-seater sofa pushed against the wall in a sorry attempt to allow for more space. But there were large windows overlooking the peaks of the city, letting in a stream of light and creating a sense of freedom. The air was cold, a musky smell lingering on the draft that crept in through the cracks around the windowpane. But otherwise, it was perfect. They had all the furniture they needed, all she'd have to buy was a small television and some fresh bedding.

And clothes. And toiletries. And food.

They had nothing, nothing at all but the roof over their heads and the clothes they stood in. Yet Amber was able to ignore the weight of what needed to be done, and revel in the light of what she'd already achieved. She had her son, and they had a home.

'Come on little man,' she said, turning to Alfie and stroking a finger over his smooth cheek, before poking him on the nose. 'Shall we go shopping?'

Now - Austin

Austin caught up with Amber, who was pacing down the street red faced, her fists swiping at her tearful eyes. He reached out to grab her shoulder, causing her to whip around in alarm. She softened when she saw him, but the devastation was still clear in the way her features sagged, her face crumpled under the pressure.

'Where's my son, Austin?' she cried. 'I have nowhere else to turn now!'

'Let's not give up,' Austin said. Without thinking he pulled Amber into a hug. He was even more surprised when she relaxed into him, her head resting against his chest. It had been a long time since he'd held a woman, since he'd held anybody. There was nothing romantic about it. They stood as still and as stiff as statues, on a grey high street, side by side with pedestrians and traffic. The air was heavy with the fug of car fumes and sirens blared in the distance. But a warmth stirred in his heart as he looked down at his arms clasped tight around Amber's trembling shoulders.

'We'll think of something. I know we will,' he murmured into her hair, determined to be the strong one, to stay positive.

'But I can't wait much longer.' Amber shuddered. 'It's killing me.'

'I know. Look, we won't go back to Bath tonight. You're exhausted. And maybe it's a good idea to stay in Manchester anyway. Maybe we need to keep an eye on Dean, and Ray too if we can. If you're right, and Ray's known where Alfie is all this time, one of them is bound to visit soon. Or even have Alfie with them at some point. If it happens we can act on it. What do you think?'

Amber sniffed, pulling out of Austin's embrace. Her cheeks were stained with tears, her lips quivering. She nodded, but there was no conviction left in her. She was deflated, all her hope drained away leaving an empty shell, like an actor without a mask to hide behind.

'I'll book us a hotel. But it's not late yet. Is there anything you want to do, while we're here?'

'Can we...can we drive to Ray's?' Amber asked. She closed her eyes and shook her head, as though she couldn't believe she'd even asked it. 'I...I just want to know if Alfie is living there with him, now that I've gone. I need to know. Ray might've moved him back in now that I'm not there?'

It wasn't what Austin had in mind. The thought of driving out toward the very man who had caused so much damage and pain made Austin's stomach bubble with hot acid. His mind settled on the two notes that had been posted through his door. The fact Ray had watched them, followed them, set his heart into a fury. Had he followed them up to Manchester too? Would he follow them as they staked out his home?

Don't be such a bloody wimp, Austin.

'Well...we can,' he agreed, shrugging as though he didn't mind either way. 'But what are we going to do? We can't just march up to the front door.'

Amber's body jerked as a sharp shiver rocked her. 'No. Of course not...I couldn't...I wouldn't risk it. But I want to be near the house. No, not the house. I want to be near Alfie. If he's there I'll sense it, I know I will.'

Austin frowned. He did not believe in the parental sixth-sense mothers and fathers gushed about, as though having a child had given them superpowers. He didn't doubt the bond between Amber and Alfie, but he did find it hard to believe Amber would feel Alfie's presence through the solid brick walls of the house.

'Amber, I don't know. I'm sorry but I don't think you'd sense him.'

'Because I'm not really his mother?' Amber's face twisted, her eyes flared so the brown deepened almost to black. 'That's what you think?'

'What? No! I just meant...' Austin recoiled, trying not to let Dean's warning taunt him or skew his judgement.

I told you so, buddy. She's mad.

'You don't get it, Austin. You think I'd choose to go back there without a good reason? I'd watch that place burn to the ground without hesitation. But if there's any chance I'll find Alfie there then I'll go, and I'd run into it, fire or no fire. It's all the same level of hell without Alfie. You're not a parent, you don't understand!'

'Fine!' Austin could not be bothered to fight her, exhaustion was getting the better of him. If she wanted to stand outside her abusive ex-boyfriend's house, then who was he to stop her?

At least he'd be with her, to ensure nothing happened, to stop her from coming to harm. His stomach tied in knots with the peculiar mix of not caring anymore and at the same time, caring so much it hurt.

*

Austin drove to Amber's directions, her voice shrinking as they slipped down a lane and towards a large house looming in the distance. Even with the sudden silence, Austin knew it was the place they were headed. It was the only house visible against the expanse of countryside.

'Park down the road,' Amber said. 'If we pull onto the drive-way and Ray's in, he'll hear the tyres on the gravel. We're better off walking to the gate and looking in from there. We'll only walk right up to the house if we think it's safe to.'

'Are you okay?'

Although Amber's plan sounded solid, her voice was weak, her skin grey.

'I'll be okay. I never thought I'd come back here, not for any-thing, and certainly not by choice. But if there's any chance Alfie is here then I need to know.'

'And do you think Ray's here? He's been watching us, re-member? If he didn't see us leave, he could still be in Bath, couldn't he?' Austin had to ask it, even though he hated the way Amber grimaced.

'There's only one way to find out,' she said, her voice little more than a squeak. 'But we have to keep quiet. He can't see me here, Austin. He can't.'

Austin nodded. They left the car in silence and walked the remainder of the lane until they reached a grand iron gate. It was open, leading onto an impressive driveway, and Austin couldn't help but marvel at the sheer beauty of the place. He imagined Amber meeting Ray all those years ago and visiting his house for the first time. She must've thought she'd landed the man of her dreams. The reality sent ripples of cold through his veins.

'Ray's home,' Amber whispered. 'That's his car.' She pointed at the flash Audi parked close to the house, and then frowned as her eyes drifted to the vehicle parked beside it. 'I don't know who's that is though.'

Austin looked closer, wondering why his heart had gathered pace, threatening to gallop out of his chest and into the fields. He took in the large tyres, the shape of the silver logo, and when it hit him he reached out for Amber's hand.

Mercedes Vito.

It was the van. He'd never seen it, only a picture of the make and model in the papers around the time of Alfie's disappearance. And although the papers had used a silver van for their depiction, the one before him was the same, except for the navy-blue finish.

It was the van the police suspected drove up the track to Jasmine's house, the one that left its marks in the earth the day Alfie disappeared.

Then - Amber

Bath was a city of basements. It gave the phrase *going underground* a new meaning. There were bars, cafes and shops thriving from beneath the cobbled streets, built into what used to be cellars. It was a beautiful use of the space, so creative, and Amber found Bath was an easy place to fall in love with.

She had been worried her and Alfie's escape would mean they were destined to live a life of fear, with Amber checking over her shoulder each passing minute. But she was surprised to find she was, mostly, relaxed. She reminded herself she'd never expressed a desire to visit Bath, had never once given away anything that would cause Ray to look for her there. He wasn't a sleuth, despite his intelligence, and she had given a false name to her landlord, a precaution to ensure she could not be tracked. For the first time, she held the power, and her confidence kept her calm.

In the busy streets, battered by the ever flowing current of bodies, Amber took comfort in the crowds. If anything, it was the lonely nights in the flat that got to her. When Alfie was asleep she grew jumpy and restless in the isolation of their privacy. Several times an evening she would leap from the sofa, twist the key in the lock and throw open the door, just to be sure she could.

Then she'd force the lock back into place, hook the chain and try to settle into sleep.

The evenings were difficult, but she made up for it during the day. She took Alfie out, even if rain hailed from the clouds, determined to make up for lost time. They wandered the streets, watching performers and stopping to rest in cosy coffee shops. The mornings were quiet, and they took in the sights with little distraction, relishing the hazy sun rises over the abbey, for their eyes only. But the hush of stillness never lasted long, and by midday tides of people filled the ravines of the streets, until it was almost impossible to move.

Amber didn't mind the bustle anymore. The streets sang when they came alive, the raw soulful voices of unpolished but natural talent from the street musicians punctured the air, surrounding them in art and creativity.

It took several weeks for Amber to accept that Bath was her home, and not just a holiday. Alfie asked about his father from time to time but was easily abated with vague answers. Amber was relieved. He never seemed upset or unsettled over Ray's absence. He had spent most of his time with Amber anyway, and he was enjoying their new freedom as much as she was. Their life was good.

Despite the positives, money worries punched holes in her happiness, and Amber's mind sagged under the weight of their dwindling funds. The upfront rent she'd deposited for the flat was a huge hit to her savings, and she'd gone a little overboard buying fresh bed sheets and new clothes. She'd treated Alfie to toys and books and bought herself a mobile phone and a large set of watercolours. She needed a job, but how could she ever risk leaving Alfie with a stranger while she worked? She was already conscious she may have to home school him. He turned five next summer, but she had no paperwork to say who he was, no birth certificate. She didn't want the worries to consume her. She'd spent enough time as a prisoner, she didn't want to be held captive by her own anxiety and ruin her and Alfie's new start.

She soothed her concerns by keeping their spending to a minimum. The street performers were a blessing, free entertainment that varied in such a way it could keep Alfie entertained for a lifetime. Amber always chucked some change into the tip buckets, but it was still far cheaper than the cinema or theatre. Their other favourite pastime was sitting in a café on Grand Parade, where the hot chocolates were cheap, and the windows overlooked some of the most beautiful parts of the city. Amber would sit and paint for hours, and Alfie would copy her, making a watery mess on his page.

The café owner, Mary, was a plump old lady with a kind smile. She wore bohemian dresses and tied bandanas in her silver hair. She often refilled their hot chocolates for free, and always gave Alfie a little cupcake when they arrived.

'You are a wonderful painter, my dear,' Mary said one day, as Amber and Alfie sat in their favourite seats, looking out of the window and painting what they saw. Amber was dabbing paint onto the page, forming an image of Pulteney Bridge, the sky above the sandy bricks a dazzling sapphire blue.

'Thank you, Mary. You're too kind.'

'Have you ever thought about selling your work?'

'No-one would buy these!' Amber laughed. 'There's so much amazing art out there. I wouldn't stand a chance. And I wouldn't even know how to begin getting my work into shops or galleries.'

'Maybe you don't have to.' Mary tapped a finger against her chin, her deep-red nail polish flashing under the café's bright lights. 'Your paintings would really brighten up this old place, you know.'

Amber gazed around the café, taking it in even though it had become so familiar to her. She loved the interior, with its crooked countertop and mismatched chairs covered in bright patterned cushions. She never saw it as anything less than cosy and inviting. But as she peered closer, she noticed the chips in the sky-blue paint, the stains on the walls. She'd never say it out loud, but there was a shabbiness that had obviously come with age.

'Are you offering to buy my paintings?'

'I think I am!' Mary said with a flourish. 'And if you're able to keep them coming, we could sell them here too. I've always fancied re-branding as an art café. We could pop these in frames, price them up, and sell them on. We get a lot of tourists in here, and if you carry on painting these iconic landmarks they'll be snapped up in no time. You've a real edge to your paintings, I've never seen anything quite like them. Unique is good, my dear! The punters will love them.'

Amber dared to hope. Could she really sell her artwork? She knew it would be a slow income, an unreliable one, but it would be an income all the same. A chance to earn some money, without having to leave Alfie's side. It was perfect, too good an opportunity to miss.

'That would be amazing, Mary. Can we really do this?'

After all that had happened, Amber's life was finally going to plan. Excitement soared through her body, peaking the corners of her lips into a wide smile, flushing a warmth into her skin. She had a shot at making Alfie's life something special, a chance to keep them out of the darkness and remain forever in the light.

But even as the glowing heat radiated through her, Amber's brain could not shut off from the past. A flash of long dark hair, or an impish face in the crowds would force Sarah into her mind, as though she were following her from beyond the grave.

Amber stared at Alfie, the blue eyes he inherited from his father, the thick dark hair that resembled Sarah's. The warmth faltered, hardening into bitter cold as she thought of her friend, and she wondered if the truth about Alfie's mother would continue to haunt her, until she could stand it no more.

Now - Austin

'We have to call the police, Amber,' Austin whispered.

'No! No p—'

'Do not give me that *no police* crap! That's the van! That's the van from the police appeal. It's the same make and model, it can't be a coincidence. We have to call the police, now!'

'We do not! If we call the police Ray will make sure I'm sent down for murder. And what happens to Alfie then?'

'You can fight that! They're bound to find Ray guilty. Amber, if you want to save Alfie then this is the only safe and reasonable way to do it. Surely you can see that?'

It was only when she cowered, Austin realised he was shouting. He considered the life she'd been living, the years she spent in the hands of an abuser, and he shrank back, ashamed.

'I'm so sorry. I shouldn't have shouted. I'm not like...you know. I'm not like him.'

Amber softened. 'I know, Austin. Don't worry. Ray didn't shout anyway. His anger was more controlled. All hushed tones and blank expressions. It was scarier than shouting and screaming would've been. I never quite knew where I stood, never knew what he was thinking.'

'So, what are we going to do? That's the van. It really is.'

'Alfie must be here,' Amber sobbed. 'Or at least the person who took him is.'

'I guess so.'

Amber's eyes darted from the house to the lane, where Sam's car was waiting for them. She sunk her teeth into her bottom lip and squeezed her eyes shut.

'I can't believe I'm going to say this, but we need to go, and come back here in the morning. We have to leave now.' She trembled, pushing her hands into the pockets of her jeans.

Austin stared at her, failing to read her expression, relieved and yet dismayed she didn't want to move any closer to the house. 'Why?' he asked.

'What can we do now? We know Ray's in, and someone else could be too, because that van is there. What hope do we have of getting to Alfie? But if we wait until morning, Ray will, hopefully, have gone to work. It'll be safer to come back then.'

'That doesn't mean Alfie will be here. He must go to school or to a childminder. He won't be left on his own.'

'Maybe. But we can try and scope the place out, work out if Alfie is actually living here again.'

Austin nodded his head in agreement. If she wouldn't call the police, at least she was prepared to play it safe. It was a logical plan, the best he could hope for. They were closer now than they had ever been, but Austin was anxious. He still didn't know what they were to do if they ever did find Alfie, if he was there in the house when they came back. They couldn't just take him, could they? Would Amber and Ray be forever trapped in an off-the-radar custody battle, taking it in turns to snatch Alfie away from the other? It would be madness. And there was another thought niggling at him, one he had not wanted to voice, but he knew he would have to. As he and Amber walked towards the car, he forced the words out before they could remain cowering in the back of his mind.

'Amber, when you find Alfie...what are you going to do?'

'What do you mean?'

'I know he's better off with you than with Ray. And I know you raised him, and that you're essentially his step-mum. I'm sure you have some rights. But Alfie has a real family out there.'

Amber stopped walking, lifting a hand and holding it against her chest. Austin glanced in her direction, glad it was too dark to see the full impact of his question on her face.

'What do you mean?' she repeated.

'Sarah's family. Don't they have a right to know what happened to her? To know she had a son? He's all they'll have left of her—'

'They can't be much of a family. She was locked away, like I was! No-one ever reported her missing, you know. I searched her on the internet when I escaped the first time, but I found nothing, no sign that she'd been reported missing by anyone.'

'And maybe there is no-one, but you have to consider that there might be.'

She was silent, trembling like a bomb with its fuse burnt right down. But rather than explode Amber deflated, her whole body sinking until she was slouched, her head in her hands.

'Oh my god,' she whispered. 'What the hell have I done? I've helped covered up a murder. I've kept it quiet, all this time.'

'People will understand,' Austin said, placing an arm around Amber's shoulders. 'You did what you had to do to survive. Ray killed her, and you did everything you could to ensure you and Alfie weren't his next victims. That will all go for you, not against. I agree, we have to find Alfie and get him away from Ray, but after that we have to do the right thing. Okay?'

Amber was sobbing too hard to talk, but with his hand still resting at the base of her neck, her hair grazed his skin as she nodded.

*

The details of Amber's escape from Ray at the weekend were still sparse, but Austin knew she'd been unable to get away with any of her possessions. Not even her own shoes. She had no cash and no debit card. Austin wasn't confident about his own financial situation. His wages covered his rent, bills, food, and little else. In the past few days he'd spent more on train tickets and petrol than he'd spent on any luxuries for almost a year. As her drove into Cheadle Hulme to find a hotel his stomach churned, and he tried not to think about his overdraft.

Perhaps sensing it, when they reached a modest B&B near the small town centre, Amber took control at the reception desk. 'A twin room please.'

'Just the one room?' the receptionist asked.

'Yes, please.'

They were handed the keys and shown to a room so small the beds were almost touching. It was bleak, the orange glow from the light only highlighted the cobwebs, as the bulb dangled from the ceiling on a wire. The walls were painted a pale shade of tan, the thin carpet deeper, like dark coffee. It even smelt brown and Austin grimaced as he forced himself not to imagine why the stench reminded him of that colour.

Forty quid for a room that looks and smells like actual crap?

When the lady strode back to the reception, Austin moved his body through the thick tension in the room and turned to face Amber. 'You didn't have to do that. I would've got you your own room. Maybe you'd have gotten one that wasn't the actual embodiment of a turd.'

'It's just one night,' Amber shrugged, her lips quirking slightly at his comparison. 'It's fine. I don't expect you to keep paying out for things. Once I've found Alfie, and everything's sorted, I can focus on getting myself back on track. Earning some money. Then I'll pay you back.'

Austin shook his head. He did not want her money. He wanted the same as she did. To find Alfie, and make sure the whole crazy mess that surrounded his little life was sorted once and for all. To know he would live a safe and happy life with people who loved him was the only payback Austin needed or deserved.

*

'Austin! Austin! Wake up! We need to go.'

Austin woke to Amber's voice, frantic and fast, the pressure of her hand on his shoulder and a soft but urgent shaking that rocked him to consciousness.

'Wassamatter?' he mumbled, as his eyes adjusted the light, and Amber's colourless face loomed into his vision.

'Ray is still following us. He's left another note.'

Austin sat up, taking what appeared to be a postcard from Amber's outstretched hand. The design was a watercolour painting of Bath, the bright brush strokes forming the shape of the abbey against an orange sky. The exact spot where Alfie had been left alone after Austin's act. Austin flipped it over to the back, his throat tightening at the familiarity of what faced him. Magazine letters cut out and stuck into place.

Hidden in plain sight.

'He's in Bath! He's been there this whole time!' Amber paced at the side of Austin's bed, her hair matted, her t-shirt inside out.

'You're sure this mean he's in Bath? How? Who's been looking after him?'

'I don't know,' Amber said. 'But we've got to go back and find him. This postcard, Austin, it's *my* painting. I sold them in a coffee shop when Alfie and I were living in Bath.'

'So how did Ray get it?'

'I don't know. He always loved my paintings...maybe he...maybe he saw them and recognised they were mine. We sold one, you know. To a Manchester address.'

'Maybe...seems a bit of a stretch...' Austin's head was heavy with tiredness, he was fed up of her theories and how so far, they'd led to nothing.

'Oh my god!' Amber's hand flew up to her face. 'The lady from the cafe. Mary! What if she...she could have...'

She dissolved then, melting into the tears that consumed her. Austin did the only thing he knew would console her. He packed up their things, and walked her to the car, ready to drive them back to Bath and, hopefully, to her son.

Then - Amber

The clock struck midnight and Amber and Alfie danced around their tiny living room, Big Ben's chime ringing from the television, the flash of the fireworks making the screen-light flicker.

'I did it, mummy!' Alfie called out. 'I stayed awake! Until *midnight!*'

Amber didn't tell him that he had fallen asleep at eight, and only woken at quarter to midnight when she had nudged him back to consciousness. Instead, she picked him up and swung him around, pulling him close and kissing him on the cheeks.

'Yes, you stayed up until midnight, sweetheart! Happy New Year!'

'Happy New Year!' Alfie giggled, staring past Amber in amazement at the dazzling display that filled the screen.

It was their second new year without Ray, the first one had rolled by only two months after their escape. She'd not celebrated it, still wrapped in a haze of anxiety at the time. But a whole year had passed since then, and they were still safe. Amber was making enough money from her artwork sales to keep the flat. There was little to spare, but her mother's money was able to tide them over when it came to food and other essentials. They couldn't live on it forever, but Amber couldn't think too far ahead. She had to live day by day, focus on each minute at a time, and hope her sales increased.

Mary had insisted on putting some of Amber's artwork online. There were chic websites designed especially for independent artists and designers to sell their work. She'd been apprehensive at first, terrified Ray would stumble across the paintings and trace her to Bath. But the more she thought about it the more unlikely it seemed. She'd given a false name to Mary, and even though there were days she longed to tell her the truth, she'd kept her secrets locked well away. The artwork would be sold under the name of the café anyway, and Amber reasoned there were plenty of artists out there who dappled in watercolour. Why should she stand out from the crowd?

Besides, she had bigger worries, which drowned out the possibilities of her art being recognised, worries that kept her awake at night, until her eyes stung, and her limbs ached. Alfie would turn five in August and should be enrolled in school. He'd never attended nursery, and she was concerned about his social and academic skills. He was bright, an articulate child with a curious mind. He was a strong reader, confident with numbers. She read with him daily, took him to museums, answered his questions with depth and patience. But it wouldn't be enough forever. As he grew older he would need more. She wasn't qualified or equipped to home school him, and even if she was, he would never be given the chance to make friends or meet new people. He deserved the life other children lived, with time away from their parents to gain some independence.

All those years they'd spent locked away, she thought their escape was the gift of freedom. But without Alfie's official documents, and with no blood links between them, they had left one prison and walked right into another kind of entrapment.

*

The next morning, Amber and Alfie headed to Mary's Café. Mary had already promised she'd be open, even though many of the independent cafés closed on New Year's Day.

'This is exactly why I did it,' she said when they arrived, gesturing at the packed tables of tourists devouring breakfast. 'People come to Bath to see in the new year. They need somewhere to go in the morning and get a fry-up to soak up the booze!'

There was only one small table left unoccupied, and Amber and Alfie squeezed through the maze of chairs to reach it. Sophie, a young waitress, took their order. Amber treated herself to a full cooked breakfast, and a pile of pancakes for Alfie. It was worth celebrating the new year after all, even if her worries kept trying to break down the positive barriers she was fighting so hard to keep up.

Alfie doodled as he ate. His latest fascination was colouring and drawing with the set of pencil crayons Amber bought him for Christmas. She flushed with warmth whenever she saw him doodle, aware he was playing copy-cat to her own passion.

'Takes after his mum,' said Mary, wedging herself into the spare seat at their table. The breakfast rush had died down and she was treating herself to a coffee break.

'It seems he does,' Amber smiled, ignoring the image of Sarah's beautiful face that flashed into her memory at the word *mum*. It hurt to think of Sarah. In the early months of the escape Amber had bitten her fingernails to stubs, waiting for Ray to keep his promise and report her to the police. But he hadn't. Amber spent many evenings scrolling through the internet, searching for news stories, appeals for her whereabouts, anything. But there'd been nothing, and she assumed Ray's threat had been empty all along, that he was too cautious to get the police involved. He knew the truth; he must've been worried they'd find it too. And all the while Sarah's life became a distant memory, with nobody fighting to keep it alive. Amber thought of her daily. She still caught glimpses of her in dark haired strangers, in girls with pretty faces.

'The art is selling well,' Mary said. 'It's so popular amongst the tourists. I think we should consider branching out. Not just getting prints made for postcards but to put on mugs and things too. Tea towels, and what-have-you.'

'Tea towels?' Amber laughed.

Mary was a businesswoman through and through, always trying to work out ways to make more money and maximise profits. Amber was grateful, so pleased to have found somebody that could manage the business side while she focused on the art.

There was no shortage of inspiration in Bath, Amber was as in love with the city as she had been when she first laid eyes on it. It was not quite Rome, but it was her home from Rome, a city she knew she could live in forever and never got bored of. She adored the narrow alleyways with their quirky stores, the magnificent buildings, and grand pillars. There was always something to draw, splashes of colour coming from street performers in red velvet capes and the Christmas market stalls that streaked the streets with trails of light.

And when night fell. Bath looked like Christmas no matter what time of year it was. Warm orange glowed from square windows, fairy lights were strung up outside cute cafes and rustic gift shops. It was a city that knew of its beauty and flaunted it, unashamedly proud, and undeniably breath-taking. Nestled in a valley, when night descended, the houses on the hills lit up, so that everywhere you looked it was like a starry sky.

'The online sales are picking up,' Mary beamed, her round face rosy with pride.

'That's brilliant!'

'Yep. We even sold one to up Manchester way two days ago. One of the large canvases. I'll send over your pay early this month if you like? Because that piece was one hundred and fifty, just on its own.'

Amber grinned, forcing herself to summon the excitement Mary would expect to see after such a big sale. But her heart rate quickened, pumping painfully in her chest. Manchester? It couldn't be Ray, could it? He had the money, wouldn't think twice about spending it if it sent Amber a message...

I know where you are.

She swallowed. 'Do you know the exact address, Mary?'

'Not off the top of my head, love, and I'll have to be getting back to work now. I could check it out for you another time though. Any reason?'

'Oh, I have...friends up there. That's all.'

'I should've guessed, with your accent. I do too. Well, family.'

'Oh. Do you?'

'I do indeed! We will have to catch up about this properly at some point.'

Mary waded to the counter to relieve Sophie, leaving Amber trapped under the bubbling weight of wondering about the painting, and who had bought it.

Now - Austin

The journey to Bath was long and strained. Amber drifted between long bouts of quietness, to lengthy ramblings about how and where they might find Alfie. She hopped from hopefulness to helplessness, her voice rising in waves that crashed into hushed whispers. All the while, Austin gripped at the steering wheel, heavy with the sense they had retreated to square one. They were headed back to Bath where, less than a week ago, Amber had shown up outside his office and begged for his help. It felt impossible then, and though he didn't say it out loud, it felt impossible still. There'd been spells of optimism in between, but it was as though they'd looped full circle, and Alfie was still so far out of reach.

Austin drove to the carpark near his flat, using the guise of free parking to dispel Amber's insistence they head straight for the city centre. He was using it as an excuse, a way to make sure they went to his flat first. He wanted to sit down and work out a plan, not roam the streets or demand answers from elderly coffee shop owners. Amber wouldn't like the delay, but he was hoping he could convince her once they arrived.

They climbed out of the car, Austin braving himself to suggest his plan. But Amber spoke first. 'Um, Austin?'

She nodded towards the old Georgian town house, Austin following her gaze to the magnificent building that housed his apartment. Jasmine was sat on the doorstep, two large suitcases at her side. Austin stumbled towards her, tripping on his clumsy feet as he tried to stop his legs shaking.

What the hell is she doing here?

She saw him, raised a hand in a tentative wave, her bangles sliding down her bare arm. She was dressed for the summer in white vest and denim cut-offs, her already tanned skin darkening in the Spring sunshine. Seeing her, sat against the dusty stone, sunglasses propped on her head so her eyes could find his, it was easy to forget she wasn't his anymore. Austin longed to place his hands on her face and plant a kiss on her gloss-stained lips.

'Hi, Aus,' Jasmine smiled, using his old nickname as though no bitterness had ever passed between them.

'Jasmine. What're you doing here?' He didn't mean to sound rude, but his mind was numb, spewing out words without coherent thought.

'I came to see you. I want us to try again, I want you back. I didn't realise you were still...pre-occupied.' Her eyes shifted to Amber, who was hovering by Sam's car, chewing on her fingernails. Austin's cheeks burnt at her words.

'I'm not pre-occupied, Jasmine, whatever that means. But I'm not going to have a discussion like this on the doorstep. We can't talk about it here. Not now.'

'We can, Aus, because I don't have much time. I'm leaving.'

'Leaving?' Austin frowned at the floral-patterned suitcases, Jasmine's thin fingers curled around the plastic handles.

'Yes. I'm leaving Bath. I'm selling the house.'

'But you love that house!'

'I love a lot of things. But you know me, I can't sit still for long.'

'Where are you going?'

'I'm going to stay with my sister for a bit.'

Austin had never met Jasmine's sister. They hadn't been on speaking terms for years, and only made up in the year before he and Jasmine split up. He'd never met any of her family, and she'd only met his parents once. He sometimes wondered if that was part of their downfall. No family, just the two of them packed into a unit so tight they were suffocating each other without even realising it. Perhaps, if there'd been more people to share the burden of their troubles, they'd never have ripped apart.

'And then? Where are you going after that?' Austin asked.

She was building up to something else. Jasmine wasn't the type to move in with family, not in the long term. She craved independence and freedom, alone time, quiet.

'Well, I was going to use the house sale to fund a trip to Australia. Rent a place by the sea. I'm going to apply for a work permit, try and move my life out there. I want you to come, Aus. Isn't this what we always spoke about? Always dreamed about?'

Austin's throat squeezed, his breath catching as he struggled for air. It was true, they'd discussed it a lot in their time together. Austin's parents lived out in Melbourne, his childhood was embodied in the beaches and cliffs. He would love to move out there, away from England's grey and into Australia's daz-zling blue.

'We need to discuss this properly. We can't just move to Aus-tralia together now, without figuring out if *we* can work again.'

'Of course we can make it work. We were happy!' Jasmine's voice floated in enthusiasm, but her smile didn't reach her eyes. It lay flat on her face, her brow straining against furrowed ten-sion in an attempt to lift her expression. It didn't work. There was something false about the whole look. Or perhaps Austin was finally becoming immune to the lure of Jasmine's care-free demeanour, noticing the agitated friction she hid beneath her white-toothed smile.

'Well, that's what I thought. But you left me when I needed you most. I know it was a shit time, but I needed your support. And I'm not saying I can't forgive you for that. I'm sure I can. But now's not the time to talk about it. I have to help Amber find Alfie first.'

'So you're choosing her? Over me?'

'It's not about choice. I'm not dating her, this isn't about relationships. I'm trying to help her find her lost child. The child *I* lost. Once Alfie's safe, we can talk.'

Jasmine stared at him, her emerald eyes as deep as a forest he could become lost in. 'It wasn't your fault, you know. Alfie's dis-appearance. You were only trying to help, to do the right thing.' She'd said it to him before, in the stillness of sleepless nights when the torture of his mistake kept him awake. It had done nothing to help him then, but it was still a mild comfort, hearing the words.

'It's not your job to find him, Austin. And I don't trust that woman. Please, get away now, before something terrible happens and you get yourself in a mess again. It's not worth it.'

Austin wanted to believe her, to take her hand and jump a plane to Australia. But how could he live with himself? For the first time in almost a year some of the burden had lifted, his role in Alfie's disappearance ever so slightly diminished. Although the police had never charged him, Austin had carried a weight of guilt with him ever since, and if they found the boy he would at last be cleared of the charges his own mind had pinned on him.

'I'm so sorry, Jasmine. If you can wait for me, that'd be amazing. If you can't, then you can't. But I have to do this. I'm not choosing Amber over you. It's not about either of you. I choose Alfie. I have to find him.'

'Fine.' Jasmine straightened, pushing her sunglasses down to cover her eyes as she pulled at the suitcases. 'But I'm not going to be waiting. You can't call me up if you ever find the kid and say you're ready. I won't be looking back. Just stay safe, promise me?'

Even though her sunglasses hid her eyes, her face contorted with genuine fear, the twist of her lips making Austin panic too. Why was she so afraid of Amber?

'Promise,' Austin said. 'And you too. Stay safe.' He kept her in his sight as she sauntered away, her dark braids falling down her back, bouncing as she dragged the suitcases to her car. He should've offered to help her carry them, but he was too awkward to be a gentleman when all he wanted to do was fling his arms around her legs and beg her not to go without him.

But he'd made his choice. It *was* a choice, whether he liked it or not, just as Jasmine said it was. He had chosen Alfie. He had chosen Amber. And he had to stick to his choices, no matter what happened next.

Then - Amber

The streets of Bath were busier than usual. It was the Easter holidays and Friday was always a popular day for tourists and locals to flood the city centre. Amber had tried to avoid it, spending time with Alfie in the flat, rather than heading into the trap of the bustling centre.

By the end of the week she'd given in. Alfie had become restless, desperate to visit Mary in the café and have his favourite hot chocolate with cream and marshmallows. Amber was keen to see Mary herself. She had not yet spoken to her about the address in Manchester, and Mary hadn't bought it up since. Amber suspected she'd forgotten, and worried mentioning it again would rouse suspicion. She should trust Mary by now, she was a friend, not just a business partner. But Amber doubted she would ever allow herself to trust anybody, not fully. She'd not shared her address nor her name, and even though she often longed to, she'd kept her distance. Unburdening herself of the truth wasn't worth the risk, even though it weighed on her, and guilt stirred in her stomach whenever Mary's hard work landed a wad of cash in her hand.

When they reached the cafe it was full, every table crammed with customers and a small queue waiting outside for seats. Tourists peeked through the open door, eager to enjoy the quirky interior, all desperate for tables by the windows that offered views to Pulteney Bridge.

'I think we'll have to get a hot chocolate somewhere else today, Alfie,' Amber said.

'But I want to see Mary!'

'I know, sweetheart. But she's busy, look. No seats.'

'Oh.' Alfie's head bowed as he stared at the floor, kicking a stone into the gutter.

'Come on. I've seen another place that looks really cool!'

Amber took Alfie's hand in hers, overwhelmed by the swarm of bodies and determined not to lose sight of him amongst them. Past the abbey, towards Church Street, Amber knew of a fudge shop where the windows were always piled high with displays of colourful toffees and treats. She would take Alfie there instead and let him choose whatever he liked. They could eat outside, under the sun.

The Square in front of the abbey was hectic, tour guides marched by holding flags and trailing large groups behind them. People crouched and kneeled with expensive cameras, all trying to get a perfect shot of the gothic architecture, tutting as others stepped in front of them and spoiled their frame. She kept Alfie's hand tight in hers as they continued to walk, and her arm jerked back as he fell to a halt.

'Mummy, look! Magic!'

Her gaze followed his outstretched finger to a modest clump of the crowd, gathered in front of a street performer. He had shoulder length dark blonde hair, a sharp goatee, and tanned skin. A host of props were lined up behind him, and he was encouraging more people to watch, a thick Australian accent bouncing towards them. Alfie adored magic, and even Amber was intrigued by the magician's edgy appearance. They'd never watched him before, she was certain she'd recognise him if they had.

'Seriously, this guy is amazing!' A woman's voice drifted through the noise, cementing Amber's decision.

'Come on then, little man. Let's go see.'

They made for the crowd, Alfie darting forward so his hand slipped from Amber's. He launched himself to the front and stood with his fingers wriggling at his side. Amber apologised as she pushed past another lady to stand behind Alfie and rested her hand on his shoulder.

'Gather round, gather round! Come on, love, you're going to be missing out if you don't! Ah, ignore her ladies and gents, she doesn't know what's good! You're in for a treat, come on now, the more the merrier!' The magician worked the crowd effortlessly, even those refusing to stop and watch laughed or blew him a kiss as they walked by.

As the crown thickened Amber's palms prickled with sweat and she tilted her head to the sky, taking in more air. Alfie was transfixed, bobbing up and down on his toes. She wouldn't tear him away. She'd fight the claustrophobia for a while. The acts never lasted very long, and so she concentrated on the solid ground beneath her feet, steadying herself.

'Some of you missed the beginning, but don't you worry, the best if yet to come!' The magician's voice boomed, dominating his audience and hushing them into silence. 'For my next trick, and it's a good one, I will need a volunteer from the audience!'

'Me!'

Alfie darted forward, staggering to a stop beside the magician before the man even had time to pick out who he wanted. Amber let her arm drop to her side, though she longed to pull Alfie back and hold him. She shook her head. It was about time he showed some independence, and she couldn't bear to take that from him, under the watchful judging eyes of all those strangers. Instead, she took a small step forward, her eyes on her son and the man with the lion's mane of hair.

'And what's your name, little dude?' asked the magician.

'Alfie.'

'Okay, Alfie. And how old are you?'

'Four.'

'Wow, four! Four is the very best age to be. Did you know that, Alfie?'

Amber smiled at the interaction, amazed and proud at her little boy for volunteering and putting himself in front of all those people. Alfie's eyes were locked on the magician, the sleeves of his t-shirt rolled up, his tongue sticking out as he concentrated on his instructions.

As Amber watched, a hand pressed against her shoulder. She ignored it, aware that people often barged through crowds, forcing others to step aside. But the pressure didn't disappear, it stayed put, burning into her skin until she was agitated and nervous. She considered swatting it away or turning around to find out what their problem was, but she didn't want to take her eyes off Alfie.

The presence of the body pushed closer, until she felt the tickle of movement against her hair.

'Keep quiet, Amber. And don't look round. For Alfred's sake.'

Her body plunged into ice, the warmth from the sun disappearing as though a grey cloud had descended and cast a bitter shadow. It was a woman's voice, throaty and smooth, dripping into Amber's ear, slick like treacle. She didn't recognise it, but in her shock, she thought it might've been Sarah. Amber's knees buckled, and the grip on her shoulder tightened, holding her upright.

'If you shout, resist, or run, then you will go to jail for Sarah's murder, and Alfred will be taken into care. Do you understand?'

Alfred.

Only Ray called him that. Ray and Sarah. But it wasn't Sarah's voice. She'd thought it was at first, but Amber noticed the differences. It was too deep, too husky and hard compared to the soft silk of Sarah's. Swallowing, Amber nodded her head in response to the question, the fingers on her shoulder pinching as she moved.

'You are going to turn and walk without looking back. I'll stay behind you and direct you. Someone will bring Alfred to you, and he will be safe. But you have to come with me, exactly as I am telling you. And remember what I said before. You do the opposite of any of this and it's a life behind bars for you, and a life in care for Alfred. I'll call social services. He'll be taken away.'

Amber was paralysed. She didn't have the strength to move her legs, nor the will to turn her back on Alfie, leaving him alone and afraid. Was the woman telling the truth? Was somebody waiting for him, would somebody bring him to her? She couldn't take the risk, but she couldn't face the alternative either. Jail. She would be arrested, for kidnap as well as murder. She'd never see Alfie again.

'Promise me Alfie will be safe,' Amber whispered, keeping her voice low so the woman would know she was complying. 'Promise me.'

'Of course he'll be safe. I'm not a monster. I'm doing what needs to be done, it's the right thing. You'll see soon enough. But for now, we have to go.'

Amber wondered, for a fleeting moment, if the woman was actually on her side. Perhaps she knew the truth about Ray and what he'd done to Sarah. Maybe she'd been tipped off, told that Ray had found Amber and was coming for her. Maybe she wanted to hide Amber and Alfie away, and doing what she was doing was the only way to ensure their safety. A secret, to make sure they couldn't be traced, to make sure nobody overheard them.

But even as she thought it, doubt flooded her senses, until she could no longer breath. The threatening tone, the mention of jail, social services, Alfie being taken into care. They didn't sound like the words of somebody on her side.

'Walk away, Amber. This is your last chance.'

Amber took in every inch of Alfie, from his thick black curls to his tiny feet, bouncing in their trainers as he took on the challenge of performing magic with the Australian man at his side. It wouldn't be the last time she saw her son, whatever was happening, she would not let that be the case. She would keep him safe, and if walking away was the only way to do so, then she'd do it.

She twisted, her heart clenching as Alfie slipped from view. The person behind her moved in the same way, fluid and fast, so Amber couldn't catch so much as a glimpse. The hand remained on her shoulder and, with each step sending a stab of anxiety and guilt into her chest, Amber stumbled away, guided by her faceless captor.

Tears flooded her vision, cascading down her cheeks in hot bursts, as she pictured Alfie left behind. Her boy, on display in front of a crowd of strangers, and left in the care of the unknowing street performer, and whoever was waiting to take him from there. They'd bring him to her. The lady had promised. Amber bit down the bile punching into her throat, swallowing it so it burned into her stomach, as doubt burned into her brain.

Now - Austin

Over by Sam's car Amber lingered, pretending to tie her shoe-lace. When Jasmine pulled away, Amber walked towards him, her lips pursed tight together, her eyebrows knotted.

'Shall we go now, Austin?'

'Go?' Austin's mouth was dry, a bitter taste coating his tongue. His stomach was hollow, churning the emptiness into an ache. Jasmine was gone. Before long she'd be leaving the country. He'd never see her again. He rubbed at his eyes, scratchy and sore from a lack of sleep and the long drive from Manchester. He needed half an hour to sit with a coffee and get his head straight.

'Can we just have a minute or two?' he asked. 'I'll make us a coffee, and we can work out what we're going to do.'

'We can't wait! We're so close now, Austin. We've been blind this whole time, chasing ideas, but now we know Alfie is here, in Bath! I can't just sit still now I know that.'

'We don't even know where to begin. Sitting down and working through some options is the best and quickest way to make progress. There's no point strolling around Bath and hoping we'll spot him. It may not be the biggest city, but it's big enough.'

'I get that your stressed, and I appreciate—'

'I'm not stressed! I'm just tired. I'm fed up. Jasmine's moving away, and I've turned down the opportunity to go with her, to make sure I can stay here and find Alfie. So please, just give me a few minutes to clear my head before we start looking again.'

'Don't say all that like you staying to help is some great sacrifice! If you hadn't taken Alfie to your house that day, he might've been found by somebody else. He was *supposed* to be found by somebody else. And then none of this would've happened!'

Amber's hand shot to her mouth, as if she had any chance of clawing back her words. But she couldn't, and they hung in the air between them, jagged and dangerous. He knew he deserved it but it was still hard to look her in the eye.

'I need to go for a walk. I won't be long.' Austin unlocked the door to the flat. 'Here. Wait for me, and we'll go looking soon. But just give me twenty minutes to myself.'

'Austin, I'm so sorry. I—'

'It's nothing I've never thought myself. Just promise you'll wait here? Don't go off trying to look on your own.'

'I promise. You won't be long?'

'No.'

Austin took large strides until he was out of the car park and slipped down a narrow side street. There was a patch of peacefulness down there, a small square of grass and trees just beyond the graveyard further along the road. It was a quiet spot, exactly what he needed. He'd not had a moment to himself since Monday, and he craved some time alone with his thoughts, some time to put things into perspective.

He could've taken up Jasmine's offer. Flown out to Australia and put everything else behind him. He imagined the carefree lifestyle he remembered so well. BBQs on the beach, surfing at the weekends, beers in open bars. But he would never have absolved himself of the guilt, would never have been able to stop wondering about Alfie and what had happened to him. All that talk of choices, but really, there was no choice at all. He had to find the boy, had to know he was safe and well. It was the only way he could live his life with any sort of serenity.

Austin continued to walk, enjoying the moment of calm after his week of madness. The journeys, the people, the worry. Austin's limbs ached, his eyelids prickled each time he blinked. He longed to go back to his flat and crawl into bed for a couple of hours. He knew he couldn't, Amber would only wait so long. With a sigh he sat with a thud on the bench and rested his head in his hands, his hair coarse against his fingers. They had left the hotel that morning in such a rush he hadn't even showered.

Oh crap, Jasmine must've thought I looked a right mess.

He sat for a while, breathing deeply and fighting the heaviness in his head that threatened to lull him to sleep. Even in the outdoors, with the cold hard wood of the bench as his only comfort, he could've slept. He glanced at his watch. It'd been almost an hour since he left Amber at his flat. She'd be pacing his living room, gnawing at her fingernails, peering out the window. He didn't have the energy for company, but the search had to continue, and he knew it.

Austin heaved himself from the bench and paced back towards his home, willing his legs to move faster but struggling to find the drive. When he finally rounded the last corner, he looked towards the flat, his mind firing alert when he saw the front door was wide open.

'Amber?' he called, feet pounding on the concrete as he dived up the steps and into the hallway. 'Are you okay?'

Greeted by silence and a stillness that sent him cold, Austin darted from the living room to the kitchen. The bathroom door was open, and he was certain she wouldn't be in his bedroom. He checked anyway, peeling back the door until he was left standing alone and feeling like a prat. She wasn't there. Of course she wasn't.

'Amber!' he called again, dread crawling over his skin.

He even threw open the door to his wardrobe, like an idiot fooling himself that she could be playing some sort of game. But she wasn't in there.

Why would she be in there?

He scrambled back to the living room, hoping she'd left a note to say she'd gone into Bath to look for Alfie. He'd go and meet her, and they'd search together like he'd promised. As his eyes fell to the coffee table, he relaxed when he saw the folded piece of paper in the middle. But the moment he picked it up, blood rushed to his head, pounding in his ears and making him dizzy.

It was stiff with hardened glue, and he peeled it open to reveal cut out letters, true to their usual pattern. They were all in red this time, every letter a block capital. A warning. Austin stared at the two words, wanting to disobey them, but knowing they were a threat. He couldn't ignore them.

Because although he was sure they'd not been left by Amber, it was her words staring up at him.

No police.

Austin closed his eyes, pinching them so tightly shut that fireworks exploded into the darkness. When he forced them open, squinting into the brightness of the room, he longed to be waking up from a nightmare, one that was growing ever worse, darker and more dangerous. But he was still alone, the blood-red letters burning the bitter truth into his thoughts. Amber had been taken.

Why did I leave her on her own? What that hell was I thinking?

Once again, he had abandoned somebody he was supposed to be taking care of. But Amber wasn't Alfie. She was an adult, not a child. Yet, his mistake had been as costly as it had before. He had left Amber on her own, and now she was gone.

Then - Amber

She was guided into the back of a van that she could only see through tear-blurred eyes. She wiped at them, desperate to take note of her surroundings, to observe important details, but before she could see she was pushed into the cold darkness. For hours, it seemed, she rattled alone as the tires crunched against the road, too shocked and scared to make a noise or move.

Where is Alfie? When do I get him back? She promised me! She promised!

With Alfie's sweet face in her mind, the image of him performing with the magician, Amber grew dizzy and she fell, unconscious, to the ground.

When she finally opened her eyes again they were stiff, but she peeled them open, wincing at the light. Her head was heavy, a dull throbbing at her temple making its way to the front of her head, sending bolts of pain through her skull. Her lips were dry, her tongue too fat for her mouth and she turned to the side, relieved to see a cup of water. She gulped, drops trickling down her chin, as she adjusted to her surroundings. As soon as they came into focus, the cup fell to the floor, the remaining water pooling in the carpet.

'No!' Amber screamed, her throat burning raw with the force of her voice. 'No! Please, no!'

How could it have happened? How could she have ended up back there, in the room at Ray's, which had been her prison for so many years before?

Her head was still full of fog, and Amber tried to clear it, working at the memories swirling in the mist and sharpening them into something familiar. A woman's voice penetrated her subconscious, the heavy weight of a hand on her shoulder, fingers pinching the skin as they gripped harder and harder. Amber had been taken. Tricked. *Forced.* The woman must've been working with Ray, capturing her and Alfie after their escape and bringing them back to the house she so desperately feared.

How could I have been so stupid?

She was too stunned to cry, her eyes wide and unblinking. She had little memory of the journey. She followed the woman's directions to a van, compliant, the threat of Alfie being taken into care held to her head like a gun. But she couldn't recall much else, other than waking up on the firm mattress, the slow recognition of the room, the cup slipping from her grasp, and the hot bile that burnt in her throat.

Amber flinched as the door creaked, whipping around to face it like a beaten animal afraid of its cruel owner. The familiar outline of Ray filled the doorway, a figure she'd hoped she would never lay her eyes on again. But there it was, large and looming, a monster guarding the gates of freedom.

Without thinking Amber launched at him, her fists pummelling his chest, his stomach, pushing to force her away around him. He raised his own hands, placing them flat against her shoulders before shoving her, sending her tumbling onto the bed. The thump of the door slamming shut ricocheted around her head, sending a sharp pain rattling through her bones.

'You bitch!' Ray spat at her, towering over the bed, his face putrid, salvia flying from his lips. 'You thought you could leave and I'd never find you? Never get you back?'

'Where's Alfie?' Amber yelled. 'Where is he? Bring him to me now! I need to see him!'

'You left him, you stupid woman. He's gone.'

Amber's body convulsed. If she'd not been sprawled on the bed already she'd have collapsed in a heap. She couldn't control her movement, shockwaves coursed through her limbs, making them twitch and writhe as she clutched at her stomach and retched. Her throat was so dry, nothing came up other than a scolding ache that seared her mouth.

'What do you mean he's gone?' she gasped, her breaths coming out in short bursts, her chest swelling and collapsing.

'You left him, and now he's gone. I'll look for him, of course, clean up your mess. But right now? He's lost, Amber. You lost him.'

The room was filled with a sickening groan, a drawn-out whining that pierced the air. Amber only noticed the noise was coming from her when her throat throbbed, and the sound shuddered into silence. She couldn't see, unsure if her eyes were closed or if her brain was shutting down, the pain in her head so blinding she couldn't move.

I'm dying. Oh god, I'm dying. Make it stop. Make it all go away.

Her tense limbs slackened as she imagined slipping away, the emptiness of death, the lack of fear, the freedom. She didn't believe in a life after passing, but she still believed dying would bring her closer to her mother, in some way.

I miss you mum. I don't want to be here, I want to be with you.

Would she really die, right there on the bed? It'd be so much easier than living. And Ray would find Alfie, and Alfie wouldn't be lost any more.

Ray would find Alfie.

No!

Amber's eyes snapped open, Ray's leering face swimming into her watery vision. She couldn't give up, not while Alfie was lost and alone. Would the street performer have called the police? Were they looking after her son, trying to track down his parents?

'We have to go and find Alfie,' Amber croaked. 'Please, Ray, you have to take me with you to look for him. We're his parents!'

'No, Amber. *I'm* his parent.'

His words were a punch to the gut and Amber doubled over again, before forcing herself to sit up straight. 'You're right, you're his father,' she agreed, treading carefully. 'That's why Alfie should be here, living here, with you. And I can look after him while you work, like I used to.'

She was desperate to see Alfie, to hold him. She'd handle the entrapment, take the same set up they'd had before. As long as Alfie lived with her, spent most of his time with her. She'd sit through Ray and Alfie's Saturdays with patience, she'd cope with the long, lonely hours. But she could not sleep alone in the bedroom, could not live without kissing her boy goodnight.

'You think I'll let him live with you? You left him on the street. He could've been kidnapped. Have you any idea what danger you've put him in?'

'Me? You forced me to leave him, whoever *she* was promised me Alfie would be safe! Who was she? Who was that woman?'

'Jealousy doesn't suit you, Amber,' Ray sneered. 'But I knew you were still in love with me. I can't believe you left me, sweetheart. But you're back now. It's all okay. It's all okay.'

Amber stared at him. He was madder than before, manic with delusion. She didn't love him, was far from jealous of the mystery woman. She wanted Alfie, nothing and no-one else.

'Don't you want Alfie to live with us, Ray? We were supposed to be a family, remember? I can help you find him, and then we'll bring him back here.'

'When *I* find him, he won't be coming back here.'

Amber balked. 'What do you mean?' Her voice was thin, a whisper of lost hope.

'I'll find him. If I can. Because that's what any decent person would do. But he can live somewhere else. Not here, not with us.'

'But you love him,' Amber pleaded. 'Don't you want him to live with you?'

'I couldn't care less,' Ray snarled, and the coldness of his words matched the bitter blue of his eyes which shone like shards of shattered glass. 'I only wanted him so that you wouldn't fuck off somewhere. But you couldn't even fall pregnant, could you? I got lucky with Sarah, and then lucky again that you fell so in love with the sprog you couldn't bear to leave us. But then you did, didn't you? You pissed off, just like my pathetic excuse for a mother. It's been a year and a half, Amber. Me here alone, without you. Do you know what I've been through? It's been hell, wondering where you were.'

'Ray, listen, I won't leave. I won't even try. But please bring Alfie back here when you find him. Let him live with us. You can lock me in, I'd understand. I'll never try and escape again. Just let Alfie live here, bring him back to me, please? He's our little boy, he's our son, Ray! And I know you care about him, no matter what you're saying now.'

For one mad moment, Amber thought he was going to waver. But then he smirked, his crooked teeth flashing as though preparing to bite. 'I don't care whose son he is. All I care about is that you are mine. This is our home, and we will live in it, just you and me. And this time, I am not letting you go.'

Now - Austin

Austin tried to throw his mind into action, but it was like crawling through thick mud, his exhaustion mingling with fear until it formed an impossible sludge.

Amber had been taken. Even through the fog, he knew there was only one possible place to find her. They can't have gotten far. He'd only been gone an hour. Giving up on trying to think logically Austin ran from the house, dived into Sam's car, and revved the engine, cursing the lack of petrol and pulling out of the car park to head back to Manchester.

It took all his willpower to stick to the speed limit, a sense of urgency pushing his foot harder onto the accelerator. But Austin didn't have time to be pulled over, so he forced himself to slow, the little red dial on the speedometer quivering. He didn't know what was happening or what to do, but he had to get to Ray's house before anything happened to Amber. If her horror stories were true, Ray had already killed one woman. Would he do it again?

The thought made it hard to concentrate on the road, so Austin pushed it away. He should've called the police as soon as he'd found Amber missing. They'd have been able to send local authorities to the manor, getting there much faster than he could. But the note, stating *NO POLICE* in its blood red capitals, was a threat. What would Ray do if blue lights lit up his garden, if sirens blared from the lane beyond his house? Austin wouldn't do anything that might encourage the maniac to act under pressure.

No, he decided, no matter how hard it was, he should get to the house first. Scope out the situation. If he could just fix Amber in his sights, find out where Ray was, he could call the police then. Together, they'd get her away safely. They had to.

The words she'd shouted at him turned over in his head, as he continued to soar up the motorway.

If you hadn't taken Alfie back to your house that day, he might've been found by somebody else.

Deep down, he knew she hadn't wanted to hurt him, that she regretted the words the moment they escaped her lips. It had been obvious, in the way her warm honey eyes widened with guilt. But it was only natural she had *what ifs*. God knows, Austin had plenty of his own. It was likely they both fantasised over different scenarios, better outcomes. It was no good dwelling though. If everything went to plan, if he got to the house and got the police there too, he could end up driving away with Amber *and* Alfie at his side. There was nothing he wanted more. Not even walks on Elwood Beach with Jasmine's fingers entwined with his own.

He had to stop for fuel and food, and the queue at the till moved without haste. When he finally inched to the front, Austin threw a packaged sandwich and a bottle of coke onto the counter, jabbed his card into the machine and then bolted to his car at such a speed, people stopped to stare.

It was dark by the time he neared Manchester, the sky fading to a deep blue. He pulled over to programme his phone, using the maps to guide him to Cheadle Hulme. When he rolled into the town it didn't take long to find the country lane that would lead him to Ray's house. Austin drove at a careful speed, anxious at the lack of light, as he creeped towards the manor. It stood, a menacing shadow against the moonlit sky. In any other circumstance it'd look elegant, welcoming, an orange glow from the upstairs window suggesting warmth and safety from the night. But Austin knew different. Behind closed doors years of horror lurked undetected. It made him sick.

Following his and Amber's movements from the day before, Austin parked down the lane and walked to the house, so the lights and noise of the car would not draw attention to him. When he reached the gate he tiptoed onto the gravel, noting the same vehicles that had been there the evening before. The Audi Amber said was Ray's, and the van which had taken Alfie from Jasmine's garden.

Finally outside the house, Austin didn't know where to begin. The front door was closed, of course, and any windows he could see were shut too. Did he need a way in? Or just a view inside, to see if Ray was in there, and whether he was with Amber or if she'd been left alone elsewhere? He needed them to be apart, so Ray wouldn't be close enough to harm her if he noticed the police arrive.

The police.

It was absurd to think he could do any of it alone, the house was too big. Austin could ask the police to be subtle, urge them to do as he had and park further away. In the darkness they could slip into the garden and burst open the front door before Ray had time to take action. It was a power they had, that Austin didn't. A strength he needed.

Yes police, he thought to himself, ignoring the words he had taken as gospel from Alfie, from Amber, and from Ray's note. He pulled his phone from his pocket and typed in the three nines as he creeped around the other side of the house, wincing at every crunch of gravel beneath his sneakers. Before he could press *call,* something halted him, his finger pausing above the green button blinking up from the screen.

Austin squinted through the dark at a third vehicle parked behind the house. He took a tentative step closer, shivering despite his heavy leather jacket.

It can't be.

He tore his eyes away and re-focused his gaze, hoping to see something that would tell him otherwise. It was the right make and model, but that didn't mean much. He studied the registration number, praying for an unfamiliar combination of numbers and letters. But they weren't. He knew them.

He knew the car.

The car was Jasmine's.

Then - Amber

Eight months. Or was it nine? Amber had no sense of time to calculate the months, the days, even the hours. All she had was four walls, a bed, a desk, and a bathroom.

She had food too. She considered starving herself, but a halo of hope lingered above her head, its light weakening every day but never quite extinguishing. She wanted to live long enough to escape, to find Alfie. Every day, when Ray brought her food on the polystyrene plates, she begged for news on her son. Had he been found? Where was he living? Who was looking after him, tucking him in at night, reading his favourite stories? Each day, Ray shook his head, neither confirming nor denying her theories. His silence was the cruellest torture.

It was a daily agony. She burned with pain from the moment she woke up to the moment she fell asleep, the day drawing out in a haze of shattered memories and painful wishes.

I wish we'd never gone to Bath. I wish we'd never escaped. I wish we'd stayed put, so that I'd still have him, and he'd be safe.

Were those precious eighteen months' worth it? Amber spent most of her conscious hours sprawled on the bed, eyes fixed on the blank canvas of the ceiling, replaying her most treasured times. Alfie slurping hot chocolate in Mary's café, his nose dappled with cream. The hum of buskers' guitars filling the air with song. Alfie's curious and clumsy wandering as he gazed at great buildings, tripping on his own feet as he focused more on his surroundings than on himself. Some days, she could convince herself it was worth every smile, every laugh, every moment spent under outdoor skies. Other days, her anguish at losing Alfie tinged all the memories with an ugly stain, the hideous truth sneering at her, taunting her.

She was convinced Ray had found Alfie. Surely he'd be frantic if he hadn't, asking Amber questions about who they'd known in Bath and where Alfie might've gone. But then she recalled his indifference, his jibe at only wanting a child to keep Amber in her place. On those days, Amber would pace the room, stamping her bare feet onto the floor until they stung, forcing her fists into the walls and door until her knuckles bled. She never washed it off, she let the red dissolve to a crusty brown, her fingers stiff when she tried to unfurl them. The pain didn't help, but it was better than the emptiness. Sometimes it even hurt enough to dull her regrets.

She'd never give up on her son. She nearly gave up on herself once, the fantasy of death taking over her rational thoughts and seducing her into an unrelenting despair. She stopped eating, went three days without a bite. Ray said nothing. He took away her full plates and returned with new ones the next mealtime. He chose foods from early in their relationship, the dishes he knew she loved. Creamy pastas, spicy noodles, chips with heaps of salt and vinegar. The smells sent her stomach into a frenzy, and it gurgled and ached until she gave in, shovelling food so fast her chest stung for hours afterward.

But the food also gave her energy, and somewhere, somehow, she found enough strength to remain hopeful. She'd escaped once before, she could escape again. Her attempts were futile, but persistent. She never spoke to Ray, ignored his attempts to make small talk. He sat with her at dinner times, and she ate in silence while he tried to engage her. He was never annoyed by her silence, but if she tried to get out when he opened the door, he shoved her with a force that left her bruised.

Amber admired her bruises, spending at least an hour each day stood naked in front of the mirror in the bathroom, twisting and turning her skinny frame. Her bones protruded, sculpting ugly lumps in her paper skin. Against the milk-white of her body, the bruises bloomed and flared, the colours deepening from purple to black, before fading to yellow and wilting like flowers in the snow. They were battle wounds, proof she was doing all she could to try and get to Alfie. A rainbow of love, each blemish representing her unfaltering desire to find her son and bring him home, safe.

When one bruise faded, it wasn't long before another took its place, and Amber vowed she would never see her skin unmarked again. Not until she was free to walk through the great oak door and back into the real world, where Alfie would be waiting for her.

Now - Austin

Questions swarmed into Austin's mind, like sharks racing to a pool of blood, teeth bared. What was Jasmine's car doing parked outside Ray's house? Did she know him? How? For a moment Austin considered that she may have followed him, tried to track him down to convince him to leave for Australia with her. But it didn't make sense. She had got there first.

His lack of answers made him want to scream, but he forced himself silent as he stared down at his mobile phone. The number was still on the screen, three white nines burning into the dark. He couldn't call the police, not until he knew how Jasmine was involved. With another soundless scream, Austin erased the number and slid the phone into his pocket.

With numb legs, he stumbled towards the car, until his face was pressed right up against the window, squinting through the dark. It was without a doubt Jasmine's, not a similar car, not a coincidentally comparable registration plate. It was hers. In the dim light he could make out the pile of CDs on the passenger seat, her much loved reggae sandwiching the Justin Bieber that was her guilty pleasure. And then there was the Yankee Candle air freshener dangling from the mirror, the one she always chose because it smelt *like the sky at midnight*. Just looking at it, Austin could smell the musty sage, his mind flaring at the memories it evoked; trips to the coast with the windows rolled down and the warm air whipping their hair.

What are you doing here, Jasmine?

With his fingers crossed and his stomach tied in a knot, Austin pondered the likelihood of Jasmine knowing Amber, the secret kept close between them, away from him. Jasmine must've come to save Amber too. But even as he thought it, it made no sense. With a sharp shock of acid to the back of the throat, he realised the only logical explanation was that Jasmine knew Ray. She could've met him since she and Austin split up. Fallen for him. Ray had two girlfriends once. With Sarah gone, and Amber refusing to love him back, it wasn't so absurd to assume he'd looked for somebody else.

Oh god, Jasmine. What've you done?

Austin's face was still pressed to the window of her car, the disorganised mix of cardigans, hairbands, and CDs pulling him in. He longed to reach right through the glass and lay his hands on a piece of her. Could she really be with Ray, somehow oblivious to Amber, who'd spent every day before the start of the week trapped in one of the spare rooms?

No. Jasmine would never be interested in somebody like Ray, no matter how well he manipulated people. She was a free spirit, she did what made her heart sing before anyone else's. She wasn't selfish. She just knew how to be happy and crushed anything that might prevent positivity in her life. She'd want a relationship with somebody equally carefree, someone who didn't conform to the conventional.

Like I used to be. Before I fucked it all up. I used to be so chilled, so cool. What happened to me?

Austin leant away from the car, shaking his head. It was no use dwelling on the past, on the what-ifs and what-might-have-beens. It wasn't even worth focusing on the what-the-hell-is-going-ons. He needed to get on with it, find out where Amber was. If he found Jasmine along the way that'd be a bonus. He hoped their circumstances were someway entwined, so he could save them both, and call the police to the property without alerting Ray.

Austin crept towards the house, sneaking a glance through the lower floor windows and coming across nothing but large, empty rooms. The wind picked up as he searched, the tree branches groaning as they swayed in the cold smoky air. Crickets chirped their song from the rushes of grass beyond the gravel, and he even caught the mewls of fighting cats in the distance. Austin paused as a shrill creak cut through the background noise, indistinguishable but close. He clenched his jaw, his whole body taut as he held it still against the urge to run. Too afraid to look around, Austin let out a slow and silent breath that juddered as his heart raced.

As the last whisper of air escaped his lips, a light clicked on behind him.

Then - Amber

Amber grew tired of fighting, gave up on futile attempts to escape. For three months she did nothing but lay on the bed, curled into a ball, battered not by Ray, but by her thoughts and fears. The emptiness left by months without her son seared in constant pain, leaving her fatigued and unmotivated. Ray refused to answer her questions, her pleas for information. Alfie would never be put in her care again, she knew that, but she needed to hear that he was safe. It didn't seem like much to ask. Ray's refusal to tell her was suffocating.

She ate, only because she hoped the flavours and the act of doing something, no matter how mundane, would distract her mind. But while it gave her something to do, it did nothing to quiet the taunts her brain spewed into her thoughts. The mocking voices filled the silence and spun her into a whirlwind of self-hatred and fear.

She was going mad. She feared it but couldn't stop it. Some days, when Ray sat down to eat dinner with her, she launched the plate at his face. It never hurt, the plates were only paper or polystyrene, the food always lukewarm. Ray wouldn't even react, he'd simply walk out the room, leaving Amber alone with the mess she'd made. If she didn't clean it up, Ray would let it rot, the stench dominating the tiny room so that Amber wretched every time she breathed in. Though she couldn't resist the tantrums, she took to clearing up the aftermath right away, shovelling the food into the small plastic bin in the bathroom so Ray would empty it the following day.

It wasn't unusual for anger to consume her, and she let it, graciously accepting the hot violence, a respite from her help-lessness. She tapped her toes, stamped her feet, paced the floor. Were they signs of madness too? It crept in, curling itself around her vital organs and strangling them. Is that what happened to Sarah, before her descent into blinding obsession with Ray? Was her devotion to him the result of a mind warped by boredom, loneliness, and fear?

Amber couldn't imagine an insanity pungent enough to make her love Ray, but she was different to Sarah. Before, she'd thought herself the stronger of the two, but she'd come to realise it was Sarah who held the strength. The strength to smile and live the life Ray had chosen for her without complaint. Perhaps her blind happiness was what kept her sane. Until the end.

Thinking of Sarah was like picking at a scab that wasn't ready to drop. But Amber couldn't restrain herself from scratching the itch, until guilt bled out of the wound and drenched her in shame. What would Sarah think if she knew Amber had walked away from Alfie, leaving him lost and alone? Hadn't she vowed to look after her friend's son, to bring him up and keep him safe? Her failure was one that would never heal.

*

The day the lightbulb in the bathroom quit working Amber shrieked until Ray burst into the room. He only visited her twice a day, once with breakfast, once with tea. But she'd wailed, the ugly rasp spilling in a constant stream. Her mind was deteriorating, forcing her to overreact. But she could not bear the darkness in the bathroom. It made the room even smaller.

'What the hell is going on?' Ray's eyes were rimmed with dark circles, one side of his face pink as though he'd been laying on it.

'Were you asleep? While I'm here dealing with *that!*' Amber pointed toward the bathroom. 'The light bulb doesn't work!'

Ray's lip curled as he pinched the bridge of his nose between two fingers. 'And you're screaming because?'

'I don't like the dark.'

'Fuck, Amber. Just keep the door to the en-suite open. The light from this room will be enough for now.'

'No, Ray! No, it won't!'

She was behaving hysterically, and she knew it, but she didn't care. She wanted to scream and shout, until her all-encompassing grief was overcome by her rage.

'Oh for god's sake. Quit shrieking, will you? I've had a long day.'

'*You've* had a long day? Try sitting in silence within the same four walls for months on end!"

'If I replace the bulb will you stop your fucking wailing?' Ray snapped, rubbing at his temples.

He had a headache, she recognised the signs. Amber couldn't supress her pleasure. If he was in pain, he'd act faster.

'Yes. But if you don't, I'll just keep screaming. And stamping.'
She lifted her foot, slamming it onto the floor like a child who'd
been told they couldn't have any sweets. Ray winced as the floorboards rattled.

'You're petulant. And pathetic.'

Amber shrugged, annoying him further with her lack of
regard. But her strop worked. Ray left the room and arrived back
in minutes, dragging a chair behind him, a new bulb sticking out
of his pocket.

He replaced the bulb, balancing on the chair while Amber sat
crossed leg on the bed. She'd been told to stay away, or he would
take the bulb and leave. She knew he was worried she'd push him
off and, too afraid of how he'd react if she tried, she behaved.

'There. Happy?' Ray flicked the switch, plunging the room
into light.

Before she could answer, a mechanical beeping trilled from
Ray's pocket, and he pulled out his phone, frowning as he looked
at the screen.

'For god's sake,' he murmured, dashing from the room and
locking the door as he went.

Amber considered his reaction. Something had annoyed him.
When his eyes grazed the screen his nostrils had flared, the red
flush of his skin deepening, a vein pulsing in his neck. She wondered what had made him so angry, and she wondered why she
even cared.

At least he'd finished replacing the light bulb before the call
came through to distract him. She peered at the light, relieved
there was no longer a gaping dark abyss beyond the door frame.
It was all back to normal. Except...

The chair.

Ray had left the chair in the bathroom. She rubbed her eyes before looking again, making sure she wasn't imaging it. But no, there it was. Dark pine with a soft velvet cushion attached to the seat. She walked towards it, running her hands over the smooth wood, tracing her fingers across the red fabric. Afraid to waste time, Amber dragged it into the bedroom where she had more space.

She lifted the chair, the weight causing her muscles to groan. She barely used her body for anything anymore, her strength had depleted, her arms yelled in protest as she tried again, pulling the chair from the carpet. She practiced swinging it, the heaviness of the chair taking the lead until she almost toppled over. She sighed, straightened herself, and rubbed her sore hands together before trying again.

Was she really going to do it? It was the first time since he'd got her back that Ray had left her with anything she could use as a weapon. Her body quivered as excitement and terror played tug of war with her emotions. How much damage would she cause? She figured, with her fatigued muscles, it wouldn't be much. But would it be enough to buy her time? Enough time to get out?

She had less to her name than when she'd made her first escape, when she and Alfie had ran. No debit card, and therefore no money. No shoes. She had a jumper, and a thick pair of socks though. That would have to do. She pulled on the extra clothing, even though her skin was clammy and hot from manoeuvring the chair. But she would not remove them, and she would not sleep. She would clutch the hard wood against her soft palms until she heard the click in the lock and then...

...and then what? Was she really going to hit Ray with the chair? Could she? She didn't have much choice. It was self-defence, wasn't it? She'd swing for his legs, hoping to hurt him enough to shock him into a slow reaction as she darted past him and through the open door. And, if she was really lucky, she'd hit him hard enough to cause a limp, making it impossible for him to catch up with her.

As time creeped forward she flexed her own legs, preparing them to run. Occasionally she would lift the chair and practice a swing, confident she could keep it steady as it sliced the air.

And then, in her familiar silence, she waited.

Now - Austin

His instincts set in before he could think, and Austin ducked as light flooded the driveway. He squinted from where he crouched, taking in the large motion sensor light hooked to the wall of the house. Swallowing a curse Austin held still until his legs cramped. What would Ray do if he came out to investigate who'd set off the light and saw Austin squatting in his garden like an oversized gnome?

With another click, the bulb dimmed, and Austin breathed out as he remained crouched in the darkness, his eyes adjusting. Did anyone even care when those outdoor lights flared up? It was usually an animal, a stray cat or a nosy fox. Relaxing a little, Austin stood, massaging the ache in his back as he straightened his posture. He side-stepped to avoid triggering the light again and took another look at the house.

An open window.

Austin's heart quickened as he crept towards it, the warm glow of light from inside luring him in. He was aware of every crunch beneath his feet, the gravel groaning with each step. He kept to his toes, minimising the noise. As a magician he was light on his feet, he'd trained to be fast, subtle, to do things without being seen. And while magic wouldn't be enough to get him into Ray's house unnoticed, it gave him an advantage.

When he reached the window he peered through the open gap, terrified he'd find himself face to face, eye to eye, with Ray. Or Jasmine. What would she do if she saw him? Would she rat him out, or would she help him? His stomach folded when he realised he didn't know whose side she was on.

But nobody was inside. The window offered an open view into a grand, but empty, entrance hall. Austin noted the base of the staircase, but he was at a loss for how to reach it. The room was open plan, no walls to hide behind, no clutter of furniture. But also, reassuringly, no sign of anybody else.

He didn't know the layout of the house, didn't know how many rooms sat off the entrance hall. Was it possible for him to get through the window and up the stairs without anybody hearing him?

What choice do you really have? Get on with it.

Forcing himself to act, rather than waste any more time overthinking, Austin lifted himself over the window ledge and pushed his way through the gap, grateful the wooden frame made no noise as he slid it open further to allow himself more room.

He paused when his foot touched the floor on the other side, aware he was close to the point of no turning back. He was entering somebody's home against their knowledge, breaking the law. But worst of all, he was diving right into a vast pool of danger. Ray was a murderer. He killed the mother of his child, he wouldn't think twice about sending Austin to hell.

But what if Jasmine isn't safe? What about Amber?

Austin let out a low grunt as he lifted his other leg and pushed the rest of his body over the ledge and into the house. He paused again, aware of every whisper of breath that escaped him, his heartbeat pounding in his ears at such a volume he was surprised Ray couldn't hear it from wherever he was in the house. Austin strained to listen through the crashing flow of blood, but there was no drum of approaching footsteps, no buzz of distant voices. It was eerily silent, as though the house itself was holding its breath.

Could he really have made it in unnoticed? Part of him wondered if it was a trap, a sick trick. But what for? Austin shook his head, freeing his mind of the questions he had no answers for. He had no space for them, needed to put all his focus on making it to, and up, the stairs without being heard. He slid into the entrance hall, peering at the doors he'd suspected would be there, leading to other rooms, other areas of the immense house. None of them were open, and he wasn't prepared to wait until the brass doorknobs rattled and the door hinges creaked.

He made for the stairs without looking back, and when he reached the base of them he climbed with all the trepidation of an adventurer at the foot of Everest. With each step he expected at least one of the stairs to emit a low creak. Wasn't that what happened in old houses? But his steps were silent and when he reached the landing and saw it was empty he had to refrain from letting out a cry of relief.

But his search was far from over. The landing was long and wide, with several doors lining the walls. In the centre were two large glass doors, moonlight spilling through and illuminating the hall like a spotlight. They led out onto a balcony and though it was too dark to tell, Austin could imagine the breath-taking countryside views that'd be visible during the day. The house, and all its beauty, made the horrors that lived within it even harder to comprehend.

With quick cautious steps Austin made his way down the hall, too scared to try opening any of the doors. There was no light seeping through the cracks of any of them, but that didn't mean they were unoccupied, and he still clenched with anxiety when he considered stumbling across Ray before he'd found Jasmine or Amber.

How are you going to get her out if the door's locked?

Austin stopped, staring at one of the doors. Amber had told him that Ray always locked her in the room. Even if he found the courage to start turning handles, even if he found the right room, how would he get her out? He'd thought it'd be something dramatic, like in a movie, imagined himself kicking down the door and watching it fly off the wall in a cloud of dust, through which he would emerge as a hero.

You're a big-headed fool, Austin Jackson.

The doors were huge, grand oak, and Austin knew he had no chance of his fantasy playing out. He'd never be able to break one down, not in one swift swoop anyway. And as soon as he made that first contact, the first shuddering crash against the wood, the sound would alert Ray and it would all be over. Perhaps it was already over. Austin narrowed his eyes, checking the next door along. That's where he saw it.

A door, like the others, with the same brass handle but one major a difference; a key jutting out beneath it, peeking from the lock. There was no point overthinking, no point trying out the *what-ifs* or forming a plan for what he'd do if he turned the lock and found he was still in the wrong place. He just had to go for it.

He folded his fingers around the key. It was warm. Austin's heart jolted. Was it a good sign or a bad one that the key had been handled recently? It slid easily as he twisted it, the clunk of the lock muted but loud enough to make Austin pause and scan the hallway for signs he'd been heard. Nothing. He twisted the handle and pushed open the door, squinting as the light hit the dimmed hallway and flooded his vision.

'Austin?'

The voice that greeted him was raspy and weak. He followed it until his eyes focused on the corner of the room, where Amber sat with her knees pulled to her chest, her hands tied at the wrists.

'Amber!' He darted towards her, adrenalin fuelling him enough to not worry about the sound of his footsteps thundering through the room. He'd found her, and he was more confident now he had her at his side. Safety in numbers. He wouldn't have to fight through whatever happened next on his own. He untangled the rope from her wrists with shaking fingers, taking her hands and pulling her up to stand.

'Are you okay?' Austin gasped, seeing her properly for the first time.

She had a graze on the side of her head, a lump forming beneath it. Her lids were heavy and dark, the golden glow of her irises dulled to the shade of dirty water.

'Yeah...I...you came?'

'Of course.'

'How did you know where to find me?'

'Where else would you be? Ray left me a another one of his notes. *No police.* It was obvious it was from him, and I knew right away he'd taken you again.'

Amber shook her head, wincing as she did, her dazed eyes filling with tears. 'It wasn't him...it was...' She shuddered, her face so pale it was like staring at a ghost, a mirage of a person. 'It was a set up. She planned it all. Sarah...'

She was confused, the bump to the head must've been making her delirious. In a house full of traumatic memories, Austin wasn't surprised.

'Amber, Sarah's dead.' He was gentle with his words, afraid she was going to tumble into a state of shock. 'Ray hurt her, remember? He sent us that note, to remind you of what he'd done, what he was going to blame you for. He called you a murderer.'

'No, he didn't.' A silky voice flooded the room, drifting in from behind Austin. He whipped around, stunned to see a beautiful young woman stood in the doorway. Dark hair fell over her shoulders, her eyes sparkled beneath winged eyeliner. She wore a black silk dressing gown, clinging to her tiny frame, and though she was small, she had an air of power and importance, as though she owned the place.

'Ray didn't leave that note,' she continued, glaring in such a way it stole some of the beauty from her face and distorted it into something sinister. 'Ray's gone. He's dead. Amber killed him.'

Then - Amber

Amber's eyelids crackled when she blinked, aching with the effort to stay open. Her brain shifted from sluggish exhaustion to adrenalin-pounding awareness, all the while wishing away the minutes. Why hadn't Ray come back yet? Had he forgotten about the chair?

As time crawled on Amber suspected he remembered but was waiting until he was sure she'd be asleep before retrieving it. A shimmer of power fluttered through her as she considered it. Ray was afraid of her, had always considered her capable of using whatever means she could to escape. That's why he'd never risked leaving her with anything before. And now he'd messed up, she wasn't going to give up her opportunity for the sake of a few hours' sleep.

She switched off the light, wanting to give Ray the illusion she'd gone to bed, and to help keep her hidden when he finally broached the room. She stood in the heavy darkness, knowing if she sat her body would relax, and she'd be pulled into unconsciousness. She fought it, and every terse minute fuelled her with more adrenalin, the buzz helping her stay awake.

When the rush of anticipation ebbed, and sleepiness sent Amber's head drooping and nodding, muffled footsteps finally approached the door. Amber snapped her posture straight when the click in the lock slid with its familiar dull clunk. She gripped the chair so tight if made her palms tingle. The door inched open, and she hid herself behind it, her back pressed against the wall until her t-shirt stuck to the sweat glazing her skin. The back of Ray's head loomed into view as he peered round the door, his attention focused on the bed, obviously trying to work out if she was in it. She'd expected this, had shaped the duvet in a way that would make it appear her body was underneath.

She waited, not daring to breathe, afraid of making even the faintest sound. She held it in, until her lungs screamed for air and her head swayed with dizziness. Ray stepped into the room fully, his broad frame silhouetted against the light coming in from the hallway. She tightened her grip. Could she do it?

You have to do this Amber. You have to find Alfie. You have to get out.

It was the ache in her heart where Alfie should've been that drove her, the love for her lost boy coursing through her with a jolt of power and energy. She swung the chair with a grunt, stumbling towards Ray without balance. He turned just in time for Amber to register the shock and fear on his face.

It happened so fast Amber forgot her original plan to hit his legs, rendering him useless in the chase that would follow as she fled. Her grunt billowed into a scream of fury, the muscles in her arms strained as she forced them to lift the chair, her body spasmed as she twisted against her fatigue, landing the blow.

There was a crunch, wood on bone, and Ray slumped to the floor in one swift motion, no stumbling, just one fluid movement until he was flat on the ground. The light from the hallway illuminated his lifeless body, and Amber stared in disbelief at the smooth line of blood trailing from the back of his head, soaking into the carpet.

She had no time to care, to take in the mess she'd not expected. He was unconscious, giving her more time than she could've hoped for. Her stomach twisted at the callousness of her thoughts, but she couldn't fight the surge of excitement spurring her out of the room and down the hallway. Ray had repeatedly told her Alfie wasn't living in the house, that she'd lost him, but she'd never believed Ray would give up so easily on his son. His lack of consciousness meant she had time to check the house first.

She tore through the manor, switching on lights as she bolted into every room, scouring them for Alfie, calling out his name. There was no sign, no sleeping boy in the beds, no toys or books in the living room. He wasn't in any of the bathrooms, or even out on the balcony. Fear turned to cold hard dread as Amber realised Ray had been telling the truth all along. Alfie wasn't there.

She wanted to fall to her knees, pound her fists onto the floorboards and scream until the frustration and resentment was squashed beneath physical pain. But she didn't have time. Ray could've found Alfie and had him living elsewhere, away from Amber. But where? Amber hated herself, had always hated herself, for leaving him, oblivious to her betrayal as he performed magic with the street performer in Bath.

The street performer.

What had happened to him when Amber left? Had he stayed with Alife upon realising his mother had gone? And what had happened since, in the months that had passed?

She knew what she had to do.

Amber darted to the entrance hall, pulling on a pair of Ray's trainers. They were far too big and she tugged at the laces, tying them as tight as she could to keep them in place. She pulled some notes from the wallet on the counter top and fled the house, the shoes offering little support as she stumbled over the gravel and into the lane. The air was cool, ripe with the scent of smoke, birds were singing in the trees and Amber was, once again, free. Memories of the first time she'd escaped burst into her brain like shots from a gun. Only last time, Alfie was with her. Now, the hand that had clasped his as they ran was empty and Amber pushed herself to carry on, fuelled only by the desire to find him.

She needed an internet café, a library, anywhere she could look up the street performer, find any clue that might lead her to her son. And once she found out where the magician was, she was going to jump a train, and go straight to him.

Now - Austin

'She didn't kill him!' Austin yelled, his head teeming with confusion.

How was Sarah alive, and why was she there? If Ray was alive, where was he? And if he wasn't....

His gaze turned to Amber, who was still transfixed on Sarah, eyes wide and round as though she was staring at ghost. But it was Amber who looked ghostly, with her white-washed skin. Sarah's cheeks were pink, flushed, full of life.

'Oh, she did kill him,' Sarah smirked. 'Why don't you ask her? She hit him around the head with a chair. Didn't you Amber?'

Austin stared at her, willing her to deny it. Amber's body trembled as she dabbed her sweaty forehead with shaking fingers. 'I...I hit him with a chair to....to escape. But he...he was just unconscious...'

'You're sure about that Amber?' Sarah put her hands on her hips, leaning against the door frame and shaking her head. 'You waited for him to come around, did you?'

'No, but I...I had to leave right away. He'd have locked me back up! I had to find Alfie...'

'Enough!' Austin yelled, silencing Amber and rounding on Sarah, sickened by her smug expression. 'Amber only ever did what she had to do to survive, can't you see that? He kept her locked up! Kept her caged like an animal!'

'Like an animal?' Sarah laughed. 'Look at this room! It's beautiful. She has her own bathroom, it's like being on holiday, only every day. He never tied her up or forced her to do anything she didn't want to do. She should've been grateful for the freedom.'

'Freedom? You think because she wasn't tied up, she was free?'

'Austin, leave it,' Amber whispered. Her eyes were full of tears, her face hollow and stricken. 'She doesn't understand. She loves him—'

'I did love him,' Sarah nodded. 'You always thought I was so stupid, didn't you? Hidden away in his little outhouse, the secret lover, the one not loved enough to be granted a room in his own actual home. Even though I was here first. I loved him before you'd ever laid your eyes on him. You took him from me! And then, as if that wasn't enough, you kidnapped my son!'

'I thought you were dead!' Amber sobbed. 'Ray told me he'd killed you, that he was going to frame me for your murder. When I took Alfie away I thought you were dead, I thought I was protecting him from Ray and what he'd done. If I'd known you were alive I would never, *ever* have taken Alfie from you.'

'Cut the crap! All you cared about was yourself. You fell in love with Alfred the moment he was born. I saw the way you looked at him. You wanted him to be yours, and so it was all too convenient when Ray stole him from me and gave him to you.

Bet you're disappointed, now, aren't you? I've ruined everything for you by still being alive.'

'I'm thrilled you're alive,' Amber whispered. 'I grieved for you. You were my friend—'

'Give it a rest, Amber!' Sarah snapped.

Austin couldn't keep up with the argument. He was still expecting Ray to walk through the door at any moment, pushing Sarah aside and doing whatever he was prepared to do to silence him and Amber. He'd almost prefer his presence than for Sarah's story to be true, that Ray was dead and Amber had been the one to kill him. Even if she had, it would've been self-defence, right? But a balloon of despair inflated in Austin's stomach, crushing the air from him as he tried to accept another man's death as reasonable, as anything other than evil.

'Where's Alfie?' Amber staggered towards Sarah, grabbing at her dressing gown. 'Please. Is he okay?'

'After you left him, you mean?' Sarah pushed Amber away from her, and Austin reached out a hand to steady her. As his skin grazed Amber's, he snatched his fingers away.

She's a murderer

His cheeks flamed with shame as the thought spiralled into his brain. Luckily, Amber didn't notice. Her focus was on Sarah, and all Austin could do was look on. It was like watching a terrible soap opera, but without the television screen to separate him from the drama. He was a part of it. Not an actor, but a real man, shaken by the uncertainty and terror of the situation.

'I didn't leave Alfie!' Amber cried. 'I was taken!'

'Yes,' Sarah said, raising an eyebrow. 'And then you left my baby boy to be taken too. By your friend over there.'

'I was trying to keep him safe,' Austin insisted, fury scorching at his core. 'I called the police. But it was you, wasn't it?' Austin jabbed his finger at her, hating her for the hell she'd left him to burn in after taking Alfie without any explanation. '*You* drove up the lane at the back of my house, and you took him!'

'As if.' Sarah flicked her hair over her shoulder, folding her arms.

'But you have him now, don't you?' Amber asked, her knees weakening until she was almost knelt on the carpet, begging for answers. 'He's safe, isn't he?'

'No thanks to you. Or *him*.'

'How? How did you get him back? Who took him?' Amber's hands were clasped together, and Austin leant forward himself, desperate to hear the truth at last. '*Who took him?*'

'I did.'

Another voice, another body entering the room. *I did.* Only two short words, but enough for Austin's knees to buckle, because he would recognise her voice on only one syllable.

He couldn't look, wanted at least a minute more of ignorance, of not knowing the truth that would rip apart the last threads holding him together and scatter the remains. But there was no hiding behind the bliss of not-knowing, because with the voice, with the presence filling the remaining space in the room, it was undeniable.

Jasmine stood in the doorway, peering over Sarah's shoulder, her green eyes glazed with tears and a false determination that Austin recognised as her *game-face*. The face that meant she was not actually in control, but terrified. And there it was. The answer.

Jasmine had been the one to blow apart his world. She had taken Alfie. It had all been down to her.

Now - Amber

She was a murderer.

She twisted the words in her head, lingering on each one, trying to make them meaningless or untrue. They couldn't be right. There was no way she could be what Sarah said she was.

When Ray threatened to accuse her of killing Sarah, Amber had been terrified. Distraught for her dead friend, repulsed by the man who'd stabbed her, sick with the fear of being held responsible. But through it all she'd clung to the truth, to her innocence. The knowledge that she hadn't done it, could never do it.

That comfort shattered the moment Sarah's words littered the room, and now lay in a tattered heap, unsalvageable. Amber had killed Ray. The crack of the chair hitting his skull screamed into her memories, the sound bouncing around her own skull until she thought it would burst. Why had she never considered she may have done more than knock him out? She supposed it was because he was such a constant, a formidable force in her life. She never imagined he would die, especially not at her hand.

And Sarah. Sarah was alive. She was there, right in front of her, her black hair shining, her face as beautiful as ever. Ray hadn't killed her. It had all been a lie, a plot to give Amber the child she wanted without questioning it, to make her stay. And if Sarah was alive, then Ray wasn't a murderer, but Amber was. Did that make her worse than him? She squeezed her eyes shut.

Please don't let that make me worse than him.

Her head was reeling, the questions coming far quicker than she could answer them.

Why is Austin's ex-girlfriend here? Where has Sarah been all this time? If Ray is dead, where is his body? And, most importantly of all, *where is Alfie?*

'Where's Alfie?' Amber sobbed, breaking through her haze of disbelief and focusing on the son she no longer had a claim on, but still loved.

'You think I'd let him near you again?' Sarah's eyes bulged. 'You're a kidnapper. And a murderer.'

Amber gasped as the two words hit her in the gut and in the heart, forcing her to double over. It was a low blow but wasn't it the truth?

Kidnapper. Murderer.

'I didn't know you were alive,' Amber cried, winded, repeating what she'd already told Sarah, willing her to believe it. 'We were friends, Sarah. I loved you, I was distraught when you...when I thought you'd died.'

'But you were more than happy to take my son and start playing happy families?'

'It wasn't like that! I thought I was doing what you would've wanted...looking after Alfie—'

'*You* took him? From our house?' Austin snapped into the conversation, his voice harder than Amber had ever heard it.

She looked at him. He was staring at his ex-girlfriend, at Jasmine, his face twisted with fury. She'd never seen him like that. Though a temper had flared a few times during the past week, she'd never imagined his kind face was capable of such disgust, his nose crinkled, his mouth curled into a snarl.

'You watched me going through everything that followed!' Austin pointed his finger at Jasmine before jabbing it into his own chest. 'I was arrested, I was branded a kidnapper, a paedophile. I ended my career because of this! I've lived every day thinking Alfie had been killed, or wandered off somewhere and ended up dead, because I took too long to call the police. But all along you knew he was safe? What the hell did you do? Where did you take him?'

Amber was surprised to see Jasmine's hard features soften, her defensive glare drifted into crinkled eyebrows and down-turned lips.

'I had to, Aus,' she whispered. 'I was doing the right thing.'

'The right thing? What the hell, Jasmine?'

'I was only trying to help. I had to do what I could to give Alfie back to...to my sister.'

'Your sister?' Amber and Austin spluttered in unison.

Amber faced Sarah again. Why hadn't she seen it before? The glossy dark hair, the vivid green eyes, piercing like a cat's. Sarah was made of more edges, less of the care-free hippy vibe Jasmine embodied, but the similarities were there. And it was her, *Jasmine*, who led Amber away from the street act that day in Bath. She thought she'd heard Sarah's voice at first. It wasn't hers, but it had been close enough.

'You're the one who forced me away from Austin's act,' Amber said to Jasmine. 'You walked me to that van. You sent me back here, to Ray.'

'I was just doing what everybody thought was best.'

'What everybody thought was best?' Austin growled. 'You sent Amber to a life of a misery, into the hands of a dangerous and evil man! The same man who locked away your own *sister!* And then you took a child!'

'Alfred is Sarah's son!' Jasmine hardened again, her teeth gritted, her jaw taut. 'I hadn't seen or heard from Sarah in years, Austin. Didn't you wonder why I never spoke about her? Why I barely mentioned her? I thought she'd abandoned us when dad got ill, thought she couldn't cope with it. We'd had a row, hadn't we Sar? About who would look after him.'

'I didn't want to,' Sarah's cheeks reddened, her black hair falling like a curtain to shield her face as she dipped her head. 'I was young, I wanted to go out, drink, be with my friends. I'd just gotten a new boyfriend. I couldn't stand the thought of staying in with dad when I could be out having fun instead. I know it's awful. But I assumed dad would get better. I really believed he'd get better.'

'But he didn't,' Jasmine said, swallowing hard. 'And I thought Sarah had turned her back on us for good after the row. I told myself I'd never forgive her. That was until...until she got in touch, almost a year ago. She told me where she'd been living. *How* she'd been living, what Ray had done. I hated him, was prepared to travel here and destroy the monster who had taken my sister, prepared to call the police...but then she told me...she was fine. She was happy. Or she had been.'

'Right up until somebody took my son,' Sarah finished for her.

'So I'd found my sister and found out I had a nephew, all at the same time. I'm so sorry for what I put you through, Austin. I loved you so much, but this was my family. My blood.'

'Why didn't you tell me?' Austin didn't look angry anymore, his face sagged in defeat, his shoulders slumped. 'Why didn't you just bloody tell me?'

'We had to keep it quiet,' Jasmine said. 'It was such a mad situation. And Ray told us if we found Amber, and got her back to him, then Sarah could have Alfred back too and he wouldn't interfere. She was broken without her son. I had to help her. And I was scared of what Ray might do to my sister if we didn't do things his way.'

'But how did you find me?' Amber whispered. She thought she'd been so careful, giving false names to remain untraceable. The *what-ifs* played out in her mind. What if she'd been more cautious? What if she hadn't spoken to a single person, nor paraded around the city every day as though she had nothing to hide? But with Sarah alive, it was too selfish to contemplate the alternative scenarios. Alfie was Sarah's son, and for as long as she breathed, Amber would've had no right to stay hidden away with him.

'Ray saw your artwork being sold online,' Sarah explained. 'He knew it was yours the moment he spotted it. God, you really had no idea how much he loved you, did you? He'd recognise your watercolour nonsense amongst a whole fucking ocean of crap paintings.'

'It was being sold from a café in Bath,' Jasmine said. 'That's when Sarah got hold of me.'

'Ray had never let me contact my family. He convinced me I didn't need them,' Sarah explained. 'But when he told me about the art, said he thought he knew where you where, I told him I had a sister who lived in Bath. He let me call her. He said if she agreed to help him get Amber, he'd be able to get Alfred back for me too.'

'But how...' Amber struggled to find her words, disbelief was raining down on her, an unrelenting storm. 'How did you know exactly where I was that day?'

'I'd been watching you,' Jasmine confessed, her expression grim, her words sending a hurricane through Amber's mind. 'I went to the café that was selling your art every day, until I found you. And I'd follow you for a while, get a sense of your movements. The day Ray came down, I was anxious, I didn't know how to get to you, how to get you to him. I followed you from the café and then you walked towards where Austin was performing. I shouted something, *this guy is amazing,* or something like that. It made you look. It made you stop. I didn't expect Alfred to run and join in with the act. But when he did it was the perfect opportunity. I called Ray, told him where to park up, and then I took you to him. I went back for Alfie, but he lingered close to Austin for the rest of the show and I couldn't risk being seen. I watched them from a distance, and when they boarded the bus I knew Austin was taking him home. I called Ray and he came to pick me up. I directed him to the lane at the back of my house, hoping for an opportunity. And when Alfie ran from the back door we...we got him.'

Some of Jasmine's tension eased as she spoke, her bunched shoulders lowering and relaxing as she released the truth she'd been holding inside. Her confession was freeing her from the heavy weight of guilt, and though her fingers were still twisting the chain of her necklace, she seemed more at ease. The injustice of it sent jolts of pain into Amber's chest.

She swallowed down a scream, longing to throw her anger from inside where it burnt, and let it out. She should never have put her art out there for the world to see. She thought of the sale Mary made to *somewhere up near Manchester*. Her instincts had told her then it could've been Ray. The truth made her gut twist. One mistake and everything she'd done, her escape, her new life with Alfie, had been snatched from her. And being back in the house, back with Ray, had led to the incident with the chair...she couldn't think about it.

'So it was all planned?' Amber was numb, certain she wouldn't feel the blow of more truths stabbing into her chest. She needed all the answers. The hurt could wait.

'Yes,' Jasmine said. 'I know it's awful...'

'Don't apologise, Jas,' Sarah snapped. 'This woman took everything from me! She stole Ray from me, and then she stole my son. Well, never again. You think you're leaving here? Not this time.'

Sarah pushed Jasmine from the room, causing her to stumble into the hallway, before darting forward and pulling the door to a close. Austin shot his hand out, grabbing the edge to stop it from closing.

'Where's Ray?' he hissed at Sarah.

'What?'

'You say Amber killed Ray? Where is he then? You didn't move his body on your own. Not even the two of you could've managed that.'

Was he right? Amber tried to calculate his logic, to find some reason amongst the madness. How would they have moved Ray's body? Both women were thin, petite, their arms slender, their fingers delicate. Ray was solid, broad. Could they really have carried his body from the room, down the stairs and to wherever he was now? Why would they even want to move him? Amber's vision clouded as she considered the obvious answer. They'd called the police, the body had been taken away properly, to the coroner's office, to determine cause of death. It was less than a week ago, but surely Amber would've heard something, been tracked down and arrested?

'Let go of the door.' Sarah pulled at it, but her strength wasn't enough against Austin.

Austin yanked it backwards, so hard Sarah yelped and let go, flapping her hand.

'Sar?' called a voice from downstairs. It was low, deep, carrying up into the hallway. 'Sarah? What's going on?'

Sarah's eyed widened, blood rushed to Jasmine's cheeks, and Austin spun around to face Amber, their eyes locking. She could tell Austin thought the voice was Ray's, relief relaxed some of the tension in his face, as he fell into the belief that Ray was alive, and Amber could not possibly be a murderer.

But she knew Ray, and she knew his voice well enough to know that it wasn't him.

Now - Austin

The deep boom of the man's voice cut through Austin's anger, making his stomach clench. Ray was alive, he was there. What would he do to them? Sarah's attempt to lock him and Amber in the bedroom had failed, he'd been strong enough to overpower her. Could he take on Ray as easily?

Beneath his fear, a sharp niggle of sadness stung at his core. Would Jasmine have let her sister lock him up? Would she let Ray do the same, or worse? And if she did, what would happen next? Would they be left to die? Every instinct in Austin's body told him to run, grab Amber's hand and run. But she would not leave until she'd seen Alfie, of that he was sure. And despite the sparks of adrenalin urging his legs to move, Austin needed it to. To see the boy again and know for certain he was okay.

'Sar?' the voice called again, and through the haze of confusion and uncertainty, Austin recognised it.

Footsteps pounded up the stairs and a broad figure stepped in to fill the doorway. Not Ray but his brother. Dean.

'What the hell is going on?' Dean demanded, staring at Sarah before waving a hand towards Austin and Amber. 'What are they doing here?'

As Sarah gabbled her response Austin zoned out, his gaze focusing on Jasmine. She turned to him too, and he expected to see darkness behind her eyes, the deep-rooted wickedness she had kept so well hidden, the selfishness that led to the ruining of his life. But he couldn't find it. She was the same as she had always been, the girl he'd loved. If anything, her eyes were full of sadness, her face pinched with guilt.

Was it really so wrong of her to do unthinkable things to help her sister, to bring her nephew back to his real mother? Austin could probably forgive her for leaving him, for lying to him. In time, he might even have forgiven her for letting him believe he'd caused indirect harm to a four-year-old boy. But he could never forgive her for luring Amber away from his act, for leading her back into the abusive relationship she'd run from. Or, for undoubtedly being the one who'd taken her from Austin's flat earlier that evening and bought her to the house once more.

Austin grimaced, throwing Jasmine the strongest look of contempt he could muster. She flinched, but Austin didn't care. He turned away, looking at Amber who was stood biting her lip as she stared at Dean, her brown eyes round and full of lost hope.

'Why are you here?' Amber whispered. 'Where's Alfie? Where's Ray?'

'It's none of your business why I'm here,' Dean spat, but his body inched towards Sarah, and Austin remembered the way he'd called out her name when he arrived.

'There's something going on between you,' Austin said, looking from Dean to Sarah.

Dean scratched his chin frowning, but Sarah beamed, apparently unable to stop the smile from spreading across her face.

'So what if there is?' Dean grunted.

'She was your *brother's* girlfriend…'

'That asshole? You think keeping her locked up constitutes a relationship?'

'She loved him,' Amber said. 'She really loved him.'

'I thought I did, but I was tricked!' Sarah shrieked. 'It's Dean, it's always been Dean! Ray…he lied to me…he made me feel—'

'Ray brainwashed her,' Dean said, putting an arm around Sarah's shoulders and pulling her close.

At Austin's side Amber was nodding. He remembered what she'd told him about Sarah's blind obsession and wondered if she'd transferred her feelings onto Dean in Ray's absence. They must've formed their relationship quickly…unless…

'You and Ray fell out over a girl,' Austin said to Dean, remembering what Ray's father had told them in Portsmouth.

'Oh my god,' Amber gasped.

'Well figured out, *Sherlock*,' Dean sneered. 'Find that funny, do you? Because I don't. My girlfriend ran off with my brother. I adored her, I was devastated when she left. You can hardly blame me for wanting nothing to do with Ray after that.'

'You know I'm sorry, Dean. I don't know what I was thinking,' Sarah simpered.

'I know, babe. And if I'd known how he was treating you…' Dean's fist clenched at his side.

'But you got back in touch with Ray,' Austin said. 'You told us just yesterday. And…hang on a minute…'

Austin's mind whirred, something didn't add up. Ray couldn't be dead. Or at least, if he was, Dean had lied.

'Dean, you told me and Amber yesterday that you'd spoken to Ray. Just the night before, that's what you said. But Sarah said that Amber killed him, on Monday. If he was dead...'

'I don't know what you're talking about.' Dean folded his strong arms across his broad chest. 'Sounds to me like you're looking for a scape-goat for your murderer girlfriend.'

Jasmine winced at the word *girlfriend* and Austin couldn't help the bubble of satisfaction rising to his head. Jasmine was jealous of Amber. He didn't bother to correct Dean, there were more important things to argue about.

'No, you definitely said you'd spoken to him. And it's a bit odd isn't it? Your brother is murdered and within the week you've moved in with the mother of his child? Into his house? Is that even legal? Did he leave this place to you? Because it seems to me like Ray's death hasn't been reported and that's pretty damn suspicious. You say Amber killed him? Well, you don't need to lock her up in here. Call the police, and they'll do the job for you.'

Amber stiffened, her mouth falling open as she stared at Austin, her hands clasping together. He tried to throw her a reassuring glance but didn't want to give himself away. He was bluffing, and he hoped it would pay off. Everything about Sarah and Dean's situation screamed at him that something was up, and he would bet on his own life that if Ray was dead, it wasn't Amber who'd done it.

'I'll call them now,' Austin said, pulling his phone from his pocket and dialling 999. It happened fast. Dean lunged at him, sending the phone flying out of his hand and across the room.

His fist came down on Austin's face, the blow sending sparks spiralling behind his lids.

'No, Dean, don't! Don't!' It was Jasmine, her voice ragged as she pulled at Dean's arm, trying to yank him away. 'Dean, please! Leave him!'

'Do you still have feelings for this loser, or something?' Dean snarled, pulling away from Austin who was slumped against the bed, his head throbbing. 'Get a fucking life, Jasmine. You want to be part of this family, then you need to accept that he can't be a part of it with you. He's too involved. and he knows too fucking much.'

'So which one of you was it?' Austin mumbled through his fat throbbing lip.

They all turned to him, even Amber, who was rigid, her movements wooden.

'What do you mean?' Sarah asked.

'You say Amber killed Ray? Well we've been getting notes all week. From him. Ray's been following us. How do you explain that?'

Austin hoped he'd got them there, because there was no other way to explain the letters. The letters were proof Ray was alive, or that he at least was up until the final note had been left for them, just the night before. He tried to feel smug, but he was still slouched against the bed, his aching body resting on the floor while the others stood above him. Jasmine's cheeks brunt scarlet as she stared down at him.

'The notes were...well they were from me,' Jasmine said, her voice barely a whisper as her confession rocked Austin, like a boat on choppy seas.

'You were watching us?' Austin gaped. 'Following us? *Threatening* us?'

'I didn't want to threaten you, Austin, or scare you. I just wanted to keep you out of it. That's why I warned you off Amber, why I tried to convince you to come away with me. I just wanted you away from her, away from this mess.'

Nausea coursed through Austin, from the pit of his stomach to his thumping temple, where the blow from Dean's punches still pulsed. He'd truly believed Jasmine wanted him back, had begun to envision a future where, after Alfie was found, the two of them could reunite and try again. But it had been a ruse, an attempt to push him away from Amber and the truth they were going to uncover.

'You said you were selling the house,' Austin spoke through gritted teeth. 'You said you were selling it, so you could move to Australia. You asked me to come. What if I'd have said yes?'

'Oh, quit with the sob story, magic-man,' Dean snapped. 'Fuck, Sar, how has this bloody happened? How did he get in here? What are we supposed to do now?'

'Don't hurt him, Dean,' Jasmine begged, and Austin looked past her plea to protect him, and focused only on her dismissal of amber's freedom. To his left, Amber was still trembling, her face a mask of disbelief. Ray still hadn't made an appearance, but now they knew he hadn't written the notes. She believed she'd killed him, Austin could see that. But no...

'Amber can't have killed Ray!' Austin blurted into the tense atmosphere, pulling everyone's attention back to him. He was so sure she hadn't. 'There's no way she did. But you can't tell me he's alive and happy, that he's handed over his house to his brother, and is letting him live here, with his ex-girlfriend. So, we know that much. Ray's dead. Who did it?'

He expected a silence, the awkward stillness of his truth knocking the words from their lips. But there was no such moment of peace.

'It was me, okay?' Sarah shrieked, her voice shrill, her eyes shining.

'Don't Sar,' Dean warned, as Jasmine let out a sob.

Amber was stood stock still, and Austin stared up at Sarah, trying to ignore the pain in his face.

'I came up to the house,' Sarah said, through heaving breaths. 'I was still living in the outhouse, but I was living there with Alfred. Since Jasmine bought him back to me, I'd stayed, wanting to be close to Ray so Alfred could see his father. I knew he had Amber locked up here again, but I was determined to raise Alfred as part of a family. So, I came up from time to time, to see Ray. I came up on Monday morning, hoping to see him before he left for work. But the front door was wide open. I sat Alfred in the living room, and searched the house for Ray, until I found him crashed out on the floor up here. There was blood coming from his head. He was groggy. Alive, but dazed. I bent down to stroke his face, to help him. And he muttered...he muttered...*Amber.* And...I don't know what came over me. Realisation, I suppose. Realisation that what he'd done was wrong, that he would never love me the way he loved Amber, that I'd have been happier if I'd just stayed with Dean...'

'Oh, Sar,' Dean shook his head, putting one hand against hers and bringing the other to his face, pinching the bridge of his nose as he sighed.

'...and I knew I could never have a life with Dean, because Ray wouldn't allow it. And I realised Ray didn't love me, didn't even want me and our son to live under the same roof as him. I wanted him gone, wanted it over. So, I ran to the kitchen, grabbed a knife...I didn't think I'd actually do it. I stood over him, certain I wouldn't, just wanting to feel strong and in control. Maybe I could convince him to let me and Alfred into his life properly, you know, if I scared him enough? I don't even remember deciding to see it through...but I do remember the blood...the knife going in, and again, and again...'

She swallowed, her face contorted, torn between grief and the lightness her confession had given her.

'It was me. I killed him.'

Now - Amber

It was too much to take in.

Ray was dead. Sarah was alive. And Alfie was...

'Where's Alfie?' Amber asked. How many times had she asked and been met with no answer? She couldn't wait another minute. Not another second. 'Where is he?'

'He's *my* son, Amber!' Sarah shrieked. 'He's in bed, okay? He's safe. This is nothing to do with you anymore.'

'It is if he's being bought up by a murderer!'

It was as though the word slapped Sarah in the face, she jerked her head back as it hit her.

Murderer.

Amber had no strength for compassion, to feel guilty. She was weak with relief that she had not killed Ray, burning with anger that Sarah would have let her live with the burden had the truth not come out.

'Where's Ray's body?' Austin's words were thick, his face was swollen on one side, the marks from the punches he had taken from Dean sprawled across his cheek and lips. He trembled as he pulled himself up to stand, steadying himself by gripping the bed frame. 'There's no way you moved him on your own. We've established that. So what help did you have?'

Sarah's eyes drifted towards Dean, an involuntary reaction giving away their secret. Dean groaned as Amber gazed at him, accusing him.

'And you?' Austin pointed at Jasmine, whose pretty face was screwed up in anguish, tears trickling down her face. 'Did you know about this?'

'I...I did, but he...he was a monster, Austin...what he did to my sister...'

'You took Amber, didn't you? From my place, earlier today? You bought her back here, knowing what Sarah and Dean were capable of?'

'I panicked!' Jasmine cried, and Amber almost felt sorry for her, the tranquil calm she'd displayed at her home the other day had splintered into ugly fear. 'You wouldn't come with me, and I didn't want you caught up in it. I just wanted to get her away from you, to stop you looking for Alfred—'

'You're all criminals!' Austin shouted. 'All of you.'

'Yeah? And what are you going to do, *magic-man*?' Dean mocked.

Austin's shoulders rose as he tensed, the two men rounding on each other. Dean's fist flew through the air and collided with Austin's face again, sending him flying to the ground. Amber bent down to check on him, but as she did a cry seeped into the chaos, distant and dazed.

'Mummy?'

Amber turned to the door, her instincts pulling her towards it. It was Alfie's voice.

She didn't stop to look at Sarah. She launched herself from the room, so fast that the three pairs of outstretched reaching for her missed.

'Alfie!' she screamed, as she skidded into the landing.

There was a cool breeze flooding the corridor, a draft nipped at Amber's skin, sending her body cold.

'Mummy!'

The yell was high pitched, frightened, with an edge to it that plunged Amber into ice. She was aware of footsteps behind her, but she didn't care to see who was following. There was a whistling, the rushing sound of wind, and the curtains either side of the balcony door billowed.

Amber lunged at them, prising them apart and revealing the double doors that opened out onto the terrace. Sat shivering in the corner of the slabbed decking was Alfie, his thumb in his mouth, his body trembling in his pyjamas. His hair was cut short, his legs long and thin, a maturity had lined his face since Amber last saw him, almost a year ago. Her heart ached for the time she'd lost, as she lumbered towards his outstretched arms.

But she wasn't quick enough. A pair of hands pushed her, causing her to stumble, and Amber looked up to see Sarah dart past and scoop Alfie into her arms. He was too big to be held by her, but she clutched at his pyjamas, pressing his body to hers. 'Mummy!' Alfie wailed. He was still reaching out for Amber, his blue eyes shining, his mouth quivering as he leant away from Sarah. 'Mum!'

'Sarah, bring him inside,' Amber pleaded.

She was all too aware of how close Sarah was stood to the edge, the railing only up to her waist. It wasn't safe, and the realisation was colder than the wind-whipped air. 'Please, Sarah, bring him inside. It's freezing out here.'

'Don't tell me what to do!' she hissed. 'Alfred is *my* son.'

'Sar!' Dean appeared in the doorway, Jasmine at his side. 'What the hell are you doing?'

They stared at Sarah in horror, seeing for the first-time what Amber had seen in Sarah from the start. Captivity had driven her crazy, the turmoil of losing her son the final push towards madness. Guilt crawled over Amber's skin. She was the one who'd taken him, but she'd never have done it if she'd known the truth. And a deeper truth hung in the air, another arrow for Sarah's bow of insanity. She'd killed a man. Her poor tortured soul needed help. But Amber needed to get Alfie away from the ledge before she could even think about saving anybody else.

'Don't come near me!' Sarah shrieked. 'Any of you!'

'Sar, come on.' Dean's voice was steady. 'This is all going to be okay. I promise you.'

'He's right, Sarah,' Jasmine insisted, though the quiver in her voice betrayed her uncertainty. 'I'll never let you lose Alfred again. You know that. Just come inside.'

'I want my mummy!' Alfie screamed, squirming in Sarah's arms.

Amber's heart clenched as Sarah's balance wobbled, but she managed to hold her ground, and her grip on Alfie.

'I am your mummy, sweetheart,' Sarah cooed, nuzzling her face into Alfie's cheek. 'I've been telling you and telling you. That lady over there, she lied to you. She's not your mummy. But I am, and I'm going to look after you, forever.'

'No! Mum! Mum!'

'It's okay, Alfie,' Amber called out. 'Just stay still, Alf. Try not to wriggle, okay?'

It was all she could do to try and keep him safe. If Sarah lost her balance the two of them would topple over the edge. Amber trembled, the fear rolling over her body in waves that battered her, making her shake. She had to let Alfie go, help Sarah to recover from the darkness and then leave her to raise her son without Amber's help. If it kept him safe, she'd accept it.

'Sarah, come inside, please,' Jasmine begged. She reached out her hand, but Sarah took a step back, making everybody yelp.

'Keep away from us!' she howled. 'Leave us alone! I don't want any of you, or any of this. I just want my son.'

Alfie was sobbing, his eyes still fixed on Amber. It pained her that she couldn't reach out to comfort him, couldn't stroke his dark hair, or wipe the tears from his cheeks. Sarah was wild, her head swinging from left to right as though she were searching for an escape route.

'Do you want us to go inside, Sarah?' Jasmine asked. 'If we get out of the way you can bring Alfred back in without worrying. Does that sound okay?'

'No,' Sarah sobbed. 'You'll just be the other side of the door. Waiting. I can see it in your eyes, Jasmine. And yours, Dean. You think I'm crazy! Well, no-one's taking my son away from me. Not again.'

Sarah turned her back on them as another gust of wind swooped down, sending her hair flying behind her. She clutched Alfie to her chest and though he was still following Amber's instruction to stay still, he was crying. Sobs ripped through his body until he heaved, and Amber couldn't let him choke on his fear for a moment longer. The breeze smelt of bonfire smoke, the pungency of danger, and birds in the trees beyond the railing screeched into the dark.

She threw herself forward, determined to grab Alfie, not caring what happened, not caring if anyone went over the edge, as long as it wasn't him who fell.

But as she moved, a hand yanked at her arm, and she fell with a crack onto the patio, as Alfie disappeared from view.

Now - Austin

Austin struggled to lift his head, a crushing weight held it against the carpet. With a grunt, he forced himself from the floor, the darkness shifting from his vision until he was able to see the room through his daze. It was empty. Everybody had gone. He frowned, sending a throbbing jolt of pain through his skull. His lips were fat, his face sore.

As his head cleared, Austin became aware of voices filtering down the hallway and through the open door of the bedroom. Jasmine's voice, and the deep arrogant boom of Dean's. He staggered out of the room, following the sound, which led him to the open double doors of a balcony.

Sarah was stood at the edge, clutching Alfie. Austin's legs buckled when he saw him. Alive, after all those months, all those sleepless nights of guilt and worry. He'd grown, his hair was shorter, framing the maturity that was forming in his face. If it weren't for the red ringed eyes and the damp cheeks he'd look well. Healthy. It was a relief, but the sight of him crying tore at Austin's heart.

'Mum!' he cried, leaning away from Sarah, who kept her grasp on him tight.

Austin followed Alfie's gaze to the ground, where Amber was flat on the floor, trying to push herself up with trembling arms.

'Amber!' Austin gasped, pushing Dean out of the way and pulling Amber to her feet. 'What the hell's going on?' he demanded, circling the group.

'Please, we need to get Alfie inside,' Amber whispered.

Austin scoured the balcony, taking in the situation. Sarah was stood at the edge, too close to the low barrier, her clasp on Alfie possessive. Her eyes were wide and wild, her hair whipped around her pale face by the wind. She was crazed, and the fear from everybody on the balcony rose into the darkness and mingled with his own. Sarah could drop Alfie. She could jump.

'Sarah...' Austin tried, but she snorted when he spoke.

'Oh, shut up!' she spat, peering over her shoulder. 'You've got the least right to be here. I don't even know who you are.'

'But you know who *we* are,' Jasmine insisted, gesturing from herself to Dean. 'We love you, Sarah. And we won't let anybody take Alfred away from you, never again. We're a family, and we're all here to support each other.'

'What about them?' Sarah growled, turning and jabbing a finger at Austin and Amber. She wobbled as she did it, a collective hush descending over the balcony as everybody held their breath. The tension was still, solid against the wind battering their bodies and whistling through the trees in a low and threatening groan. The bitter air soothed Austin's bleeding lip and bruised skin, but he was still clammy all over.

'We'll go,' Amber sobbed. 'Me and Austin, we'll go, and we'll never speak of this again. Not any of it. Not Ray, not tonight...Sarah, I just want Alfie to be safe. Even if that means letting him go.'

For a moment, Austin thought she'd done it. The sacrifice made his heart swell for her, and it was obvious she meant it. Her face crumpled, tears streamed down her cheeks, her whole body slumped in defeat. She was a broken woman, using the last of her strength to keep Alfie safe. Austin couldn't imagine her going on without him, but he made a silent vow to help her through it.

But it hadn't worked. Sarah took a step closer to the edge.

'Oh god, she's mad,' Jasmine whispered, pressing her hand against her chest. She turned to Austin, her green eyes round and desperate. It was strange to see them gazing up at him. There was a time when he'd have pulled her close, kissed the top of her head, breathed in her sweet, floral smell and promised her it would all be okay. But it wouldn't be appropriate, and Austin couldn't make a promise like that. The situation was too extreme, too scary. How could it all be okay?

'I'll jump,' Sarah's voice floated on the breeze, high-pitched and emotionless, as though she were talking in her sleep. 'It's the only way me and Alfred can stay together, forever.'

Alfie wailed, his cry piercing the night, making everybody flinch. Without thinking Austin took a step forward, Amber and Jasmine mirroring his movement, their instincts the same.

Get to Alfie. Keep him safe.

Dean lurked close to the doors, the only one who hadn't made a move.

'No!' Sarah yelled. 'Take a step back! All of you!'

Nobody moved as Alfie continued to cry in his mother's arms. He wriggled, throwing his body backwards so Sarah had to reach out her arms to pull him back to her.

'Stay still, Alfie!' Amber called. 'Remember to stay still. It's all going to be okay.'

Amber exhaled as Alfie stopped squirming. She took another slow step forward, speaking before Sarah could yell in protest.

'Sarah, come on, please. You don't need to do this. All those years Ray kept us captive, me, you and Alfie. This is your chance to be free, to give Alfie a proper life. To be happy.'

'You'll take him from me,' Sarah sobbed.

'I won't. When I took him, I thought you were dead, remember? I was taking Alfie away from Ray, not you. Just come inside, Sarah. Please?'

Silence fell again, only the rustle of leaves and Alfie's sobs could be heard. Austin kept his eyes on Sarah, on Alfie, willing her to step away from the edge, at least a little. As soon as it was safe, they could reach for them both, pull them into the house, and work out what happened next. They had to decide what was best for Alfie. Nobody else mattered.

Sarah's eyes met his, moving on to Amber, then Dean, then Jasmine. She gave them all a silent stare, as though she wished to convey a message she couldn't bear to express out loud. Nobody spoke, and the quiet was agonising. When she was done, Sarah turned from the light of the house to face the darkness, lifting her leg so it was higher than the railing.

Austin screamed, but the sound was trapped in his head, not quite making it to his numb lips. He knew he had to do something, but his feet wouldn't move. He was useless and still.

But two bodies barged past. Amber, her face set into a hard, stony determination, a mother fighting for her son's life. And Jasmine, gripped in terror, her skinny arm outreached towards her sister.

They hurtled at Sarah and Austin saw fingers grappling, legs moving. The bodies collided, the three women and Alfie merged into a bundle that Austin couldn't distinguish.

And then, through the blur, a body, toppling over the edge, falling so fast it was impossible to tell who it was, but large enough to know it was an adult.

With a sharp pain searing his heart, Austin pressed his hands to his chest and prayed it wasn't Amber.

Now - Amber

She was falling.

Her body was light, weightless, a feather fluttering through a gentle breeze. How wonderful, after everything, to feel so insubstantial, so unimportant. The relief grazed her skin in a brush of cold air.

But a weight descended upon her and Amber rushed to the ground, plummeting like a rock dropped into the ocean, sinking, drowning, until everything faded to black.

*

She came around to the sound of rushing air, to bitter cold, and an ache in her back. She could not open her eyes, did not want to. What had happened? It pained her to recall it. What had she seen?

It took her a while to notice a warmth on her right hand, skin on skin. Her eyelids fluttered open, and she took in the blonde beard, messy hair, and flushed skin.

'Austin,' she croaked.

'You fainted,' he said, giving her a grim smile. 'Fell to the ground like a sack of spuds!'

He was trying to make light of the situation, but his jaw was clenched. Something was troubling him. She'd fainted, the empty, elegant freefall had gripped her and dragged her crashing to the stone slabs of the balcony's patio.

'If you can move, we should get you inside. It's cold out here.'

Amber nodded, accepting Austin's hand as he pulled her to her feet. She wobbled, but he put his arm around her. She leant into him, grateful for something solid, and allowed him to guide her into the warmth of the house.

'Where's Alfie?' Amber whispered, terror flooding into her veins as her head cleared.

Austin didn't say anything, remaining silent as they walked down the hallway and into the master bedroom. It was a different lifetime, those days when Amber shared the room with Ray, dizzy in her new relationship. As she stepped into the scene of so many happy memories her eyes drifted to the bed and her head spun for a different reason.

Alfie was sat on the bed, his eyes heavy with tired, swollen and red from crying. He was drinking from a mug, the sweet scent of chocolate filling the room. He looked up from his drink as Amber stepped towards him.

'Mummy!' he cried, as Amber sat down and pulled him into a cuddle.

She couldn't imagine how confusing his life had been, all those months he'd spent without her, having to adjust to Sarah. A stranger who should never have been a stranger, insisting she was his mother. Their bond had been so severed, had he ever felt safe with her? Had Sarah ever felt loved by him? Amber blinked back tears as she considered it, not knowing how bad it'd been or if the future would be worse. What would Alfie go through next? Her questions were impossible to answer.

Amber peered over Alfie's dark fluffy hair at Jasmine, who had taken his mug and was sat beside him, her face stricken. They sat in silence, until Alfie's head fell heavily into Amber, and his breathing confirmed he was asleep.

'She's gone,' Jasmine whispered into the silence. 'I ran down, outside, I checked her pulse but...Sarah, she's...'

Amber pieced together the moments before she fainted, slotting them into place like a puzzle, all the parts she could remember. Lunging for Alfie, desperate to keep him from going over the edge. The struggle, the uncertainty, the three pairs of arms entangled until two hands slipped away and a body hurtled over the edge.

'We have to call an ambulance,' Austin said.

'Yes,' Jasmine sobbed. 'But there's going to be so many questions...'

'It's time to tell the truth.' Amber stroked her hand over Alfie's hair. Would she ever be allowed to see him again? What would happen with both his parents dead? Amber had no rights to custody, she was of no relation to him. She hadn't even been married to Ray. But there could be no more lies, no more fighting over who was best placed to raise Alfie. It would have to be settled, and properly. Officially.

Austin and Jasmine left the room, and Amber kissed Alfie on the head before joining them in the hallway. She pulled the door so it was almost shut, not wanting to risk Alfie hearing any of the conversation they had to have.

'Where's Dean?' Amber asked, glad he was gone, but afraid of his absence and what it might mean.

'He fled,' Jasmine groaned, her face contorted in anger. 'At first I thought he was running down to check on Sarah, like I was. But he made for the driveway and I heard his car start up, and the bastard drove away. I suppose he knew we'd have to call an ambulance. And then the truth...all of it...he knew it'd come out.'

'Well, he was right,' Amber said, her heart heavy at the injustice of Dean escaping the horror. 'The truth does have to come out. It's going to be hard on all of us. We've all messed up. I took Alfie away from his father. From his mother too...although I didn't know it at the time. I didn't...'

'Sarah murdered Ray,' Jasmine whispered. 'She and Dean buried him, on his own land. I suppose she can't answer for that now.'

'Dean can though,' Austin said. 'He helped move and hide the body. He'll be held accountable for it now. The police will find him.'

'But I knew he was dead,' Jasmine wept. 'I know where his body is. And I've kept it quiet.'

'You had your reasons,' Amber said, the same sinking dread pummelling her own thoughts. 'When I thought Ray had killed Sarah, I kept it quiet too. We all do stupid things, to escape the truth, to try and live with some peace.'

'I took you back to Ray, Amber. I helped him lock you away. And then I helped Sarah take Alfie,' Jasmine coughed. 'Will I be arrested for kidnap? I mean, he's my nephew...'

'You didn't seem to be quite so bothered when *I* was arrested for kidnap!' Austin murmured. 'It was alright then, was it? For me to be branded as some sort of criminal?'

'Austin, I'm sorry...I was trying to do right by my sister...'

'No arguing.' Amber screwed up her eyes in an attempt to stem the pounding in her head. 'The police are going to be called. It all comes out. Tonight.'

'But what about Alfie?' Jasmine asked. 'He's all that's left of Sarah. I can't lose him too.'

She sobbed as she said it, and Amber could tell the sharp shock of what had happened was all that was keeping her mind working. Amber had already grieved for Sarah once, she would have to go through it again. But it was new for Jasmine. Her sister was dead. Alfie's mother was dead.

'The police will know what to do,' Amber said, the overflowing love in her heart losing its fight against her brain and its logic. Somehow, she was seeing clearly for the first time in years. 'They'll make sure Alfie's safe...happy...'

'After everything he's been through!' Jasmine wailed, and Amber shushed her, not wanting Alfie to wake. Jasmine lowered her tone as she continued. 'Hasn't he been pulled from person to person enough? Everything I did, I did to reunite him with Sarah, with his real mum. He's been so unsettled, bless him. I called her every day, I even visited a few times in that outhouse Ray had her living in. She couldn't get Alfred to call her 'mum'. She couldn't get him to feel at home.'

Pain shot through Amber's chest, like bullets from a great gun of truth. Alfie had been unhappy.

'At least he was with Sarah, and not Ray,' Austin said, and Amber tried to see the positive. Yes, it was better that he was with Sarah, no matter how unsettled he was. At least she loved him. At least her intentions were good.

'Why did you stay Jasmine?' Austin said. 'Why did you stay in Bath after you returned Alfie to Sarah? Why didn't you go with her or make her stay with you?'

'She wouldn't leave Ray. I tried, I really did. She wanted to stay, to try and encourage Ray to move them into this house, to be a family. She was delusional, and I knew it. I should've done something. Even called the police. But Amber was locked away up here, and I'd been the one to make that possible, and I couldn't handle it. Sarah insisted it was what she wanted. I couldn't argue forever. We stayed in touch, but I had to stay in Bath, to find some peace again. It's my spirit city. It's where I'm happiest. Safest.'

Amber bit back a sigh, the phrase *spirit city* making her frown. But then, she'd felt safe in Bath too. It was Sarah who'd given her the place to consider, it was a city she'd loved as well. She turned down moving there with her sister, to stay with Ray. And he didn't even want her. Didn't want Alfie. Hatred bubbled through Amber's veins, hot and heavy. She was glad he was dead. No matter how much she tried to be repulsed by the bitterness of her thoughts, she couldn't pretend otherwise.

'I'm going to call for the ambulance,' Austin said. 'All this talking, it's not helping anything.'

Amber looked at him, then glanced back at the crack in the door, to the light emitting from the bedroom where Alfie lay, asleep. The complications adults in his life had caused had ruined his childhood. How would he cope with a new set of strangers? A whole new life to adjust to?

'Sarah killed Ray,' Amber said, teasing the words slowly, her mind stirring into a frenzy as she considered her a plan. Austin and Jasmine leaned in, their frowns identical as they narrowed their eyes and listened. 'It's true. And the more truths we tell, the easier it'll be to hide the rest. Sarah killed Ray, Dean helped her hide the body. Jasmine, you didn't know anything about that, until tonight.'

'But I—'

'You knew nothing. You helped Sarah find Alfie when she got in touch with you eleven months ago, but that's it. She didn't tell you about the murder. Not until tonight, when you showed up to visit, and asked where Ray had gone, and why Dean was here. You threatened to call the police. Dean fled, and Sarah jumped.'

'Amber, what—' Austin interrupted.

'How exactly does this help?' Jasmine asked, her fingers clasping at her golden necklace as she fiddled with the chain.

'Because it makes you innocent. I'll tell the truth about what Ray did to me. About how I thought Sarah was dead, and I took Alfie. I'll say I left Alfie after finding out the truth about Sarah, I'll say I couldn't cope with the guilt, so I ran and left him. That way, Austin, your story stays the same. What you told them doesn't need to change, and so it won't be questioned.'

'And how do we explain being here tonight?' Austin asked, his face streaked with sweat and confusion, his complexion paling beneath his tanned skin.

'You don't. You're going to leave. You were never here. I'll call for the ambulance, I'll speak to the police.'

'But where does that leave you?' Jasmine asked, her eyes glazed as she tried to process it all. 'What if they don't believe you? They might think you pushed Sarah...they might not believe you thought she was dead before, when you took Alfie. You could be arrested.'

The plan was flawed, Amber knew it, but it was a risk she was prepared to take for Alfie. Jasmine had betrayed her, and Austin, in the worst possible ways, but Amber could finally understand why. Jasmine was looking out for her sister, for Alfie. And Jasmine's preference for peace, for calm, would be exactly what Alfie needed after the chaotic start to his young life. If there was any chance of keeping them together, Amber had to take it.

'And Alfie? If this all goes wrong, you'll never get to see him again,' Austin said, reaching out a hand and placing it on Amber's shoulder. It was the stillness of his touch that made her realise she was trembling.

'This isn't about me. It's about doing what's right. We're telling the truth, almost all of it. We're just leaving out the part where Jasmine took me, from your act back then, and from your apartment today. And once the truth's out, I move on, in whatever circumstances my honesty lands me in. It'll be like Ray never happened.'

It was empowering, knowing she was going to erase Ray from her life, wiping the memories away. Like chalk on a chalkboard, a messy scrawl, swiped away to leave a clear slate. Not so much as a smudge to stain it. It was harder to accept that she was also erasing herself from Alfie's life, ensuring she had no place in his future. But it had to be done.

'You go,' she said, stopping Austin as he opened his mouth to speak. She turned to Jasmine, and though she was still pale, still sagging under the weight of it all, she managed a tight nod.

'What if none of this works?' Austin blurted. 'What if they don't buy it, Amber? What if they don't believe Jasmine was uninvolved? We could be sending her down by doing this.'

'I'm a witness to what happened tonight. I witnessed Sarah's confession and her fall...her *jump*.' Amber insisted. 'I can defend Jasmine.'

'It's okay, Austin,' Jasmine said, reaching out for his hand.

Amber was amazed that after all Jasmine had put him through, Austin was still desperate to save her.

'I fucked up, big time,' Jasmine sighed. 'But you and Amber have no claim to look after Alfie. If you stay, it doesn't change the odds of him ending up in care, with strangers. But if we do as Amber says, if you go, it simplifies the story. It makes it easier to explain. And Amber's right, if I leave you out of it, then I don't have to admit what I did to Amber. How I took her, enabled her...her imprisonment.' Jasmine swallowed, guilt crawling into a blush that flooded her cheeks. 'If you stay, if we tell the whole truth, Alfie doesn't get to stay with any of us. If we do *this*, at least there's a chance.'

Amber nodded, grateful for Jasmine's compliance. Her sacrifice, her risk, more than made up for what she'd done to Amber. All that mattered was Sarah's son. The boy Amber loved so much. She slipped into the bedroom, and tiptoed towards Alfie, kissing him on the head. The silent goodbye tugged at her heart as she accepted it was time to let him go.

All she'd ever wanted for him was freedom, to grow up in a world of unlocked doors. She only hoped, agony pounding at her soul as she prepared to make her role in his life vanish, that she was giving him exactly that chance.

Now - Austin

Austin stepped out the front door, the fresh air rushing to greet him. His footsteps crunched over the gravel as he walked through the gate and into the dark lane. He took large strides as he made his way to Sam's car, parked further down. He was walking away, and he had no idea how to feel about it.

Alfie is alive. He's safe. He's safe!

Overcome by a surge of adrenalin Austin jumped, kicking his feet and punching the air. A manic laugh escaped him, high pitched, just one shrill bark that cut into the night-time peace. He knew there was nothing to celebrate, that Alfie's future was, in that moment, just as uncertain and complicated as his past. But knowing he was alive, that he had been looked after and loved, pulled a weight from Austin that left him floating, his eyes fixed on the stars in the sky.

They blurred as a mist of tears descended over his vision. They were a bizarre cocktail, a sharp shot of relief mixed with tears of sadness and shock. A woman had died, toppled over the railing before his eyes. He wasn't sure if the sickening crack in his memory was something he'd really heard at the time, or if he had created it himself. It had happened so fast. Alfie could've gone over with her. Or Amber. Or Jasmine.

Oh, Jasmine.

Austin realised he was walking away not only from Ray's house and the investigation that would start when the police arrived, but from Jasmine too. There was no way he'd see her again after this, even if Amber's plan worked. How could he? A huge part of him was still burning with bitter resentment, over the lies she'd told and the pain she'd caused. Another part of him pitied her. Her care-free lifestyle had stopped her from being able to handle the situation with her sister rationally. In trying to keep the peace, she'd abandoned all logic.

No police.

What was it with everybody and that bloody phrase? But that had changed now. He wondered if he should go back, speak to the police too, tell the whole truth and not Amber's re-worked version. But then he thought of Alfie, the boy he was when he'd volunteered for the act, chubby-cheeked and wide eyed. And he thought of the boy he'd become in the months since, long skinny legs, an anxiety in his features that had the maturity of an adult, rather than the innocence of a child. Amber's plan was for him. And Austin could finally move on, now that he knew Alfie was okay and the only lies going forward had been put in place to give him the best chance of a steady future.

He climbed into the car and started the engine. On the blackened lane he slipped away, leaving the house behind him. By the time he reached the town, sirens were blaring, and he kept going, until their shrill wail faded into the distance.

On the motorway Austin drifted with the traffic, back into normal life, where he was inconsequential. Just another car, another set of headlights, another man scratching his too-thick stubble and yawning. He'd return the car to Sam, go back to work. He'd return to live in his flat alone, there'd be no more Amber, no more weird letters. It would be boring, mundane, insignificant.

Everything you never wanted, mate.

Against the steering wheel Austin's fingers twitched. He turned on the radio, allowing his spirits to soar with the volume as he tweaked the dial. Alife was alive, and for the first time in eleven months, Austin felt alive too. He wound down the window despite how fast he was driving, and the wind rushed in, whipping his hair. In the distance headlights shone, like a galaxy of shooting stars, beacons of hope dotting the horizon. It was only cars, he knew it. Only the motorway at night, long and tiresome.

Yet somehow, for some reason, it felt a little like magic.

12 Months Later

The following year was a circus of solicitors and lawyers, social workers, and police. It went around and around, like the whirling colours of theatre lights or the dazzling dresses of ballerinas in a show. It was dizzying.

Twelve months on, Amber sat on a park bench, laughing as Alfie Tallon hopped through the grass, trying not to get his school uniform muddy. His Aunty Jasmine was following him, shaking her head and groaning about having to do more laundry.

'She used to be so laid back,' Austin grinned, slumping onto the bench beside Amber. 'Who'd have thought she'd have gotten so uptight about doing the washing?'

Amber laughed. 'No-one likes doing the laundry. She's doing really well though. Considering...'

She left the words hanging in the air. There were too many ways to finish the sentence, and none of them sounded right out loud.

Considering her sister died.

Considering she is raising a damaged boy, from an extremely broken home.

Amber sighed, her eyes still on Alfie.

'Yeah, she is doing well,' Austin smiled. 'But what about you?'

Amber looked at him. She saw him every day, had been sharing his flat since she'd been set free from police questioning. She'd answered many questions about that night at Ray's, when Sarah had toppled over the balcony and their broken lives had shattered into even smaller shards. And she'd answered them honestly, *almost* honestly, including telling the truth about how she ran away with Alfie, and about the abusive relationship with Ray. She only emitted Jasmine's involvement, claiming it was Sarah who had helped Ray to capture her.

The lie was like a dishonour, tarnishing Sarah's name, but Amber and Jasmine agreed she wouldn't mind if it meant Alfie was bought up by his family. And when they'd been free to leave the police station, Jasmine had driven Amber back to Austin. She didn't have anything of her own, no money, no possessions. Austin had been generous enough to move her in without a second thought, buying a pull-out bed for the living room. A year on and Amber was nearly ready to claim back her independence and rent a place of her own.

'I'm fine. Better than I have been in ages,' Amber told Austin, truthfully.

Was it that time was healing her? She wasn't sure about that. She still woke in sweaty panics in the night, still felt the agony of every second she spent alone. No, it was probably Alfie, little Alf, and her regular visits to see him, keeping her strong.

*

'The art's going well,' Austin said, his eyes fixed on Amber as she leant back on the bench, relaxed and happy.

It wasn't a question, he knew it was true. Amber had filled his living space with her paintings, while she waited for the ones in Mary's café to sell. His tiny flat was cluttered, cramped enough with two of them living there, let alone having to side-step canvases to make a cup of tea, or go to the toilet. Austin didn't mind. He was out most of the day anyway, performing his magic on the streets, with a new-found flare that was drawing in bigger crowds. Amber often went to watch him, and sometimes Jasmine took Alfie.

He didn't perform outside the abbey though. A pitch had opened up further along the High Street, where the crowds still flocked, and the bad memories stayed away.

'It is going well,' Amber agreed. 'I'll be out of your hair soon.'

'There's no rush,' Austin said. 'To be honest, it's nice. Having you around.'

'I'll still be around,' Amber promised. 'But I'll just have my own room. And space for all my canvases and paint pots.'

Austin laughed, relieved he'd be able to take a pee without the eyes from Amber's portraits on him.

From across the playground Alfie waved his arms. 'Come and play, Aunty Amber!' he called, clambering onto the see-saw and pointing at the other end.

'That's my cue.' Amber beamed, lifting herself from the bench and darting over to take the empty seat opposite Alfie.

Jasmine walked away, taking Amber's place beside Austin. 'It's exhausting, raising a child,' she said, breathing out so her fringe fluttered above her eyes. 'I'm lucky, I guess, that he's such a good kid.'

'You're doing brilliantly, Jas. And thank you. For letting Amber see him. I don't think she'd cope without him in her life.'

Jasmine waved a hand. 'It was the least I could do. I don't know what would've happened if the police knew what I'd done. I can't believe it myself, not now. What was I thinking? But Sarah was in such a state over Alfie, and it disturbed my balance, you know? I was living entirely for her, acting out what she wanted and needed. I can't believe she's gone.'

Austin lowered his eyes, the sorrow on Jasmine's face reminding him of that night at Ray's when he'd discovered her shocking secrets. He didn't like to think of her as who she was then, only wanted to remember the free spirit who'd whooped and cheered through his magic act on the streets of London, before insisting she took him for dinner.

'Anyway,' Jasmine breathed. 'I'm glad to have Amber around. When things have died down, and the police have stopped asking us in every few weeks, she can see Alfie more. He loves her, I'd never take that from him. Man, we are one fucked up family, aren't we?'

Austin laughed. 'Yes. We really are.'

Jasmine smiled, and Austin noted his stomach no longer flipped at the sight of her white teeth against the deep purple lipstick. He admired her, perhaps more than ever, but he didn't love her anymore. He was her friend, and he had no intentions of becoming her lover. Things were too different, and he was happy with life as it was. But when her expression darkened, the weight of her worries playing across her features, he did feel a twinge in his heart.

'The sentencing is next week,' Jasmine said. 'I can't believe it's taken this long.'

'Oh god,' Austin groaned. 'I'm sorry. I didn't realise it was so soon, now. What do you reckon?'

'They'll find Dean guilty, I know they will. I've seen it in the stars.'

'Oh, don't give me that crap, Jas,' Austin said, nudging her and winking.

'Okay, okay. But I just have a feeling. Things haven't gone well for him in court. And once they recovered Ray's body well...' she shuddered. 'It'll all be over soon, Aus. It'll all be over.'

Austin nodded. The nightmare was going to end, and it was about bloody time too.

And as he looked at Amber, her hair fluttering in the breeze as she pushed herself into the air on the see-saw, Alfie squealing in delight opposite, he knew their freedom had only just begun. And between the four of them, no matter how dysfunctional their family unit, they'd find ways to grow stronger. Together.

No more lies, no more secrets, no more vanishing acts.

About the Author

M.L. Davis

M.L. Davis is a novelist from South West England.
She has a passion for writing thriller/crime novels and finds inspiration in big cities, long train journeys, and the vulnerability of human nature.
In 2022 she graduated with a degree in Literature and Creative Writing and is now studying for a Masters in Health and Wellbeing. She works as an Operations Manager in a busy NHS GP Practice.

M.L. Davis also runs a blog with advice, tips, and inspiration on writing;
www.mldavis.co.uk

Vanishing Act is M.L. Davis' debut novel.

ACKNOWLEDGEMENTS

Writing a novel is, in many ways, a solo venture. But at the same time it is a product of the support, encouragement, commitment, and love of those around you.

Thank you to my husband, Toby, who read this story first and never faltered in his belief it would one day be published.

Vanishing Act would not be what it is today without the help of my friends and fellow authors K.M. Allan (Kate) and Lorraine Ambers (Rainy), who beta-read and critiqued the story, which helped me shape it from messy drafts to finished manuscript.

To my amazing family, for always supporting me, including my Dad, Gary, for his generosity and determination to see my work published.

My best friend, Shanice, who is my number one book buddy.

A huge thank you to three of my secondary school English teachers, who never gave up on me; Ben Hutchins, Katie Lambert, and Nick Wells.

And finally, my writing buddy and companion, Nymeria - my perfect pooch! Thank you.

Milton Keynes UK
Ingram Content Group UK Ltd.
UKHW012250110624
443988UK00005B/313